# 英語輕鬆學

## Speak English Like a Native: Beginner Level

### 學好 初級口語

### 就靠這本！

# Preface 序

　　《英語輕鬆學》是一套專門訓練英文口語能力的系列書籍。包含下列
四本：

❶ 《英語輕鬆學：學好 KK 音標就靠這本！》

❷ 《英語輕鬆學：學好入門會話就靠這本！》

❸ 《英語輕鬆學：學好初級口語就靠這本！》

❹ 《英語輕鬆學：學好中級口語就靠這本！》

　　我們從 KK 音標開始，幫助讀者打好發音基礎，而後三本則各自以最
貼近讀者的生活經驗為主題架構編寫。《英語輕鬆學：學好入門會話就靠
這本！》以日常實用基礎會話為主，《英語輕鬆學：學好初級口語就靠這
本！》、《英語輕鬆學：學好中級口語就靠這本！》除了會話之外，更進階
到題材新穎的短文，讓學習不只輕鬆，還妙趣橫生。

　　內容大題的設計則有以下特點：

❶ 暖身單元我們結合聽力訓練，以重複聆聽並且搭配關鍵字詞與簡單問
　 題的方式訓練讀者開口說。

❷ 正文使用中英對照的方式，幫助讀者快速理解內容，其後則列出該課
　 重點單字片語，幫助讀者記憶與運用。

❸ 會話單元搭配口語新技能，補充英文口語的相關進階說法，後再使用
　 該課相關內容設計聽力簡短對答，幫助讀者同時訓練聽力及口語。

❹ 短文單元則搭配實用詞句，補充更多相關字詞或文法；並且歸納出該
　 課的重要音標做練習並朗讀課文加強發音。最後鼓勵讀者以自己對課
　 文的印象及該課習得的單字、用語，用自己的話將課文換句話說，測
　 驗自身對課文及相關重點的了解程度，進而活用。

**5** 最後討論題目的單元，鼓勵讀者與一同學習的夥伴分享自身相關經驗。而全書所有單元皆附參考答案，提供讀者練習、對照。

　　本套書為彩色編排，搭配精美的圖片，讓學習賞心悅目。同時為了讓讀者能更完整且有效率地學習，除了全系列套書附贈免費專業外師朗讀音檔之外，更請本公司王牌講解老師之一奚永慧（Wesley）老師搭配 Stephen、Jennifer 老師，分別錄製講解《英語輕鬆學：學好入門會話就靠這本！》、《英語輕鬆學：學好初級口語就靠這本！》、《英語輕鬆學：學好中級口語就靠這本！》這三本書，歡迎讀者們上「常春藤官方網站」（ivy.com.tw）及「博客來」（books.com.tw）訂購。

　　祝大家學習成功！

# Contents 目錄

**Chapter ③** 休閒娛樂 Leisure Activities

# Chapter ④ 職場與教育 Work and Education

# User's Guide 使用說明

全書朗讀
音檔下載

**Lesson 19**
Lesson 19

## What Do You Do on Sundays?
### 你週日都做什麼？

**搭配筆記聆聽會話** Listen to the text with the help of the notes given

| | |
|---|---|
| on Sundays | 每週日 |
| market | 市場 |
| favorite | 最喜歡的 |
| What about you? | 你呢？ |
| That's too bad! | 太不幸了！ |

**再次聆聽並回答問題** Listen again and answer the questions below

Questions for discussion:

1. What time does the man wake up on Sundays?
2. Where does the man meet his friends?
3. What does the woman do on Sundays?

掃描 QR Code 聆聽
專業外師朗讀音檔。

暖身單元結合聽力訓
練，以重複聆聽並且
搭配關鍵字詞與簡單
問題的方式訓練讀者
開口說。

---

**實用會話** Dialogue

Ⓐ Hey, Ron! What do you do on Sundays?
Ⓑ I sleep until nine o'clock. And then I walk to the market. I like to buy fruit and vegetables at the market. Later, I meet my friends for lunch at our favorite restaurant. What about you?
Ⓐ Oh, I work on Sundays.
Ⓑ That's too bad!

Ⓐ 嘿，榮恩！你週日都做什麼？
Ⓑ 我會睡到九點鐘。然後我會走到市場。我喜歡在市場買蔬菜水果。接著，我會與我朋友在我們最喜歡的餐廳吃午餐。你呢？
Ⓐ 喔，我週日都要工作。
Ⓑ 太不幸了！

**短文聽讀** Text

Jonas will have saved $5,000 by the end of the year. He will have put aside enough money to buy his girlfriend a beautiful engagement ring. He plans to take her to Paris on a weekend and propose under the Eiffel Tower. He then plans to take her for a candlelit dinner on a cruise on the Seine. Jonas is such a romantic!

到今年年底前，喬納斯就會存好五千美元。他將存到足夠的錢買一隻漂亮的訂婚戒指給他女友。他計劃在一個週末要帶她去巴黎，並在艾菲爾鐵塔下求婚。他接著計劃要帶她到塞納河的遊船上享用燭光晚餐。喬納斯真是個浪漫的人！

正文使用中英對照的方式，幫助讀者快速理解內容。

### 單字片語 Vocabulary and Phrases

**1** **sleep** [ slip ] *vi.* 睡覺 (三態為：sleep, slept [ slɛpt ], slept ) &
*n.* 睡覺，睡眠 (不可數)
Sleep tight!　　　睡個好覺！
go to sleep　　　去睡覺

**2** **until** [ ən'tɪl ] *prep.* 直到……為止 (= till [ tɪl ])
Charlie has to wait here until 3 o'clock.
= Charlie has to wait here till 3 o'clock.
查理要在這裡等到三點鐘。

**3** **walk** [ wɔk ] *vi.* & *vt.* 走路 & *n.* 散步，步行
go for a walk　　　去散步
take / have a walk　散步
I walk to my office every day.
我每天都走路到辦公室。
Let's go for a walk after dinner.
晚餐後我們去散步吧。

**4** **market** [ 'mɑrkɪt ] *n.* 市場；超市
supermarket [ 'supə,mɑrkɪt ] *n.* 超市

> 正文後列出該課重點
> 單字片語，幫助讀者
> 記憶與運用。

### 口語新技能 New Skills

**1** What do you do on Sundays?　　你週日都做什麼？

on Sundays　　　每週日
= every Sunday
Rita tends to sleep in on Sundays.
= Rita tends to sleep in every Sunday.
麗塔每週日通常會睡懶覺。
**比較**
on Sunday　　　在週日
I have to study on Sunday.
我週日得要讀書。

**2** What about you?　　你呢？

What about...?　　那……呢 / 如何？
= How about...?

> 會話單元搭配口語新
> 技能，補充英文口語
> 的相關進階說法。

會話單元

### 簡短對答 Quick Response

◆ Make quick responses to the sentences you hear.

> 使用該課相關內容設
> 計聽力簡短對答，幫
> 助讀者同時訓練聽力
> 及口語。

### 討論題目 Free Talk

🖊 Talk on the following topic:

◆ Where do you like to go on Sundays?

> 討論題目的單元，鼓
> 勵讀者與一同學習的
> 夥伴分享自身相關經
> 驗。

## 實用詞句 Useful Expressions

**❶** 表示「在……之前」的說法

by + 時間　　在某時間之前

We have to arrive there by 3 p.m.
= We have to arrive there no later than 3 p.m.
我們下午三點前要抵達那裡。

The students should hand in their reports by this Friday.
= The students should hand in their reports no later than this Friday.
學生們應在本週五以前繳交報告。

**比較**

by the time...　　等到……的時候

**🖋 Notes**

by the time 可引導副詞子句，修飾主句，但須注意句子時態的變化。

By the time I arrived, the plane had already taken off.
等到我抵達時，飛機已經起飛了。
By the time you come home, I will have prepared dinner.
等你回到家時，我將已弄好晚餐了。

短文單元搭配實用詞句，補充更多相關字詞或文法。

## 發音提示 Pronunciation

| **❶** [ o ] | Jonas [ˈdʒonəs] | romantic [roˈmæntɪk] |
|---|---|---|
| | propose [prəˈpoz] | |

| **❷** [ dʒ ] | Jonas [ˈdʒonəs] | engagement [ɪnˈgedʒmənt] |
|---|---|---|

## 朗讀短文 Read aloud the text

🖋 請特別注意 [ o ]、[ dʒ ] 的發音。

Jonas will have saved $5,000 by the end of the year. He will have put aside enough money to buy his girlfriend a beautiful engagement ring. He plans to take her to Paris on a weekend and propose under the Eiffel Tower. He then plans to take her for a candlelit dinner on a cruise on the Seine. Jonas is such a romantic!

歸納出該課的重要音標做練習並朗讀課文加強發音。

## 換句話說 Retell

🖋 Retell the text with the help of the words and expressions below.

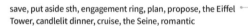

save, put aside sth, engagement ring, plan, propose, the Eiffel Tower, candlelit dinner, cruise, the Seine, romantic

## 討論題目 Free Talk

🖋 Talk on the following topic:

◆ Have you ever saved money in order to buy something expensive?

鼓勵讀者以自己對課文的印象及該課習得的單字、用語，用自己的話將課文換句話說，測驗自身對課文及相關重點的了解程度，進而活用。

短文單元

# Chapter 1

# 日常生活
## Daily Life

# Ask for Directions
## 問路

**搭配筆記聆聽會話** **Listen to the text with the help of the notes given**

| a convenience store | 便利商店 |
| --- | --- |
| go straight | 直走 |
| turn right | 右轉 |
| app | 應用程式 |
| Thanks for your help. | 謝謝你的幫助。 |

**再次聆聽並回答問題** **Listen again and answer the questions below**

 Questions for discussion:

❶ Where does the woman want to go?

❷ What is next to the convenience store?

❸ Does the woman have a map?

**實用會話 Dialogue**

Ⓐ Excuse me. Could you tell me where a convenience store is?

Ⓑ There is one on High Street. It is next to the police station. Go straight for about 50 meters, and then turn right. Do you have a map?

Ⓐ There is an app on my cell phone. Thank you for your help.

Ⓐ 不好意思。你可不可以告訴我哪裡有便利商店？

Ⓑ 高點街上有一家。它就在警察局隔壁。直走大約五十公尺，然後右轉。你有地圖嗎？

Ⓐ 我的手機有下載應用程式。謝謝你的幫助。

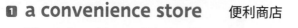 

**❶ a convenience store** 　便利商店

There is a convenience store around the corner.
轉角處有家便利商店。

**❷ a police station** 　警察局
a fire station 　消防隊
a gas station 　加油站

The policeman seized the bad guy by the arm and took him to the police station.
員警抓住那個壞蛋的手臂，把他帶往警局。

**❸ straight** [ stret ] *adv.* 直直地 & *a.* 直的

Go straight ahead for three blocks, and you'll see the store on your right.
往前直走三個街區，你就會看到那家店在你的右手邊。

**❹ meter** [ ˋmitɚ ] *n.* 公尺，米 (本字亦可寫成 m)
a square meter 　一平方公尺
a cubic meter 　一立方公尺

The swimming pool is 25 meters long and 4 meters deep.
那個泳池長二十五公尺，深四公尺。

**❺ right** [ raɪt ] *adv.* 向右；在右邊 & *a.* 右邊的 & *n.* 右邊
turn right (right 是副詞) 　向右轉
= turn to the right (right 是名詞)

Turn right at the next block, and you'll see the store.
= Turn to the right at the next block, and you'll see the store.
在下一個街區右轉，你就會看到那家店了。

**❻ app** [ æp ] *n.* 應用程式 (為 application [ ˌæpləˋkeʃən ] 的縮寫)

## 口語新技能 New Skills

🎙 問路的說法

◆ 問路可使用下列問句：

**Could you tell me where + 地點 + is?**
你可以告訴我⋯⋯在哪裡嗎？

**Do you know where the nearest + 地點 + is?**
你知道最近的⋯⋯在哪裡嗎？

**How do I get to... ?**
我要怎麼去⋯⋯？

**I'm going to... Could you show me the way?**
我要去⋯⋯。你可以告訴我怎麼去嗎？

◆ 針對上述問句，可以這樣回答：

**Go (straight) down this road.**
沿著這條路直走。

**Turn right / left at the next intersection.**
下個路口右轉／左轉。

**You can get there by bus / subway / train.**
你可以搭公車／地鐵／火車抵達。

🄰 Do you know where the nearest hospital is?

🄱 Turn right at the next intersection. It'll be on your left.

🄰 你知道最近的醫院在哪裡嗎？

🄱 下個路口右轉。醫院會在你的左手邊。

◆ 替換看看：

| post office　郵局 | bus stop　公車站 |
|---|---|
| police station　警局 | train station　火車站 |
| bank　銀行 | supermarket　超市 |

## 簡短對答 Quick Response

◆ Make quick responses to the sentences you hear.

## 討論題目 Free Talk

Talk on the following topic:

◆ Where is your school? How do you get there?

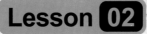

朗讀 ▶
Lesson 02

## Lesson 02

# I Must Clean My Room
## 我必須打掃我的房間

搭配筆記聆聽短文 **Listen to the text with the help of the notes given**

| | |
|---|---|
| I have a day off work. | 我不用上班。 |
| play video games | 打電動 |
| empty | 空的 |
| garbage | 垃圾 |
| order | 訂購 |

再次聆聽並回答問題 **Listen again and answer the questions below**

🎙 Questions for discussion:

**1** Does the speaker have to work today?

**2** What must the speaker do first?

**3** What does the speaker want to order?

Today is Sunday. I have a day off work. I can play video games and watch TV all day, but first I must clean my room. There are so many empty pizza boxes that I can't see the TV! I must take out the garbage, too. Then, I can play video games and watch TV. I can also order pizza.

今天是星期日。我不用上班。我可以整天打電動並看電視,可是首先我必須打掃我的房間。披薩的空盒子多到我看不見電視機了!我也必須把垃圾丟掉。然後我才可以打電動跟看電視。我也可以訂披薩。

## 單字片語 Vocabulary and Phrases

**❶ a video game** 電動遊戲，電玩
video [ ˈvɪdɪˌo ] *a.* 影像的；錄影的 & *n.* 錄影帶；影片
play video games 打電動

**❷ TV** 電視 (為 television [ ˈtɛləˌvɪʒən ] 的縮寫)

**❸ all day (long)** 一整天
all night (long) 一整晚
I was busy all day (long).
我一整天都很忙。
The baby was awake all night (long).
小寶寶一整晚都醒著。

**❹ clean** [ klin ] *vt. & vi.* 清理，打掃 & *a.* 乾淨的
You should clean your desk. It's a mess.
你應該清理你的桌子。它一團亂。
Nathan's home is basic and clean.
納森的家簡約又乾淨。

**❺ empty** [ ˈɛmptɪ ] *a.* 空的
Please recycle these empty bottles.
請回收這些空瓶。

**❻ pizza** [ ˈpitsə ] *n.* 披薩

**❼ box** [ baks ] *n.* 盒子，箱子

**❽ garbage** [ ˈɡɑrbɪdʒ ] *n.* 垃圾 (不可數，美式用法)
= rubbish [ ˈrʌbɪʃ ] (英式用法)
= trash [ træʃ ]
take out the garbage / rubbish / trash 倒垃圾
a piece of garbage / rubbish / trash 一件垃圾
talk garbage / rubbish / trash 說廢話

**❾ order** [ ˈɔrdɚ ] *vt.* 訂購；點餐；命令 & *n.* 訂單；命令；順序
I want to order a new laptop.
我想訂購一臺新的筆記型電腦。

Are you ready to order?
您準備好要點餐了嗎？

## 實用詞句　Useful Expressions

**❶ I have a day off work.**　我不用上班。

have a day off (work)　放一天假
We have a day off this Friday.
這週五我們放假一天。

比較

take a day off (work)　請一天假
Tom took a day off today to see the doctor.
湯姆今天請了一天假去看醫生。

**❷ There are so many empty pizza boxes that I can't see the TV!**
披薩的空盒子多到我看不見電視機了！

so... that...　如此……以致於……
Tracy is so rich that she can buy anything she wants.
崔西很有錢，她可以買任何想買的東西。
Roy is so shy that he has trouble talking to strangers.
羅伊很害羞，以致於他很難跟陌生人談話。

### 🔑 Notes

英語母語人士有時在口語會話中會將 that 省略，改用逗號取代，因此上列例句亦可改為：
Tracy is so rich, she can buy anything she wants.
Roy is so shy, he has trouble talking to strangers.
根據上述，本課句子亦可改寫為：
There are so many empty pizza boxes, I can't see the TV!

## 發音提示　Pronunciation

| ❶ [ɑ] | watch [ wɑtʃ ] | box [ bɑks ] |
|---|---|---|
| | are [ ɑr ] | garbage [ ˈgɑrbɪdʒ ] |

| ❷ [ɔ] | off [ ɔf ] | also [ ˈɔlso ] |
|---|---|---|
| | all [ ɔl ] | order [ ˈɔrdɚ ] |

## 朗讀短文　Read aloud the text

🔖 請特別注意 [ɑ]、[ɔ] 的發音。

Today is Sunday. I have a day off work. I can play video games and watch TV all day, but first I must clean my room. There are so many empty pizza boxes that I can't see the TV! I must take out the garbage, too. Then, I can play video games and watch TV. I can also order pizza.

## 換句話說　Retell

🔖 Retell the text with the help of the words and expressions below.

video game, TV, all day, clean, empty, pizza, box, garbage, order

## 討論題目　Free Talk

🔖 Talk on the following topic:

◆ What do you like to do on weekends?

# A Little Food in the Fridge
## 冰箱裡的一點食物

---

**搭配筆記聆聽會話** | **Listen to the text with the help of the notes given**

| | |
|---|---|
| Let's eat out tonight. | 我們今天晚上去外面吃吧。 |
| fridge | 冰箱 |
| dine out | 外出用餐 |
| mushroom | 洋菇，蘑菇 |
| I love your omelets! | 我愛吃你做的歐姆蛋！ |

---

**再次聆聽並回答問題** | **Listen again and answer the questions below**

Questions for discussion:

1 Why can't the couple dine out?

2 What does the couple have in their fridge?

3 What does the man like to eat?

## 實用會話　Dialogue

Ⓐ Sweetheart, let's eat out tonight. There's only a little food in the fridge.

Ⓑ It would be nice to dine out, but we don't have much money.

Ⓐ We have a few eggs, mushrooms, and vegetables. Shall I make an omelet and salad?

Ⓑ That sounds great! I love your omelets!

Ⓐ And I love you!


Ⓐ 親愛的，我們今天晚上去外面吃吧。冰箱裡只剩一點食物了。

Ⓑ 去外面吃是很好，不過我們沒什麼錢。

Ⓐ 我們有一些雞蛋、蘑菇和蔬菜。我來做個歐姆蛋和生菜沙拉如何？

Ⓑ 聽起來很不錯！我愛吃你做的歐姆蛋！

Ⓐ 而我愛你！

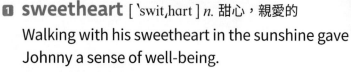

**❶ sweetheart** [ ˈswit͵hɑrt ] *n.* 甜心，親愛的

Walking with his sweetheart in the sunshine gave
Johnny a sense of well-being.

強尼跟他的愛人在陽光下散步，這讓他有一股幸福感。

＊ well-being [ ͵wɛlˈbiɪŋ ] *n.* 幸福

**❷ fridge** [ frɪdʒ ] *n.* 冰箱 (= refrigerator [ rɪˈfrɪdʒə͵retə ])

**❸ dine out** 在外面吃飯 (= eat out)

dine in 在家裡吃飯 (= eat in)

Would you like to dine out with me tonight?

今天晚上你要不要跟我去外面吃飯？

**❹ mushroom** [ ˈmʌʃrʊm ] *n.* 洋菇，蘑菇

**❺ omelet** [ ˈɑmlət ] *n.* 歐姆蛋 (英式拼法為 omelette)

**❻ sound** [ saʊnd ] *vi.* 聽起來；好像 & *n.* 聲音 & *a.* 健全的

Your idea sounds good. Let's try it out!

你的點子聽起來不錯。咱們試試吧！

口語新技能 **New Skills**

🎤 助動詞 shall 的用法

◆ 助動詞 shall 有下列幾種用法：

**ⓐ** 徵求對方意見時：

Shall I...? 要不要我……？

Shall I turn on the air conditioner?

= Would you like me to turn on the air conditioner?

要不要我開冷氣呢／你想要我開冷氣嗎？

**ⓑ** 請求對方合作時：

Shall we...? 我們……，好嗎？

Shall we leave for the airport now?

= Let's leave for the airport now, shall we?

我們現在就出發前往機場，好嗎？

**c** 命令對方時：

You shall...　　你必須……

= You must...

You shall complete the task before receiving the payment.

你必須在收到款項前完成該任務。

**d** 向對方保證遵守某承諾時：

You shall...　　你一定會……

You shall receive the payment within a week.

我保證你將在一週內收到款項。

## 簡短對答　Quick Response

◆ Make quick responses to the sentences you hear.

## 討論題目　Free Talk

🖉 Talk on the following topic:

◆ What do you have in your fridge? What can you make out of the food in your fridge?

# I Have a Sweet Tooth
## 我喜歡吃甜食

| | |
|---|---|
| I have such a sweet tooth. | 我很喜歡吃甜食。 |
| sugar | 糖 |
| dentist | 牙醫 |
| I can't help it. | 我忍不住。 |
| everything | 所有事物 |

Questions for discussion:

**1** Does the speaker like sweet food?

**2** What does the speaker like to eat the most?

**3** What does the dentist say to the speaker?

短文聽讀 **Text**

I have such a sweet tooth. I will eat anything with sugar in it— chocolate cake, ice cream, or fruit salad—but my favorite is tiramisu. My dentist tells me to eat less sugar, but I can't help it. I just want everything to be sweet. Maybe I don't have a sweet tooth. Maybe I have sweet teeth!

我很喜歡吃甜食。我會吃任何含糖的食物 —— 巧克力蛋糕、冰淇淋、水果沙拉 —— 不過我最喜歡的是提拉米蘇蛋糕。我的牙醫告訴我要少吃一點糖，可是我忍不住。我就是想要每樣食物都吃起來是甜的。我可能不只是喜歡吃甜食。可能我愛吃甜食愛到瘋了！

**❶ have a sweet tooth**　　愛吃甜食

= enjoy sweets

sweet [ swit ] *a.* 甜的 & *n.* 甜食 (常用複數)

tooth [ tuθ ] *n.* 牙齒 (複數為 teeth [ tiθ ])

Penelope has a sweet tooth.

= Penelope enjoys sweets.

潘妮洛普喜歡吃甜食。

**❷ sugar** [ ˋʃʊgɚ ] *n.* 糖 (不可數)

Would you like some sugar in your tea?

你的茶裡想要加點糖嗎？

**❸ chocolate** [ ˋtʃɑklɪt ] *n.* 巧克力

**❹ ice cream**　　冰淇淋 (不可數)

cream [ krim ] *n.* 奶油；乳脂；乳霜

a scoop [ skup ] of ice cream　　一勺冰淇淋

I bought two scoops of chocolate ice cream.

我買了兩勺巧克力冰淇淋。

**❺ salad** [ ˋsæləd ] *n.* 沙拉

**❻ tiramisu** [ ˌtɪrəmiˋsu ] *n.* 提拉米蘇蛋糕 (為義大利甜點)

**❼ dentist** [ ˋdɛntɪst ] *n.* 牙醫

the dentist's　　牙醫診所

= the dental clinic

dental [ ˋdɛnt!̩ ] *a.* 牙醫的，牙科的

clinic [ ˋklɪnɪk ] *n.* 診所

I need to go to the dentist's today.

= I need to go to the dental clinic today.

我今天需要去牙醫診所。

**8 tell sb to V**　　叫 / 吩咐某人做……

The guard told us to show him our IDs.

警衛叫我們給他看身分證件。

Teresa was told to come here.

泰瑞莎被吩咐來到這裡。

## 實用詞句　Useful Expressions

**1 I have such a sweet tooth.**　　我很喜歡吃甜食。

such + a(n) (+ 形容詞) + 單數可數名詞 / 複數可數名詞 / 不可數名詞

非常……，如此……

Vera is such a lovely girl.
　　　　　　單數可數名詞

薇拉是個非常令人喜愛的女孩。

Apes are such intelligent animals.
　　　　　　複數可數名詞

黑猩猩是很聰明的動物。

I'm tired of such lousy weather.
　　　　　　不可數名詞

我真是受夠這種爛天氣了。

**2 I can't help it.**　　我忍不住。

can't help it　　忍不住 / 無法抑制

Molly is not supposed to eat deep-fried food, but she can't help it.

莫莉不應該吃油炸食物，可是她忍不住。

◆ 以下列舉與本片語相似的用法：

　**a** can't help + V-ing　　忍不住 / 無法克制做……

　= can't help but + V

　= can't but + V（較少用）

　　I couldn't help laughing when I heard the joke.

　= I couldn't help but laugh when I heard the joke.

　= I couldn't but laugh when I heard the joke. （較少用）

　　我聽到笑話就忍不住笑了。

**b** can't help oneself　　某人忍不住 / 無法抑制
John is supposed to quit smoking, but he can't help himself.
約翰應該要戒菸，可是他忍不住。

**c** It can't be helped.　　別無選擇。
Andy doesn't want to go on the business trip, but it can't be helped.
安迪不想出差，可是他別無選擇。

## 發音提示　Pronunciation

| **1** [θ] | tooth [ tuθ ] | everything [ ˈɛvrɪˌθɪŋ ] |
|---|---|---|
| | anything [ ˈɛnɪˌθɪŋ ] | teeth [ tiθ ] |

| **2** [e] | cake [ kek ] | favorite [ ˈfev(ə)rɪt ] |
|---|---|---|
| | maybe [ ˈmebɪ ] | |

## 朗讀短文　Read aloud the text

請特別注意 [θ]、[e] 的發音。

I have such a sweet tooth. I will eat anything with sugar in it—chocolate cake, ice cream, or fruit salad—but my favorite is tiramisu. My dentist tells me to eat less sugar, but I can't help it. I just want everything to be sweet. Maybe I don't have a sweet tooth. Maybe I have sweet teeth!

## 換句話說 Retell

Retell the text with the help of the words and expressions below.

have a sweet tooth, sugar, chocolate, ice cream, salad, tiramisu, dentist

## 討論題目 Free Talk

Talk on the following topic:

◆ Do you have a sweet tooth? What is your favorite dessert?

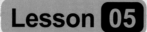

# Lesson 05

# Too Much Coffee
## 喝太多咖啡

**搭配筆記聆聽短文** **Listen to the text with the help of the notes given**

| | |
|---|---|
| awake | 清醒的 |
| I was very tired today. | 我今天很累。 |
| a large cup of coffee | 一大杯咖啡 |
| asleep | 睡著的 |
| wide awake | 非常清醒 |

**再次聆聽並回答問題** **Listen again and answer the questions below**

 Questions for discussion:

**1** Why was the speaker awake last night?

**2** What did the speaker drink?

**3** Why can't the speaker sleep today?

I was awake last night because our new baby was crying. I was very tired today, so I had a large cup of coffee. And then another. And then another. And then another! Now, the baby is asleep, but I am wide awake. Why, oh why, did I drink so much coffee?

昨天夜裡我都是醒著的,因為那時我們剛出生的寶寶一直在哭。我今天很累,所以我喝了一大杯咖啡。接著再一杯。然後又一杯。繼續又再一杯!現在寶寶睡了,但我卻非常清醒。唉,我為什麼要喝這麼多咖啡呢?

**❶ awake** [ əˈwek ] *a.* 清醒的 & *vi.* 醒來
（三態為：awake, awoke [ əˈwok ], awoken [ əˈwokən ]）

Gina was wide awake the whole night, fearing the worst.
吉娜徹夜未眠，擔心最壞的情況會發生。

**❷ cry** [ kraɪ ] *vi.* & *vt.* 哭（三態為：cry, cried [ kraɪd ], cried) & *n.* 哭泣
cry oneself to sleep　　哭到睡著
burst out crying　　突然大哭
= burst into tears

As soon as the mother left the room, her baby began to cry.
那個媽媽一離開房間，她的寶寶就哭了起來。

**❸ asleep** [ əˈslip ] *a.* 睡著的
fall asleep　　睡著了

The baby fell asleep in the crib.
那個寶寶在嬰兒床裡睡著了。

＊ crib [ krɪb ] *n.* 嬰兒床

**❹ wide** [ waɪd ] *adv.* 十分地 & *a.* 寬的 (= broad [ brɔd ])
be wide awake　　十分清醒

Diana couldn't fall asleep and was wide awake all night.
戴安娜睡不著，整夜都十分清醒。

**❶ 介紹代名詞 another 的用法**

代名詞 another 表示「另外一個」先前已提過的人或物 (如本文的 another
= another cup of coffee)，可作主詞、受詞或表語：
Karen has bought many stuffed toys like this—another of them
came today.
凱倫已經買了許多像這樣的絨毛娃娃 —— 今天又多了一個。
（another 作主詞）

The flu is transmitted from one person to another through the air.

流行性感冒藉由空氣在人與人之間互相傳染。

（another 作受詞）

To know is one thing; to do is another.

知道是一回事，做又是另一回事。

（another 作表語）

**2** 表示「非常累」的說法

tired [ taɪrd ] *a.* 感到疲倦的；感到厭煩的

be tired out　　累壞了

= be worn out

= be exhausted

Harry was so tired that he fell asleep at once.

哈利累壞了，所以馬上就睡著了。

Kevin was tired out after the basketball game.

= Kevin was worn out after the basketball game.

= Kevin was exhausted after the basketball game.

凱文在籃球比賽結束後整個人累垮了。

比較

**a** be tired from...　　因……而勞累

Jack was tired from working.

傑克因工作而疲累。

**b** be tired of...　　對……感到厭煩

= be bored with...

The traveler is tired of staying in hotels.

這個旅人厭煩了住在飯店裡。

## 發音提示 Pronunciation

| | | | | |
|---|---|---|---|---|
| **❶ [ aɪ ]** | I [ aɪ ] | | tired [ taɪrd ] | |
| | night [ naɪt ] | | wide [ waɪd ] | |
| | cry [ kraɪ ] | | why [ (h)waɪ ] | |

| | |
|---|---|
| **❷ [ dʒ ]** | large [ lɑrdʒ ] |

## 朗讀短文 Read aloud the text

📍 請特別注意 [ aɪ ]、[ dʒ ] 的發音。

I was awake last **night** because our new baby was **crying**. I was very **tired** today, so I had a **large** cup of coffee. And then another. And then another. And then another! Now, the baby is asleep, but I am **wide** awake. **Why**, oh **why**, did I drink so much coffee?

## 換句話說 Retell

📍 Retell the text with the help of the words and expressions below.

awake, cry, asleep, wide

## 討論題目 Free Talk

📍 Talk on the following topic:

◆ Do you like to drink coffee? How many cups of coffee do you drink a day?

## Lesson 06

# It's Only a Nightmare
## 那只不過是場夢魘

**搭配筆記聆聽會話** Listen to the text with the help of the notes given

| | |
|---|---|
| cockroach | 蟑螂 |
| having a bad dream | 做惡夢 |
| scary | 恐怖的 |
| sweat | 流汗 |
| What a nightmare! | 真是場惡夢！ |

**再次聆聽並回答問題** Listen again and answer the questions below

📍 Questions for discussion:

**1** What did the boy dream of?

**2** Were there any cockroaches?

**3** What did the boy think of the dream?

Ⓐ Mommy, Mommy! There are cockroaches in the bed!

Ⓑ Argh! Where? Where?

Ⓐ Everywhere! You have to get them off me!

Ⓑ I don't see any. I think you were just having a bad dream, darling.

Ⓐ Oh! That was so scary. I'm sweating. What a nightmare!

Ⓑ Relax. You're awake now.


Ⓐ 媽咪，媽咪！床上有蟑螂！

Ⓑ 呃！哪裡？在哪裡？

Ⓐ 到處都是！妳必須把它們從我身上趕跑！

Ⓑ 我沒有看到蟑螂。親愛的，我想你剛才做惡夢了。

Ⓐ 噢！好恐怖。我在流汗。真是場惡夢！

Ⓑ 放輕鬆。你現在醒了。

## 單字片語　Vocabulary and Phrases

**1 mommy** [ ˈmɑmɪ ] *n.* 媽咪 (= mom，美式用法)
mummy [ ˈmʌmɪ ] *n.* 媽咪 (= mum，英式用法)

**2 cockroach** [ ˈkɑkˌrotʃ ] *n.* 蟑螂 (常簡寫成 roach [ rotʃ ])

**3 everywhere** [ ˈɛvrɪˌwɛr ] *adv.* 到處都是，處處
= everyplace [ ˈɛvrɪˌples ]

It's getting hotter and hotter everywhere in the world.
世界各地天氣正變得愈來愈熱。

**4 get... off...**　　(使……) 從……去掉；(使……) 從……下來
Please get the cat hair off the sofa for me.
請為我把貓毛從沙發上清除掉。

**5 have a dream**　　做夢
I had a sweet dream last night.
昨天夜裡我做了個美夢。

**6 darling** [ ˈdɑrlɪŋ ] *n.* 親愛的 (對配偶、情人或家人的暱稱)

**7 scary** [ ˈskɛrɪ ] *a.* 可怕的，恐怖的，令人害怕的

**8 sweat** [ swɛt ] *vi.* 出汗 & *n.* 汗
sweat heavily / a lot　　大量流汗

I sweat a lot on hot days.
大熱天我會流很多汗。

**9 nightmare** [ ˈnaɪtˌmɛr ] *n.* 惡夢；不快的預感
have a nightmare　　做一場惡夢 (非 dream a nightmare)
a recurring nightmare　　一再出現的夢魘

Billy had a nightmare last night. He dreamed he was being chased by a wolf.
比利昨夜做了場惡夢。他夢到自己正被一隻狼追趕。

**10 relax** [ rɪˈlæks ] *vi.* 放鬆；休息 & *vt.* 使放鬆
It's the weekend, and I can finally relax.
週末來臨了，我總算可以放鬆了。

**❶ 表示「必須」的說法**

has / have to + V    必須……

If you want to lose weight, then you have to eat less.

如果你想減肥，就必須吃少一點。

**比較**

**ⓐ** must [ mʌst ] *aux.* 必須

🔑 **Notes**

用於有義務性、強制性的情況，通常可與 have to 相替換。

You must be at least 150 cm tall to go on this ride.

= You have to be at least 150 cm tall to go on this ride.

你必須至少一百五十公分高才能坐這個遊樂設施。

**ⓑ** need to V    需要……；必須……

🔑 **Notes**

表「需要……」時，通常是為了達成某種目的而需要從事某件事；表「必須……」時，則通常為生理需求或較不緊急的情況。

Ben needs to get a visa to go to the US.

班需要拿到簽證才能去美國。

The little girl needs to go to the bathroom.

那個小女孩需要去上廁所。

**❷ 以 what 引導的感歎句**

◆ 以 what 引導的感歎句句型如下：

What + 名詞 + 主詞 + be 動詞!    好一個……啊！

What a delicious meal it was!

好可口的一餐啊！

What nice people they are!
他們人真好！
What great music it is!
這音樂真棒！

### 📌 Notes

實際使用時，通常將「主詞＋be 動詞」予以省略，而採用下列化簡的說法：

What a delicious meal!
好可口的一餐啊！
What nice people!
他們人真好！
What great music (it is)!
這音樂真棒！

## 簡短對答  Quick Response

◆ Make quick responses to the sentences you hear.

## 討論題目  Free Talk

📌 Talk on the following topic:

◆ When was your last nightmare?
What was the dream about?

# Don't Walk and Text
## 不要邊走邊傳訊息

| | |
|---|---|
| be people watching | 觀察形形色色的路人 |
| checking his phone | 看他的手機 |
| a trash can | 垃圾桶 |
| trip | 絆倒 |
| bump into a tree | 撞到一棵樹 |
| bang | 撞擊 |

 Questions for discussion:

**1** Where was the speaker?

**2** What was the guy doing?

**3** What did the guy bump into?

短文聽讀 **Text**

I was sitting in the park, people watching and waiting for my friend to arrive. There was a guy in the park checking his phone while walking. First, he nearly walked into a trash can; then he tripped over a seat; then he bumped into a tree and banged his head! And, all the time, he was still using his phone. There's a lesson in there somewhere!

我坐在公園裡觀察形形色色的路人，並等待我的朋友抵達。公園裡有一個男生邊走邊看他的手機。首先，他幾乎快要撞到一個垃圾桶；接著他被一個座椅絆倒；然後他撞到一棵樹還敲到頭！而且，他仍一直在使用手機。這還真是給人上了一課！

**❶ be people watching** 觀察形形色色的人
= be crowd watching

**❷ wait** [ wet ] *vi.* 等候
wait for sb/sth 等待某人 / 某事
wait to V 等著做⋯⋯

We're waiting for the bus.
我們正在等公車。

I'm waiting to see the doctor.
我正在等著看醫生。

**❸ guy** [ gaɪ ] *n.* 男人，傢伙
比較
guys [ gaɪz ] *n.* 大家，各位 (不分男女，用於稱呼一群人時)

**❹ nearly** [ ˈnɪrlɪ ] *adv.* 幾乎
= almost [ ˈɔl͵most ]

**❺ trash** [ træʃ ] *n.* 垃圾 (不可數)
a piece of trash 一件垃圾

**❻ can** [ kæn ] *n.* 圓罐，圓桶
a trash can 垃圾桶

**❼ trip** [ trɪp ] *vi. & vt.* (使) 絆倒 (三態為：trip, tripped [ trɪpt ], tripped)
trip over / on... 被⋯⋯絆倒

I tripped over the curb and fell onto the sidewalk.
我被路緣絆倒，跌倒在人行道上。

**❽ seat** [ sit ] *n.* 座位

Have / Take a seat, please.
請坐。

**❾ bump** [ bʌmp ] *vi. & vt.* 撞擊
bump into sth/sb 撞到某物 / 某人
bump into sb 巧遇某人

The drunk guy bumped into lots of people
on the dance floor.

那位喝醉的男士在舞池中撞到許多人。

I bumped into an old friend at the supermarket yesterday.

我昨天在超市巧遇了一位老朋友。

⑩ **bang** [ bæŋ ] *vt. & vi.* 撞擊

Angie fell and banged / bumped her head against / on the ground.

安琪跌了一跤,頭撞到地上。

⑪ **somewhere** [ ˈsʌm‚wɛr ] *adv.* 某處

## 實用詞句 Useful Expressions

🔑 與傳訊息相關的用語

ⓐ text [ tɛkst ] *vi. & vt.* 傳訊息 & *n.* 訊息;簡訊 (= a text message)

text sb　　傳訊息給某人
= send sb a text
get / receive a text　　收到訊息
Rita spends hours texting her boyfriend.
= Rita spends hours sending texts to her boyfriend.

麗塔花好幾個小時與她的男友互傳訊息。

I got a text from Kenny last night telling me to meet him here.

我昨晚收到來自肯尼的訊息,他叫我在這與他會面。

ⓑ 下列為發訊息時常用的縮寫:

BRB (= be right back)　　　　馬上回來
BTW (= by the way)　　　　順帶一提,對了
ASAP (= as soon as possible)　儘快
FYI (= for your information)　供您參考
LOL (= laugh out loud)　　　哈哈大笑
TTYL (= talk to you later)　　晚點聊

CH
1

日常生活

| | | |
|---|---|---|
| ❶ [ ɛ ] | friend [ frɛnd ] | head [ hɛd ] |
| | there [ ðɛr ] | lesson [ ˈlɛsn̩ ] |
| | check [ tʃɛk ] | somewhere [ ˈsʌmˌwɛr ] |
| | then [ ðɛn ] | |

| | | |
|---|---|---|
| ❷ [ ð ] | there [ ðɛr ] | then [ ðɛn ] |

## 朗讀短文 Read aloud the text

🔑 請特別注意 [ ɛ ]、[ ð ] 的發音。

I was sitting in the park, people watching and waiting for my friend to arrive. There was a guy in the park checking his phone while walking. First, he nearly walked into a trash can; then he tripped over a seat; then he bumped into a tree and banged his head! And, all the time, he was still using his phone. There's a lesson in there somewhere!

## 換句話說 Retell

🔑 Retell the text with the help of the words and expressions below.

be people watching, wait, guy, nearly, trash, can, trip, seat, bump, bang, somewhere

## 討論題目 Free Talk

🔑 Talk on the following topic:

◇ Have you ever walked and texted at the same time?

# Lesson 08

# Moving Out
## 搬出去

朗讀 ▶
Lesson 08

## 搭配筆記聆聽短文 Listen to the text with the help of the notes given

| | |
|---|---|
| move out | 搬出去 |
| history | 歷史 |
| miss | 想念 |
| leave | 留下 |
| after all | 終究 |

## 再次聆聽並回答問題 Listen again and answer the questions below

Questions for discussion:

1. Who is Mandy?
2. Why is Mandy moving out?
3. What will Mandy leave behind?

My sister, Mandy, is going to move out next month. She is going to university to study history. She asked if I will miss her. I said, "Of course I will miss you. Will you be leaving your big bed and big desk?" She said she would. I guess I'm not going to miss her that much after all!

曼蒂是我姊姊，她下個月將搬出去。她將到大學攻讀歷史。她問我是否會想念她。我說：「我當然會想妳。妳會留下妳的大床和大書桌嗎？」她說會。我想我不見得會那麼想念她！

## 單字片語 Vocabulary and Phrases

**1 move out** 搬出去，遷走

move out of + 地方 搬離某地

Don't forget to clear your closet when you move out.
你搬走時別忘了把衣櫃清空。

**2 university** [ ˌjunəˈvɝsətɪ ] *n.* 大學

**3 study** [ ˈstʌdɪ ] *vt. & vi.* 攻讀，學習
（三態為：study, studied [ ˈstʌdɪd ], studied）

study + 科目 + at + 學校 在某學校攻讀某科目

**4 history** [ ˈhɪst(ə)rɪ ] *n.* 歷史

**5 miss** [ mɪs ] *vt.* 想念，思念

I missed my family terribly when I studied abroad.
我出國念書時很想念我的家人。

**6 after all** 終究，還是

The fog is gone, so our flight will leave as scheduled after all.
濃霧已散，所以我們的班機還是會準時起飛。

## 實用詞句 Useful Expressions

📍 表示「我想……」的常見說法

◆ 英語的口語表達中有多種方式可表示「我想……」，通常意思相通可互相替換使用，但在某些狀況下語意會稍有不同，因此需要特別注意。

**a** I guess... 我想……；我猜……

📍 **Notes**

使用 "I guess..." 時，說話者往往有些不確定，甚至有點猜測、揣測的意涵。

**ⓑ  I suppose...　　我想……；我料想……**

📌 **Notes**

使用 "I suppose..." 時，除了可單純表示「我想……」，亦可表示說話者的推測或預測。

**ⓒ  I think...　　我想……，我認為……**

📌 **Notes**

"I think..." 在使用時，說話者若是在表達自己的主觀想法，通常可與 "I believe..." 相替換，但不宜替換為 "I guess..." 或 "I suppose..."。

　　I think Jim has been badmouthing me behind my back.
= 　I believe Jim has been badmouthing me behind my back.
　　我認為吉姆在背地裡講我的壞話。

**ⓓ  I reckon...　　我想……；我認為……**

📌 **Notes**

"I reckon..." 為較非正式的說法，在美國南方或英國較常使用。通常可將 "I reckon..." 替換為 "I think..."，皆用於表達自己的想法。

　　I reckon the home team will win the game today.
= 　I think the home team will win the game today.
　　我認為今天這場比賽主隊會獲勝。

---

**發音提示 Pronunciation**

| ❶ [ ɝ ] | university [ ˌjunəˈvɝsətɪ ] |
| --- | --- |
| ❷ [ ʊ ] | would [ wʊd ] |

## 朗讀短文 Read aloud the text

📌 請特別注意 [ ʒ ]、[ ʊ ] 的發音。

My sister, Mandy, is going to move out next month. She is going to **university** to study history. She asked if I will miss her. I said, "Of course I will miss you. Will you be leaving your big bed and big desk?" She said she **would**. I guess I'm not going to miss her that much after all!

## 換句話說 Retell

📌 Retell the text with the help of the words and expressions below.

**move out, university, study, history, miss, after all**

## 討論題目 Free Talk

📌 Talk on the following topic:

◇ Have you ever moved out of your house before?

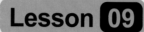

朗讀

# A Heavy Sleeper
## 睡得真沉

搭配筆記聆聽會話 **Listen to the text with the help of the notes given**

| | |
|---|---|
| answer my calls | 接我的電話 |
| You really are a heavy sleeper. | 你睡得真沉。 |
| wake up | 醒來 |
| dream | 做夢 |
| one million dollars | 一百萬美元 |

再次聆聽並回答問題 **Listen again and answer the questions below**

Questions for discussion:

**1** Did the woman answer her phone?

**2** What was the woman doing?

**3** What was the woman dreaming about?

## 實用會話 Dialogue

🇦 I was calling you all morning. Why didn't you answer my calls?

🇧 Sorry! I was sleeping.

🇦 Wow! You really are a heavy sleeper.

🇧 I know. I didn't want to wake up.

🇦 Why?

🇧 I was dreaming about winning one million dollars.

🇦 我整個早上都在打電話給你。你為什麼不接我的電話？

🇧 抱歉！我那時正在睡覺。

🇦 哇！你睡得真沉。

🇧 我知道。我不想醒來。

🇦 為什麼？

🇧 我夢到中了一百萬美元。

**❶ answer** [ ˈænsɚ ] *vt.* 回應 (電話、門鈴等)

answer the phone / door     接電話 / 應門

I rang the doorbell, but no one answered the door.
我按了門鈴，但是沒有人應門。

**❷ wake up**     醒來 (已從睡覺狀態中醒來，但不一定起身下床)
(wake 的三態為：wake, woke [ wok ], woken [ ˈwokn̩ ])
比較

get up     起床 (已從睡覺狀態中醒來，也已起身下床)

**❸ dream** [ drim ] *vi.* & *vt.* 做夢
(三態為：dream, dreamed / dreamt [ drɛmt ], dreamed / dreamt)
dream about sth     夢見某事物

I dreamed about my favorite singer last night.
我昨晚夢見了我最喜歡的歌手。

Sarah dreamed that she was getting married to John.
莎拉夢見她要跟約翰結婚了。

**❹ win** [ wɪn ] *vt.* 贏得，獲得 (獎品) & *vi.* 獲勝，贏
(三態為：win, won [ wʌn ], won)
win the prize / lottery / game     獲獎 / 中樂透 / 贏比賽

Who do you think will win?
你認為誰會贏？

**❺ million** [ ˈmɪljən ] *n.* 百萬
millions of + 複數名詞     好幾百萬的……

The earthquake left millions of people homeless.
地震造成數百萬民眾無家可歸。

## 口語新技能　New Skills

🔖 與睡覺相關的各種說法

**a** 表示「去睡覺」可以這樣說：

| | |
|---|---|
| go to sleep | 去睡覺 |
| hit the hay / sack | 去睡覺 |
| get some shuteye | 去睡一會兒 |
| take a nap | 去小睡一會兒 |

**b** 表示睡眠品質好或睡得很沉，可以這樣說：

| | |
|---|---|
| a heavy / deep sleeper | 熟睡的人 |
| go out like a light | 立即入睡 |
| pass out | 昏睡 |
| be out cold | 睡死了 |
| sleep like a log / baby | 睡得安穩 |

**c** 表示睡眠品質不好，可以這樣說：

| | |
|---|---|
| a light sleeper | 淺眠的人 |
| have trouble sleeping | 難以入睡 |
| toss and turn | 輾轉難眠 |
| do not sleep a wink | 一刻也睡不著 |

## 簡短對答　Quick Response

◈ Make quick responses to the sentences you hear.

## 討論題目　Free Talk

🔖 Talk on the following topic:

◈ Do you usually have trouble sleeping? What do you do to help you sleep?

45

# Andy's Dream
## 安迪的夢

**搭配筆記聆聽短文** **Listen to the text with the help of the notes given**

| | |
|---|---|
| wizard | (男) 巫師 |
| predict the future | 預知未來 |
| someday | 將來有一天 |
| one day | 總有一天 |
| realize his dream | 實現他的夢想 |

**再次聆聽並回答問題** **Listen again and answer the questions below**

📌 Questions for discussion:

1️⃣ Who was in Andy's dream?

2️⃣ Where did the wizard say Andy would go?

3️⃣ What does Andy want to be?

Andy has had many strange and crazy dreams. Last night, he dreamed about a wizard who could predict the future. The wizard said that Andy would catch a spaceship to Mars someday. The wizard also said that he would be the first president of Mars one day. Andy now wants to be an astronaut and realize his dream!

安迪做過許多奇異又瘋狂的夢。昨晚,他夢到了可以預知未來的巫師。那位巫師說安迪將來有一天會搭太空船到火星。巫師還說安迪總有一天會成為火星的第一位總統。安迪現在想要成為一名太空人並將夢境化為現實!

1. **strange** [ strendʒ ] *a.* 奇怪的，不尋常的
2. **crazy** [ ˋkrezɪ ] *a.* 瘋狂的
3. **wizard** [ ˋwɪzɚd ] *n.* (男) 巫師
4. **predict** [ prɪˋdɪkt ] *vt.* 預測
   Everything the fortune-teller predicted has come true.
   算命師預言的每件事都成真了。
5. **future** [ ˋfjutʃɚ ] *n.* 未來
6. **catch** [ kætʃ ] *vt.* 搭乘；趕上 (飛機、火車等交通工具)
   (三態為：catch, caught [ kɔt ], caught)
   catch the bus / train / airplane　　趕上公車 / 火車 / 飛機
7. **spaceship** [ ˋspesˌʃɪp ] *n.* 太空船
8. **Mars** [ mɑrz ] *n.* 火星
9. **president** [ ˋprɛzədənt ] *n.* 總統；董事長，總裁
   vice [ vaɪs ] president　　副總統；副董事長，副總裁
10. **astronaut** [ ˋæstrəˌnɔt ] *n.* 太空人
11. **realize** [ ˋrɪəˌlaɪz ] *vt.* 實現
    realize one's dream / ambition　　實現某人的夢想 / 抱負

實用詞句 **Useful Expressions**

1. 數量形容詞的用法

   數量形容詞無法修飾所有的名詞，而是會依照名詞可數或不可數的性質來選擇用以修飾該名詞的數量形容詞，如下列用法：

   a. | many / few | + 複數可數名詞　　許多的……
   　　 少數的……(幾乎沒有)

   The writer has written <u>many</u> books.
   這位作家已撰寫許多本書。

   The writer has written <u>few</u> books.
   這位作家幾乎沒寫幾本書。

📌 **Notes**

few 作數量形容詞表「少數的；幾乎沒有」，但 a few 則表示「一些」，其後亦接複數可數名詞。

a few + 複數可數名詞　　　一些……

a few books　　幾本書

a few days / months / years ago　　幾天 / 幾個月 / 幾年前

**b** │ much │
　　 │ little │ ＋ 不可數名詞　　許多的……

　　　　　　　　　　　　　　少量的……（幾乎沒有）

We have much work to do today.

我們今天有許多工作要做。

We have little work to do today.

我們今天的工作量很少。

📌 **Notes**

同 few，little 作數量形容詞時均表「少數 / 量的；幾乎沒有」，但 a little 則表示「一些」，其後亦接不可數名詞。

a little + 不可數名詞　　　一些……

a little sugar / salt　　一些糖 / 鹽

a little time　　一些時間

**c** 以下數量形容詞則能與可數或不可數名詞並用：

some　　　一些

lots of　　許多

a lot of　　許多

all　　　全部

Tristan always gives me a lot of useful advice.

崔斯坦總是給予我許多有用的建議。

Ross has traveled to lots of places around the world.

羅斯已到過世界上許多地方旅遊。

**2** 重要時間副詞的說法

**ⓐ** someday　　將來有一天（與未來式並用）

You will find your Prince Charming someday.
將來有一天，你會遇見理想的對象。

**ⓑ** one day　　過去某一天；將來有一天

◆ 表「過去某一天」時，類似 the other day，與過去式並用：
I ran into Max at the movie theater one day.
I ran into Max at the movie theater the other day.
有一天我在電影院碰見了麥克斯。

◆ 表「將來有一天」時，等於 someday，與未來式並用：
Blair will become a great dancer one day.
= Blair will become a great dancer someday.
總有一天，布萊兒會成為一位很棒的舞者。

**ⓒ** the other day　　前些時候（與過去式並用）

I went to the flower market the other day.
前陣子我去了花市。

**ⓓ** some other day　　改天（與未來式並用）

I have to work overtime tonight; I'll join you for dinner some other day.
我今天得加班，我改天再和你們一起吃晚餐。

發音提示　**Pronunciation**

| **1** [ ɔ ] | also [ ˋɔlso ] | astronaut [ ˋæstrəˌnɔt ] |
|---|---|---|

| **2** [ ʃ ] | future [ ˋfjutʃɚ ] | first [ fɝst ] |
|---|---|---|

## 朗讀短文 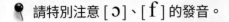 Read aloud the text

🔖 請特別注意 [ɔ]、[f] 的發音。

Andy has had many strange and crazy dreams. Last night, he dreamed about a wizard who could predict the future. The wizard said that Andy would catch a spaceship to Mars someday. The wizard also said that he would be the first president of Mars one day. Andy now wants to be an astronaut and realize his dream!

## 換句話說 Retell

🔖 Retell the text with the help of the words and expressions below.

strange, crazy, wizard, predict, future, catch, spaceship, Mars, president, astronaut, realize

## 討論題目 Free Talk

🔖 Talk on the following topic:

◆ Would you like to travel to space someday?

Lesson 11

# Look Before You Leap
## 謀定而後動

**搭配筆記聆聽短文** **Listen to the text with the help of the notes given**

| | |
|---|---|
| apartment | 公寓 |
| consider | 考慮 |
| conveniently | 方便地 |
| the catch is... | 問題是…… |
| affordable | 可負擔的 |
| cost an arm and a leg | 貴得要命 |

**再次聆聽並回答問題** **Listen again and answer the questions below**

Questions for discussion:

1 What is Jane looking for?

2 What are the apartments close to?

3 What is the problem with both apartments?

My friend, Jane, is looking for a new apartment. There are two apartments that she is considering. Both of them are conveniently located; one is close to a subway station, and the other is close to a park. However, the catch is that neither of the two apartments is affordable. Apparently, the rent for either one would cost an arm and a leg. She should think about the decision carefully and look before she leaps.

　　我的朋友珍正在找新房子。有兩間公寓是她正在考慮的。這兩間公寓的地點都很方便；一間是在地鐵站附近，另一間是在公園附近。不過，問題是，這兩間公寓的租金都不是她負擔得起的。顯然，不管是哪間公寓，租金都貴得嚇死人。她應該要審慎考慮再做決定，並且三思而後行！

**❶ look for...**　　尋找……

Johnny emptied his backpack to look for his keys.
強尼為了找他的鑰匙，把背包裡的東西都倒出來。

**❷ apartment** [ ə`pɑrtmənt ] *n.* 公寓

**❸ consider** [ kən`sɪdɚ ] *vi.* & *vt.* 考慮；衡量；認為；把……視為
consider + V-ing　　考慮……（consider 之後接動名詞作受詞）
consider sth　　考慮某事
= take sth into consideration [ kən,sɪdə`reʃən ]
= take sth into account [ ə`kaʊnt ]

Peter is considering taking a trip to Europe.
彼得正考慮到歐洲旅行。

**❹ conveniently** [ kən`vinjəntlɪ ] *adv.* 方便地；便利地
inconveniently [ ,ɪnkən`vinjəntlɪ ] *adv.* 不方便地；帶來麻煩地

**❺ locate** [ lo`ket / `loket ] *vt.* 使位於 (= situate [ `sɪtʃʊ,et ])
be located in / on / at...　　位於……
= lie in / on / at...

Our school is located in the suburbs.
我們的學校位於近郊。

**❻ close to sth**　　靠近某物 (= near sth)

Jill lives close to the subway station.
吉兒住在地鐵站附近。

**❼ catch** [ kætʃ ] *n.* 隱患；圈套；詭計；陷阱

But the catch is that when brought in from the wild, pandas lose their natural desire to reproduce.
但難題是，將熊貓從野外帶回飼養後，牠們失去了繁殖的欲望。

＊ reproduce [ ,riprə`djus ] *vi.* & *vt.* 繁殖

Ⓐ I'm going to give you $10,000.
Ⓑ No way! There must be a catch somewhere.

Ⓐ 我要給你一萬美元。
Ⓑ 不會吧！這其中一定有鬼。

**8 apparently** [ ə`pærəntlɪ ] *adv.*
顯然；表面上；似乎
Apparently / Obviously, 主詞 + 動詞　　很明顯地，……
= It is apparent / obvious + that 子句

Apparently / Obviously, John didn't tell the truth.
= It was apparent / obvious that John didn't tell the truth.
顯然約翰並未說實話。

**9 rent** [ rɛnt ] *n.* 房租；租金 & *vt.* 租用；出租
I don't own the house—I rent it.
我並不擁有這棟房子 —— 我是用租的。

**10 leap** [ lip ] *vi.* & *vt.* & *n.* 跳
(三態為：leap, leaped / leapt [ lɛpt ], leaped / leapt)
Look before you leap.　　三思而後行。(諺語)

You'd better look before you leap. I don't think you really
understand the situation.
你最好三思而後行。我覺得你還沒真的了解狀況。

---

**實用詞句　Useful Expressions**

**1** both、neither、either 作代名詞的用法

**a** both of + 數量是兩個的名詞或代名詞　　兩者都……
I have read both of these novels.
我已經讀了這兩本小說。

🔑 **Notes**

代名詞 both 形成的詞組在句中可作主詞或受詞，作主詞時，後面接複數動
詞。

**b** neither of + 數量是兩個的名詞或代名詞　　兩者都不……
Neither of the two books is / are suitable for children to read.
這兩本書都不適合給小孩子讀。

**☉** either of + 數量是兩個的名詞或代名詞　　兩者其一……

Either of these shirts would be suitable for the interview.

這兩件襯衫當中的任何一件都適合穿去面試。

**2** 表示很昂貴的說法

表示「昂貴的」除了用 very expensive 之外，亦有下列說法：

cost an arm and a leg　　貴得要命

cost a (small) fortune　　花一大筆錢

be steep　　價格貴得離譜

＊ steep [ stip ] *a.* 價格過高的

be pricey　　很貴

＊ pricey [ `praɪsɪ ] *a.* 價格高的

be daylight robbery　　光天化日之下搶錢 (喻價格貴得離譜)

＊ robbery [ `rɑbərɪ ] *n.* 搶劫

I'd love to buy that dress, but it costs an arm and a leg.

= I'd love to buy that dress, but it costs a (small) fortune.

= I'd love to buy that dress, but the price is too steep.

= I'd love to buy that dress, but it is too pricey.

我很想買那件洋裝，但是它貴得要命。

That dress costs $100! That's practically daylight robbery!

那件洋裝要價一百美元！簡直是光天化日之下搶錢！

## 發音提示　Pronunciation

| ❶ [ i ] | conveniently [ kənˈvinjəntlɪ ] | either [ ˈiðɚ ] |
|---|---|---|
| | neither [ ˈniðɚ ] | leap [ lip ] |

| ❷ [ ɚ ] | consider [ kənˈsɪdɚ ] | neither [ ˈniðɚ ] |
|---|---|---|
| | other [ ˈʌðɚ ] | either [ ˈiðɚ ] |
| | however [ hauˈɛvɚ ] | |

## 朗讀短文　Read aloud the text

🎤 請特別注意 [ i ]、[ ɚ ] 的發音。

My friend, Jane, is looking for a new apartment. There are two apartments that she is considering. Both of them are conveniently located; one is close to a subway station, and the other is close to a park. However, the catch is that neither of the two apartments is affordable. Apparently, the rent for either one would cost an arm and a leg. She should think about the decision carefully and look before she leaps.

## 換句話說　Retell

🎤 Retell the text with the help of the words and expressions below.

look for, apartment, consider, conveniently, locate, close to, catch, apparently, rent, leap

## 討論題目　Free Talk

🎤 Talk on the following topic:

◇ What are the factors you would consider when renting an apartment?

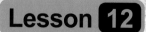

# Easier Said Than Done
## 說比做容易

**搭配筆記聆聽會話** **Listen to the text with the help of the notes given**

| box | 箱子 |
|---|---|
| easily | 輕鬆地 |
| lift | 扛起 |
| struggle | 掙扎 |
| unpack | 打開箱子取出東西 |

**再次聆聽並回答問題** **Listen again and answer the questions below**

📍 Questions for discussion:

**1** Is the man stronger than the woman?

**2** Can the man lift the box by himself?

**3** What does the woman suggest?

## 實用會話 Dialogue

Ⓐ This box is heavier than the others.

Ⓑ I can easily lift that! I'm stronger than you.

Ⓐ You're struggling with it, aren't you?

Ⓑ Err... I guess it was easier said than done!

Ⓐ Let's unpack it. Two smaller boxes will be lighter.

Ⓐ 這箱子比其他箱子都還要重。

Ⓑ 我可以輕鬆扛那個箱子！我比你壯。

Ⓐ 你扛得很吃力，對不對？

Ⓑ 哦⋯⋯。我想這真是說比做容易！

Ⓐ 咱們來拿出裡面的東西。兩個小箱子會比較輕。

❶ **heavy** [ ˈhɛvɪ ] *a.* 重的，沉重的

❷ **easily** [ ˈizɪlɪ ] *adv.* 容易地；輕易地
easy [ ˈizɪ ] *a.* 容易的

Howard could not make friends easily.
霍華無法輕易地交到朋友。

❸ **lift** [ lɪft ] *vt.* 扛起，舉起

John helped me lift the furniture up.
約翰幫我把傢俱扛起來。

❹ **struggle** [ ˈstrʌgl̩ ] *vi.* 掙扎；努力
struggle with sth　　艱難地處理……；對抗……
struggle to V　　努力……

The girl struggled with her poor health for many years.
這位女孩長年飽受病痛之苦。

The family struggled to survive on such a low income.
這個家庭努力靠微薄的收入過活。

❺ **It is easier said than done.**
說比做容易／說起來容易做起來難。（諺語）

 Notes

本句原為：

It is easier to be said than to be done.
句中 said 與 done 分別為動詞 say（說）與 do（做）的過去分詞，其前加上 be 動詞即形成被動語態。習慣上會將兩個過去分詞之前的 to be 予以省略，形成我們常見的諺語。

Ⓐ Why don't you ask your manager for a raise?
Ⓑ It's easier said than done.
Ⓐ 你為什麼不向經理請求加薪？
Ⓑ 說起來容易做起來難。

**6 unpack** [ ʌnˋpæk ] *vt. & vi.* 打開箱子取出東西
**pack** [ pæk ] *vt. & vi.* 打包

We unpacked our luggage as soon as we went home.
我們一回到家就打開行李箱拿出東西。

Remember to pack light.
記得行李帶輕便一點。

**7 light** [ laɪt ] *a.* 輕的 & *adv.* 輕便地
**pack / travel light**　　輕便旅行

## 口語新技能　New Skills

🔑 介紹反問句的用法

◆ 反問句又稱附加問句，反問句的原則即：敘述句若為肯定時，須接否定反問句；敘述句若為否定時，則須接肯定反問句。下列為常見的反問句句型：

**a** 句中有 be 動詞時，反問句則亦使用 be 動詞。

肯定句：Mike was late again, wasn't he?
　　　　麥克又遲到了，對不對？

否定句：You aren't afraid of heights, are you?
　　　　你沒有懼高症，對不對？

**b** 句中有助動詞時，反問句則亦使用助動詞。

肯定句：You have been to the US before, haven't you?
　　　　你有去過美國，對不對？

否定句：They can't catch the train in time, can they?
　　　　他們無法及時趕上火車，對不對？

**c** 句中有一般動詞時，反問句則使用 do、does、did。

肯定句：Louis speaks French, doesn't he?
　　　　路易會說法語，對不對？

否定句：You didn't tell anybody, did you?
　　　　你沒告訴任何人，對不對？

◆ Make quick responses to the sentences you hear.

討論題目 **Free Talk**

🔑 Talk on the following topic:

◆ Do you usually ask for help when you're struggling with things?

# Lesson 13

# Dreams of Flying
## 夢見搭飛機

## 搭配筆記聆聽短文　Listen to the text with the help of the notes given

| | |
|---|---|
| nightmare | 惡夢 |
| be scared of flying | 害怕搭飛機 |
| total | 完全的 |
| be used to flying | 習慣搭飛機 |
| terrify | 使害怕 |

## 再次聆聽並回答問題　Listen again and answer the questions below

Questions for discussion:

**1** What did the speaker dream about last night?

**2** What is the speaker scared of?

**3** Why does the speaker have to travel a lot?

短文聽讀 **Text**

Last night, I had a dream about flying. Actually, it was more of a nightmare, because I am scared of flying. In the dream, I was the only one on board the plane, and it was in total darkness. You would think I would be used to flying by now, as I have to travel a lot for business, but it still terrifies me!

昨晚，我做了有關搭飛機的夢。事實上，不如說這是場惡夢，因為我很怕搭飛機。在夢裡，我是唯一在飛機上的人，而且一片漆黑。因為我很常到國外出差，你可能會覺得我現在習慣搭飛機了，但這對我來說還是很可怕！

## 單字片語 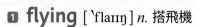 Vocabulary and Phrases

**1** **flying** [ 'flaɪɪŋ ] *n.* 搭飛機

**2** **actually** [ 'æktʃuəlɪ ] *adv.* 其實，事實上

**3** **nightmare** [ 'naɪt,mɛr ] *n.* 惡夢

> 🔑 **Notes**
>
> 做惡夢要用動詞 have，而非 dream。
> have a nightmare　　做惡夢

**4** **scared** [ skɛrd ] *a.* 感到害怕的
　　be scared of + N/V-ing　　害怕……
= be afraid of + N/V-ing

　　Benson is scared / afraid of talking to that serious-looking teacher.
　　班森很害怕跟那位表情嚴肅的老師講話。

**5** **plane** [ plen ] *n.* 飛機
= airplane [ 'ɛr,plen ]

**6** **total** [ 'totl̩ ] *a.* 完全的，徹底的

**7** **darkness** [ 'dɑrknɪs ] *n.* 黑暗
　　in darkness　　黑暗中
　　比較
　　dark [ dɑrk ] *n.* 暗處；天黑
　　after dark　　天黑後

**8** **business** [ 'bɪznəs ] *n.* 商務，公事；商業；公司
　　on / for business　　為了公事；出差
　　比較
　　for pleasure　　為了消遣；旅遊

**9** **terrify** [ 'tɛrə,faɪ ] *vt.* 使害怕，使恐懼
　　（三態為：terrify, terrified [ 'tɛrə,faɪd ], terrified）

　　The thriller terrified Amber.
　　這部驚悚片把安柏嚇壞了。

　　＊ thriller [ 'θrɪlɚ ] *n.* 驚悚片；驚悚小說

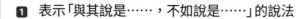

實用詞句 **Useful Expressions**

**❶** 表示「與其說是……，不如說是……」的說法

be more of a(n) + 名詞 + than a(n) + 名詞

= be not so much a(n) + 名詞 + as a(n) + 名詞
與其說是……，不如說是……

To us, Mr. Parkins is more of a friend than a teacher.

= To us, Mr. Parkins is not so much a teacher as a friend.
對我們來說，與其說帕金斯先生是位老師，不如說他是位朋友。

**❷** 表示「習慣」的說法

be used to + N/V-ing　　已習慣於……

= be accustomed to + N/V-ing
＊以上 used 及 accustomed 均為過去分詞作形容詞用，表「習慣的」。
Pauline is used / accustomed to living alone.
寶琳已習慣獨自一人生活。

---

 **Notes**

上述用法與下列三個片語有所不同，使用時應多加留意：

**ⓐ** be used to V　　被用來……
This pair of garden shears is used to trim the hedge.
這把園藝剪刀是用來修剪樹籬的。

**ⓑ** used to V　　過去常常……
Claire used to walk her dog in the afternoon.
克萊兒過去常在午後遛狗。

**ⓒ** get used to + N/V-ing　　逐漸習慣……
= get accustomed to + N/V-ing
Pauline got used / accustomed to living alone.
寶琳逐漸習慣獨自一人生活。

## 發音提示 Pronunciation

| ❶ [ ɔ ] | because [ bɪˋkɔz ] | for [ fɔr ] |
|---|---|---|
| ❷ [ tʃ ] | actually [ ˋæktʃʊəlɪ ] | |

## 朗讀短文 Read aloud the text

🔖 請特別注意 [ ɔ ]、[ tʃ ] 的發音。

Last night, I had a dream about flying. Actually, it was more of a nightmare, because I am scared of flying. In the dream, I was the only one on board the plane, and it was in total darkness. You would think I would be used to flying by now, as I have to travel a lot for business, but it still terrifies me!

## 換句話說 Retell

🔖 Retell the text with the help of the words and expressions below.

flying, actually, nightmare, scared, plane, total, darkness, business, terrify

## 討論題目 Free Talk

🔖 Talk on the following topic:

◆ Describe one of your fears. What are you scared of?

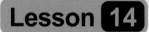

# A Picky Eater
## 挑食的人

| 搭配筆記聆聽短文 | **Listen to the text with the help of the notes given** |
| --- | --- |

| | |
| --- | --- |
| picky | 挑剔的 |
| habit | 習慣 |
| healthy | 健康的 |
| a positive effect | 良好的影響 |
| deep down | 在內心深處 |

| 再次聆聽並回答問題 | **Listen again and answer the questions below** |
| --- | --- |

🎙 Questions for discussion:

1 What does Jordan dislike?

2 Why is Jordan often sick or tired?

3 Does Jordan agree with his mother?

Jordan is a picky eater. He likes neither fruit nor vegetables. Because of his bad eating habits, he is often either sick or tired. His mother told him that he should make himself eat healthy foods. She said fruit and vegetables would have a positive effect on his health when he gets older. Deep down, he knows his mother is right.

喬丹很挑食。他不喜歡吃水果，也不愛吃蔬菜。因為不好的飲食習慣，他經常生病，不然就是感到疲憊。他媽媽告訴他應該要讓自己吃健康的食物。她說當喬丹年紀漸長時，蔬果會為他的健康帶來良好的影響。喬丹內心深處知道媽媽說的是對的。

**❶ a picky eater**　挑食者
picky [ `pɪkɪ ] *a.* 挑剔的
eater [ `itɚ ] *n.* 吃……的人

**❷ fruit** [ frut ] *n.* 水果
fresh fruit　　新鮮水果
fruit and vegetables　　蔬果

**❸ vegetable** [ `vɛdʒ(ə)təbl̩ ] *n.* 蔬菜

**❹ eating habit**　飲食習慣
habit [ `hæbɪt ] *n.* 習慣

**❺ healthy** [ `hɛlθɪ ] *a.* 健康的

**❻ positive** [ `pɑzətɪv ] *a.* 有幫助的，好的；正面的，積極的
negative [ `nɛgətɪv ] *a.* 負面的，消極的
a positive / negative effect　　良好 / 負面的影響

**❼ effect** [ ɪ`fɛkt ] *n.* 影響；結果

**❽ health** [ hɛlθ ] *n.* 健康 (狀況)

**❾ deep down**　在內心深處
Deep down, Andy was thankful to those who had once helped him.
在心底深處，安迪感激那些曾經幫助過他的人。

🖋 介紹常見的使役動詞

◆ 常見的使役動詞有 make (叫)、have (叫) 及 let (讓)，使役動詞之後使用原形動詞作受詞補語，使用方法如下：

ⓐ 使役動詞 make、have 表「叫……」：

| make |
| have | ＋受詞＋原形動詞　　叫……

Ross made his daughter cook dinner.
　　　　　受詞　　受詞補語
羅斯叫他女兒煮晚餐。

The boss had Jill organize a meeting.
　　　　　　　受詞　受詞補語
老闆叫吉兒籌備一場會議。

 **Notes**

get 亦可表「叫……」，惟其後只能接不定詞片語：
**get sb to V**　　叫某人……
I got Jessie to buy me a cup of coffee.
　　　受詞　　　　受詞補語
我叫潔西去幫我買一杯咖啡。

**b** 使役動詞 have 若為「把……」之意，其後須接過去分詞作受詞補語：
**have sb/sth + 過去分詞**　　把某人 / 某物 (請某人) 處置
Eric had his bed sheets washed.
　　　　　　　受詞　　　受詞補語
艾瑞克把床單拿去送洗。
Bella just had her hair cut.
　　　　　　　　受詞　　受詞補語
貝拉才剛剪過頭髮。

**c** 使役動詞 let 表「讓……」：
**let + 受詞 + 原形動詞**　　讓……
My parents let me stay at my friend's place.
　　　　　　　　受詞　　　　受詞補語
我父母讓我待在朋友家。

 **Notes**

使役動詞 let 之後亦可接作副詞用的介詞，以作受詞補語：
**let + 受詞 + 作副詞用的介詞（如 in、out、down 等）**　　讓……
The host let the guests in.
　　　　　　　　受詞　　受詞補語
主人讓賓客進來。

## 朗讀短文　Read aloud the text

🔖 請特別注意 [ u ]、[ θ ] 的發音。

Jordan is a picky eater. He likes neither fruit nor vegetables. Because of his bad eating habits, he is often either sick or tired. His mother told him that he should make himself eat healthy foods. She said fruit and vegetables would have a positive effect on his health when he gets older. Deep down, he knows his mother is right.

## 換句話說　Retell

🔖 Retell the text with the help of the words and expressions below.

a picky eater, fruit, vegetable, eating habit, healthy, positive, effect, health, deep down

## 討論題目　Free Talk

🔖 Talk on the following topic:

◈ Are you a picky eater? What food or vegetable do you dislike?

# Lesson 15

# As Pale As a Ghost
## 臉色蒼白

**搭配筆記聆聽會話** **Listen to the text with the help of the notes given**

| | |
|---|---|
| pale | (臉色) 蒼白的 |
| feel as sick as a dog | 病得不輕 |
| a pounding headache | 劇烈的頭痛 |
| go funny | 變得奇怪 |
| blind | 看不到的，盲的 |

**再次聆聽並回答問題** **Listen again and answer the questions below**

🔑 Questions for discussion:

1️⃣ Why is the man's face as pale as a ghost?

2️⃣ Can the man see?

3️⃣ Where is the woman taking the man?

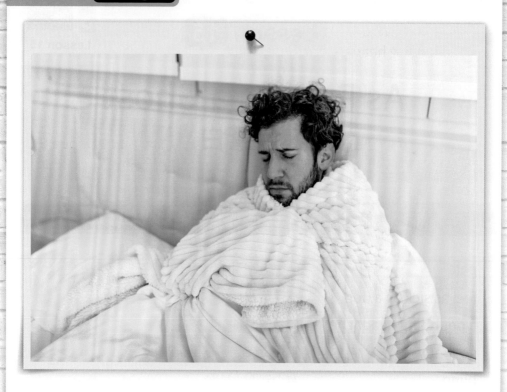

🅐 Are you OK? You look as pale as a ghost.

🅑 I feel as sick as a dog.

🅐 What's wrong?

🅑 I've got a pounding headache and my eyes have gone funny. I'm as blind as a bat!

🅐 Let me take you to the doctor's. You'll be as right as rain in no time.

🅐 你還好嗎？你臉色真蒼白。

🅑 我感覺病得很嚴重。

🅐 怎麼了？

🅑 我頭痛得很劇烈，而且我的眼睛感覺怪怪的。我看不清楚了！

🅐 我帶你去看醫生。你很快就會好起來的。

**❶ pound** [ paʊnd ] *vi.* (頭) 劇烈疼痛；(心臟) 劇烈跳動 & *vt.* 猛擊

a pounding headache　　劇烈的頭痛

I can't take this pounding headache anymore.
我受不了這劇烈的頭痛了。

Sarah's heart pounded as she ran away from the man.
莎拉跑離那位男子時心跳得很劇烈。

The angry man pounded his fist on the table.
怒氣衝天的男子用拳頭往桌上猛力一敲。

**❷ headache** [ ˈhɛdˌek ] *n.* 頭痛

ache [ ek ] *n.* & *vi.* 疼痛

toothache [ ˈtuθˌek ] *n.* 牙痛

stomachache [ ˈstʌməkˌek ] *n.* 胃痛；腹痛

backache [ ˈbækˌek ] *n.* 背痛

Cindy called in sick this morning because she had a headache.
辛蒂今早因為頭痛請病假。

**❸ funny** [ ˈfʌnɪ ] *a.* 不舒服的；古怪的，滑稽的

go funny　　變得奇怪；出問題

feel funny　　感覺不舒服

Using smartphones all the time can make your eyes go funny.
無時無刻都在使用智慧型手機會讓你的眼睛很不舒服。

My cell phone went funny after I accidentally dropped it on the floor.
我手機不小心掉到地板上後就出了點問題。

I feel funny after eating at that restaurant.
我去那間餐廳用餐後就感到不太舒服。

**❹ in no time**　　很快地

You can assign this job to Mike. I'm sure he will finish it in no time.
你可以把這份工作分配給麥克。我相信他很快就會完成。

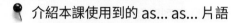

介紹本課使用到的 as... as... 片語

**ⓐ** look / be as pale as a ghost　　臉色蒼白

pale [ pel ] *a.* 蒼白的

ghost [ ɡost ] *n.* 鬼

I think there's something wrong with John. He's as pale as a ghost.

我覺得約翰有點不對勁。他臉色很蒼白。

**ⓑ** feel / be as sick as a dog　　病得不輕；感覺不舒服

sick [ sɪk ] *a.* 生病的；噁心的

比較

be as sick as a parrot　　十分失望

parrot [ ˋpærət ] *n.* 鸚鵡

Simon was as sick as a dog, so I took him to the hospital.

賽門病得不輕，所以我送他去醫院了。

I was as sick as a parrot when I didn't win the game.

我沒在比賽勝出時，我失望透頂了。

**ⓒ** be as blind as a bat　　視力不佳，看不清楚

blind [ blaɪnd ] *a.* 盲的；盲目的

bat [ bæt ] *n.* 蝙蝠

Jeremy would be as blind as a bat without his glasses.

傑瑞米沒有眼鏡就看不清楚了。

**ⓓ** be / feel as right as rain　　十分健康，完全康復

After a few days' rest, I feel as right as rain.

休息幾天之後，我感到十分健康。

## 簡短對答　Quick Response

◆ Make quick responses to the sentences you hear.

## 討論題目　Free Talk

🎤 Talk on the following topic:

◆ When was the last time you went to see a doctor? What happened?

# As Good As New
## 如新的一樣

### 搭配筆記聆聽短文 | Listen to the text with the help of the notes given

| graduate | 畢業 |
| --- | --- |
| be as dead as a doornail | 顯然地壞掉了 |
| panic | 驚恐，慌張 |
| watchmaker | 鐘錶匠 |
| fix | 修理 |

### 再次聆聽並回答問題 | Listen again and answer the questions below

Questions for discussion:

1. Who gave the speaker the gold watch?
2. Why was the battery in the watch damaged?
3. Did the watchmaker fix the watch?

My dad gave me an expensive gold watch when I graduated. Two days later, I dropped it in the bath. The battery was as dead as a doornail. I was panicking when I took it to the watch shop, but the watchmaker said it wasn't as bad as all that. The next day, he called and said the watch was fixed. It was as good as new!

　　我畢業時，老爸給我一隻昂貴的金錶。兩天後，我把它掉在浴缸裡了。電池很顯然地壞掉了。我把它拿去鐘錶行時，我很驚慌失措，不過鐘錶匠說情況並沒有那麼糟。隔天，他打電話來並說手錶修好了。它就如新的一樣！

**❶ gold** [ gold ] *a.* 金的 & *n.* 黃金，金子
**golden** [ ˋgoldṇ ] *a.* 金色的；美好的

Grandpa had a gold tooth implanted in his mouth.
爺爺在嘴裡植入一顆金牙。

The princess has beautiful golden hair.
公主有一頭美麗的金髮。

**❷ watch** [ watʃ ] *n.* 手錶

**❸ graduate** [ ˋgrædʒʊˏet ] *vi.* 畢業 & [ ˋgrædʒʊɪt ] *n.* 畢業生
**graduate from...**　　從……畢業

Tracy graduated from our country's top university.
崔西從我們國內最好的大學畢業。

I am a recent graduate.
我剛從大學畢業。

**❹ battery** [ ˋbætərɪ ] *n.* 電池

The flashlight doesn't work because the battery is dead.
手電筒無法用因為電池沒電了。

**❺ be as dead as a doornail**　　顯然地壞掉了／死掉了

From the looks of it, the animal is as dead as a doornail.
從外表看起來，這動物很顯然地死掉了。

**❻ panic** [ ˋpænɪk ] *vi.* & *n.* 驚恐
（三態為：panic, panicked [ ˋpænɪkt ], panicked，現在分詞為 panicking
[ ˋpænɪkɪŋ ]）

Vera panicked at the sight of the snake.
薇拉一看到蛇就嚇得驚慌失措。

**❼ watchmaker** [ ˋwatʃˏmekɚ ] *n.* 鐘錶匠

**❽ be not as bad as all that**　　沒有想像中糟

I don't think the weather will be as bad as all that.
我覺得天氣不會如想像中糟。

Ⓐ Everything is ruined!

Ⓑ Come on. It can't be as bad as all that.

Ⓐ 全都毀了！

Ⓑ 少來了。情況不可能那麼糟。

**9** **fix** [ fɪks ] *vt.* 修理

= repair [ rɪ`pɛr ]

Can you call the repairman to fix the sink?

你可以打給維修人員來修理水槽嗎？

## 實用詞句　Useful Expressions

🔑 介紹原級比較句構

◆ 本課旨在介紹原級比較句構。本課課文中，as dead as a doornail (顯
然已經壞掉了)、as good as new (如新的一樣) 及 as bad as all that
(沒有那麼糟) 即使用原級比較句構。此句構為：

as... as...　　和……一樣地……

Sam is as intelligent as Dahlia.

山姆跟黛莉雅一樣聰明。

Aaron is as careless as Yvonne (is).

艾倫和伊芳一樣冒失。

Helen can paint as well as a professional artist (can).

海倫畫得和專業畫家一樣好。

Tim practices as often as the team captain (does).

提姆和隊長一樣經常練習。

◆ 以下列舉一些與 as... as... 相關的常用用語：

ⓐ as... as one can　　盡可能地……

= as... as possible

　Please be as quiet as you can when you are in the library.

= Please be as quiet as possible when you are in the library.

在圖書館時，請盡可能地保持安靜。

**b** as... as any 　　與任何一樣⋯⋯

This is as good a plan as any.

這計畫和任何計畫一樣好。

（意即該計畫不差，但也非最好的。）

**c** as... as ever 　　與往常一樣⋯⋯

Long time no see. You look as young as ever!

好久不見。你看起來跟以前一樣年輕！

**d** as many / much as... 　　多達⋯⋯

There were as many as two thousand people at the protest.

抗議集會有多達兩千人。

John has as much as two hundred dollars with him.

約翰身上有多達兩百美元。

**e** as long as... 　　長達⋯⋯；只要⋯⋯

Willy has been learning English for as long as 20 years.

威利學英文已有二十年之久。

I'll go anywhere as long as there's free food and drink.

只要有免費的食物和飲料，我去哪都可以。

---

發音提示 **Pronunciation**

| ❶ [ æ ] | dad [ dæd ] | as [ æz ] |
| | an [ æn ] | panic [ ˋpænɪk ] |
| | graduate [ ˋgrædʒʊˌet ] | bad [ bæd ] |
| | bath [ bæθ ] | that [ ðæt ] |
| | battery [ ˋbætərɪ ] | and [ ænd ] |

| ❷ [ tʃ ] | watch [ watʃ ] | watchmaker [ ˋwatʃˌmekɚ ] |

## 朗讀短文　Read aloud the text

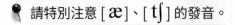

🔍 請特別注意 [ æ ]、[ tʃ ] 的發音。

My dad gave me an expensive gold watch when I graduated. Two days later, I dropped it in the bath. The battery was as dead as a doornail. I was panicking when I took it to the watch shop, but the watchmaker said it wasn't as bad as all that. The next day, he called and said the watch was fixed. It was as good as new!

## 換句話說　Retell

🔍 Retell the text with the help of the words and expressions below.

gold, watch, graduate, battery, be as dead as a doornail, panic, watchmaker, be not as bad as all that, fix

## 討論題目　Free Talk

🔍 Talk on the following topic:

◆ Have you ever broken something that was valuable to you?

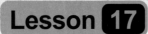

## Lesson 17

# Moving into a New House
## 搬進新家

**搭配筆記聆聽短文** **Listen to the text with the help of the notes given**

| twice | 兩倍 |
|-------|------|
| current | 目前的 |
| unfortunately | 可惜地，不幸地 |
| double | 兩倍 |
| housemate | 室友 |

**再次聆聽並回答問題** **Listen again and answer the questions below**

📌 Questions for discussion:

1️⃣ When will the speaker move into the new house?

2️⃣ Is the new house bigger than the old one?

3️⃣ Is the rent for the new house cheaper than the old one?

I will move into my new house next week! It is more than three times the size of my old house. It has twice the number of bedrooms and twice as many bathrooms. Its kitchen is four times as big as my current kitchen. Unfortunately, the rent is double the amount I am paying now. Maybe I need to find a housemate to share the cost.

　　我下週要搬進新家！我的新家大小比我舊家大三倍不止。它的臥房與浴室的間數是舊家的兩倍。廚房大小是我現在廚房的四倍。可惜的是，房租是我現在支付的兩倍。或許我應該要找個室友來分攤費用。

**❶ move into...** 搬進……

move in 搬入

move out 搬出

I'll move into the dorm next week.
我下週會搬進宿舍。

Our new roommate moved in yesterday.
我們新的室友昨天搬進來了。

My sister moved out to live with her boyfriend.
我姊姊搬出去跟她男友住了。

**❷ bedroom** [ ˋbɛd͵rum ] *n.* 臥室

**❸ bathroom** [ ˋbæθ͵rum ] *n.* 浴室

**❹ current** [ ˋkɝənt ] *a.* 目前的，當前的

currently [ ˋkɝəntlɪ ] *adv.* 目前，當前

Are you satisfied with your current salary?
你滿意目前的薪水嗎？

This product is currently selling in Japan only.
這項產品目前只在日本販賣。

**❺ rent** [ rɛnt ] *n.* 房租；租金 & *vt.* & *vi.* 租用，租借

**❻ double** [ ˋdʌbḷ ] *a.* 雙倍的；雙人的 & *vt.* & *vi.* (使) 加倍

Gary's salary doubled after he got promoted.
蓋瑞升職後薪水就加倍了。

**❼ amount** [ əˋmaʊnt ] *n.* 量

a large / small amount of + 不可數名詞　　大量 / 少量的……

a large / small number of + 複數可數名詞　　大量 / 少量的……

I deposited a large amount of money into my account.
我將很多錢存進戶頭。

A small number of students protested against the new policy.
有少數學生抗議新的政策。

**8 housemate** [ ˈhaʊsˌmet ] *n.* (分租同一棟房子的) 室友
flatmate [ ˈflætˌmet ] *n.* 室友 (英式用法)
roommate [ ˈrumˌmet ] *n.* 室友 (美式用法)

**9 share** [ ʃɛr ] *vt. & vi.* 分攤;分享
share sth with sb      與某人分擔 / 分享某物

I share the bills with my roommates.
我與我的室友們分攤水電費。

**10 cost** [ kɔst ] *n.* 費用 & *vt.* 花費 (三態同形)
at the cost of...      以……為代價
sth cost sb + 錢      某物花某人若干錢

I bought this car at the cost of three months' salary.
我花了三個月的薪水買了這輛車。

The new car cost me a lot of money.
= The new car cost me a fortune.
= The new car cost me an arm and a leg.
新車花了我很多錢。

**實用詞句** **Useful Expressions**

🖋 介紹用倍數詞句構表「……的幾倍」

**a** 下列字詞均為倍數詞:

| | |
|---|---|
| one-fifth | 五分之一 |
| one-third | 三分之一 |
| half | 一半;二分之一 |
| two-thirds | 三分之二 |
| three-fourths / three-quarters | 四分之三 |
| two times / twice | 兩倍 |
| three times | 三倍 |
| four times | 四倍 |
| ten times | 十倍 |

**b** 常用的倍數詞句構有下列四種：

1) more than + 倍數詞 + the / 所有格 + 名詞
   是……的幾倍還不止
   John is more than twice my size.
   約翰體型比我大兩倍還不止。

2) 倍數詞 + the / 指示形容詞 / 所有格 + 名詞　　是……的幾倍
   The old man is three times my age.
   那位老先生的年齡是我的三倍。

3) 倍數詞 + as... as...　　是……的幾倍
   I'm only half as old as you.
   = I'm only half your age.
   我的年齡只有你的一半。

4) more than + 倍數詞 + as... as...　　是……的幾倍還不止
   This rock weighs more than twice as much as that one.
   = This rock is more than twice the weight of that one.
   這塊大石重量是那塊的兩倍還不止。

## 發音提示　Pronunciation

| ❶ [ u ] | move [ muv ] | bedroom [ ˋbɛd‚rum ] |
|---|---|---|
|  | into [ ˋɪntu ] | bathroom [ ˋbæθ‚rum ] |
|  | new [ nju ] | to [ tu ] |

| ❷ [ ɝ ] | current [ ˋkɝənt ] |  |
|---|---|---|

## 朗讀短文　Read aloud the text

🎙 請特別注意 [ u ]、[ ʒ ] 的發音。

I will **move into** my **new** house next week! It is more than three times the size of my old house. It has twice the number of **bedrooms** and twice as many **bathrooms**. Its kitchen is four times as big as my **current** kitchen. Unfortunately, the rent is double the amount I am paying now. Maybe I need **to** find a housemate **to** share the cost.

## 換句話說　Retell

🎙 Retell the text with the help of the words and expressions below.

move into, bedroom, bathroom, current, rent, double, amount, housemate, share, cost

## 討論題目　Free Talk

🎙 Talk on the following topic:

◆ Have you ever moved into a new house? What was the difference between the new house and the old one?

# Notes

# Chapter  2

## 溝通與社交 Communicating and Socializing

# Lesson 18

# Choosing Presents
## 挑選禮物

**搭配筆記聆聽短文** **Listen to the text with the help of the notes given**

| | |
|---|---|
| birthday | 生日 |
| somehow | 不知怎地 |
| end up | 最後 |
| dislike | 不喜歡，討厭 |
| choosing presents | 挑選禮物 |

**再次聆聽並回答問題** **Listen again and answer the questions below**

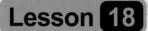 Questions for discussion:

1 What does the speaker's wife like?

2 Who does the speaker want to ask?

3 Is the speaker good at choosing presents?

I don't know what to get my wife for her birthday. She likes bags and shoes, but I don't know what color to buy. She likes wine and chocolates, but I don't know what type to buy. Somehow, I always end up buying the ones she dislikes. Maybe I should ask her sister. Why am I so bad at choosing presents?

我不知道要給我太太什麼生日禮物。她喜歡包包和鞋子,可是我不知道要買什麼顏色的。她喜歡葡萄酒和巧克力,可是我不知道要買哪種。不知怎地,我最後總會買到她不喜歡的東西。或許我應該請教她妹妹。為什麼我這麼不會挑選禮物呢?

**❶ bag** [ bæg ] *n.* 包包；袋子
handbag [ ˈhændˌbæg ] *n.* 手提包

**❷ shoe** [ ʃu ] *n.* (一隻) 鞋子
a pair of shoes　　一雙鞋子

**❸ color** [ ˈkʌlɚ ] *n.* 顏色 & *vi.* & *vt.* 著色
The children are coloring on the wall with crayons.
孩子們在用蠟筆塗鴉牆壁。

**❹ type** [ taɪp ] *n.* 種類
= kind [ kaɪnd ]
= sort [ sɔrt ]

**❺ end up + V-ing**　　到頭來……，最後……
end [ ɛnd ] *vi.* & *vt.* 結束 & *n.* 最後；結尾
Kelly and Henry ended up getting a divorce.
凱莉與亨利最後以離婚收場。

**❻ dislike** [ dɪsˈlaɪk ] *vt.* 討厭 & *n.* 厭惡
have a dislike for...　　厭惡……

🔖 **Notes**

like (喜歡) 作及物動詞時，之後可接名詞、動名詞或不定詞作受詞。然而，dislike 作及物動詞時，其後只可接名詞或動名詞作受詞，不可接不定詞。

　John dislikes to wake up early. （×）
→ John dislikes waking up early. （○）
= John does not like to wake up early.
= John does not like waking up early.
　約翰不喜歡早起。

**❼ be bad at + N/V-ing**　　拙於……，不擅長……
Kevin is bad at following commands.
凱文不擅於遵循命令。

**8 choose** [ tʃuz ] *vt.* 選擇
（三態為：choose, chose [ tʃoz ], chosen [ ˈtʃozn̩ ]）

= **select** [ səˈlɛkt ]

= **pick** [ pɪk ]

I had trouble choosing the best shirt for the interview.

= I had trouble selecting the best shirt for the interview.

= I had trouble picking the best shirt for the interview.
我難以選出最適合面試的襯衫。

**9 present** [ ˈprɛzənt ] *n.* 禮物 (= **gift** [ gɪft ]) & [ prɪˈzɛnt ] *vt.* 發表
a birthday present / gift　　生日禮物

## 實用詞句　Useful Expressions

**1 介紹副詞 somehow**

**somehow** [ ˈsʌmˌhaʊ ] *adv.* 不知怎麼地；設法

The exam was difficult, but somehow I managed to pass it.
那個考試很難，不過不知怎地我成功考過了。

I overslept today, but I still got to work on time somehow.
我今天睡過頭了，可是我還是設法準時到辦公室了。

比較

**somewhat** [ ˈsʌmˌ(h)wɑt ] *adv.* 稍微，有幾分

James was somewhat nervous when doing the presentation.
詹姆士報告時有點緊張。

**2 介紹代名詞 one 與 ones**

本課課文中的 ones 是代名詞，用以代替前述的 bags（包包）、shoes（鞋子）、wine（葡萄酒）及 chocolates（巧克力）。口語會話中經常利用代名詞 one 或 ones 來代替重複出現的可數名詞或名詞片語。one 可以用來代替先前提過的單數名詞；ones 則可以用來代替先前提過的複數名詞。

Andrew wants a new camera, but he doesn't know which camera to buy.（劣，camera 重複）

→ Andrew wants a new camera, but he doesn't know which one to buy.（佳）
安德魯想買新的相機，可是他不知道要買哪一臺。

95

The flowers in the garden are beautiful, especially those yellow flowers. (劣，flowers 重複)
→ The flowers in the garden are beautiful, especially those yellow ones. (佳)

花園裡的花很美，特別是那些黃色的。

## 發音提示 Pronunciation

| ❶ [ o ] | don't [ dont ] | so [ so ] |
|---|---|---|
| | know [ no ] | |
| ❷ [ ŋ ] | buying [ ˈbaɪɪŋ ] | choosing [ ˈtʃuzɪŋ ] |

## 朗讀短文 Read aloud the text

🎙 請特別注意 [ o ]、[ ŋ ] 的發音。

I **don't know** what to get my wife for her birthday. She likes bags and shoes, but I **don't know** what color to buy. She likes wine and chocolates, but I **don't know** what type to buy. Somehow, I always end up **buying** the ones she dislikes. Maybe I should ask her sister. Why am I **so** bad at **choosing** presents?

## 換句話說 Retell

🎙 Retell the text with the help of the words and expressions below.

bag, shoe, color, type, end up, dislike, be bad at, choose, present

討論題目 **Free Talk**

🎙 Talk on the following topic:

◆ If you have to buy a birthday present for your best friend, what would you buy?

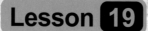

# Lesson 19

# What Do You Do on Sundays?
## 你週日都做什麼？

---

**搭配筆記聆聽會話** | **Listen to the text with the help of the notes given**

| | |
|---|---|
| on Sundays | 每週日 |
| market | 市場 |
| favorite | 最喜歡的 |
| What about you? | 你呢？ |
| That's too bad! | 太不幸了！ |

---

**再次聆聽並回答問題** | **Listen again and answer the questions below**

📌 Questions for discussion:

1️⃣ What time does the man wake up on Sundays?

2️⃣ Where does the man meet his friends?

3️⃣ What does the woman do on Sundays?

## 實用會話 Dialogue

Ⓐ Hey, Ron! What do you do on Sundays?

Ⓑ I sleep until nine o'clock. And then I walk to the market. I like to buy fruit and vegetables at the market. Later, I meet my friends for lunch at our favorite restaurant. What about you?

Ⓐ Oh, I work on Sundays.

Ⓑ That's too bad!

Ⓐ 嘿，榮恩！你週日都做什麼？

Ⓑ 我會睡到九點鐘。然後我會走到市場。我喜歡在市場買蔬菜水果。接著，我會與我朋友在我們最喜歡的餐廳吃午餐。你呢？

Ⓐ 喔，我週日都要工作。

Ⓑ 太不幸了！

**❶ sleep** [ slip ] *vi.* 睡覺（三態為：sleep, slept [ slɛpt ], slept ) &
　　　　 *n.* 睡覺，睡眠（不可數）

Sleep tight!　　睡個好覺！
go to sleep　　去睡覺

**❷ until** [ ənˋtɪl ] *prep.* 直到……為止 (= till [ tɪl ])

Charlie has to wait here until 3 o'clock.
= Charlie has to wait here till 3 o'clock.
查理要在這裡等到三點鐘。

**❸ walk** [ wɔk ] *vi. & vt.* 走路 & *n.* 散步，步行
go for a walk　　　去散步
take / have a walk　　散步

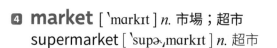

I walk to my office every day.
我每天都走路到辦公室。

Let's go for a walk after dinner.
晚餐後我們去散步吧。

**❹ market** [ ˋmarkɪt ] *n.* 市場；超市
supermarket [ ˋsupɚ͵markɪt ] *n.* 超市

**❺ buy** [ baɪ ] *vt.* 買，購買（三態為：buy, bought [ bɔt ], bought)

I would like to buy a birthday cake.
我想要買一個生日蛋糕。

**❻ fruit** [ frut ] *n.* 水果

---

**🔑 Notes**

fruit 通常為集合名詞，不可數。但若指一種或多種水果時，則為可數名詞。
This salad has plenty of fresh fruit in it.
　　　　　　　　　　　　　不可數名詞
這份沙拉裡有許多新鮮水果。

Is a tomato a fruit?
　　　　　可數名詞
番茄是一種水果嗎？

**7 vegetable** [ ˈvɛdʒ(ə)təbl̩ ] *n.* 蔬菜
fruit and vegetables　　蔬菜水果

**8 favorite** [ ˈfev(ə)rɪt ] *a.* 最喜愛的 & *n.* 最喜愛的人 / 物

**9 restaurant** [ ˈrɛstrant / ˈrɛstərənt ] *n.* 餐廳

## 口語新技能　New Skills

**1 What do you do on Sundays?**　你週日都做什麼？

　on Sundays　　每週日
= every Sunday
　Rita tends to sleep in on Sundays.
= Rita tends to sleep in every Sunday.
　麗塔每週日通常會睡懶覺。

　on Sunday　　在週日
　I have to study on Sunday.
　我週日得要讀書。

**2 What about you?**　你呢？

　What about...?　　那……呢 / 如何？
= How about...?

---

📌 **Notes**

本句常使用於口語會話中，是為了避免重複字詞而省略的簡化句型。
　I like to play basketball. Do you like to play basketball, too?
= I like to play basketball. What about you?
= I like to play basketball. How about you?
　我喜歡打籃球。你也喜歡打籃球嗎 / 那你呢？

---

**3** 表示遺憾或同情的句子

◆ 本課會話中使用下列句子以表示同情：

**That's too bad!** 太不幸了！

◆ 除了上列句子之外，也可以這樣說：

**How unfortunate!**

**What a pity!**

**What a shame!**

＊unfortunate [ ʌnˋfɔrtʃənɪt ] *a.* 不幸的；倒楣的

pity [ ˋpɪtɪ ] *n.* 遺憾，可惜

shame [ ʃem ] *n.* 遺憾，可惜

---

## 簡短對答 Quick Response

◆ Make quick responses to the sentences you hear.

---

## 討論題目 Free Talk

Talk on the following topic:

◆ Where do you like to go on Sundays?

# I Need to Borrow Money
## 我需要借錢

---

**搭配筆記聆聽短文** **Listen to the text with the help of the notes given**

| | |
|---|---|
| borrow some money | 借一點錢 |
| book a table | 訂位 |
| the rest of | 剩餘的 |
| pay you back | 還錢給你 |
| promise | 保證 |

---

**再次聆聽並回答問題** **Listen again and answer the questions below**

Questions for discussion:

❶ Is this the first time the man has asked to borrow money?

❷ Why does the man need to borrow money?

❸ What did the man spend his money on?

Hi, Dad, it's Nick. I know I said I wouldn't ask again, but I need to borrow some money! It's Sally's birthday next week. I'd like to book a table at a nice restaurant for the night, but I spent the rest of my money on new clothes. I will pay you back this time; I promise! Hope Mom is well. Love you!

嗨，老爸，我是尼克。我知道我說過我不會再開口借錢，但是我需要向你借一點錢來用！莎莉下個星期要過生日。我想要去訂一家不錯的餐廳吃晚餐，可是我把剩餘的錢花在買新衣服了。我保證，這次我會還你錢！希望老媽身體健康。我愛你們！

**❶ book** [ bʊk ] *vi.* 預訂 (= reserve [ rɪˋzɝv ])

I would like to book a room for two nights.

我想要訂房，住兩個晚上。

**❷ spend** [ spɛnd ] *vt.* 花費 (金錢)；度過，花 (時間)

(三態為：spend, spent [ spɛnt ], spent)

spend + 若干金錢 + on sth　　在某物上花費若干金錢

Alvin spent $300 on a new suit.

艾爾文花了三百美元買一套新西裝。

**❸ the rest of...**　　剩餘的……

Sophie took a trip to Japan for the rest of the holidays.

蘇菲用剩餘的假期去日本旅行。

**❹ pay** [ pe ] *vt.* & *vi.* 付 (三態為：pay, paid [ ped ], paid) & *n.* 薪水

pay sb back　　還錢給某人

Can you lend me five dollars? I'll pay you back tomorrow.

你可以借我五塊美金嗎？我明天會還給你。

**❺ promise** [ ˋprɑmɪs ] *vt.* 承諾；答應 & *n.* 諾言

promise to V　　承諾從事……

= make a promise to V

Harry promised to come with me.

哈利答應跟我來。

**❻ well** [ wɛl ] *a.* 身體好的 & *adv.* 很好地

John is not well because he has the flu.

約翰因為得了流行性感冒，所以身體不舒服。

**❶** 介紹動詞 borrow 與 lend

borrow [ ˋbɑro / ˋbɔro ] *vt.* (向某人) 借

borrow sth from sb　　向某人借某物

**比較**

lend [ lɛnd ] *vt.* 借給 (三態為：lend, lent [ lɛnt ], lent)

lend sth to sb    借東西給某人，將某物借給某人

= lend sb sth

Johnny had to borrow some money from his father to buy new clothes.

強尼必須向他爸爸借錢去買新衣服。

Can you lend me some money? Otherwise, I cannot afford it.

你可以借我一些錢嗎？不然我買不起那樣東西。

**❷ 「我想要」的說法**

I'd like to...    我想要……

= I would like to...

I'd like to sing a song for you.

我想要為各位唱首歌。

**比較**

I want to...    我 (想) 要……

"I'd like to..." 與 "I want to..." 均表示說話者的意願，但 "I'd like to..." 的語氣較為委婉、客氣，而 "I want to..." 的語氣則較為直接。

I'd like to see you tonight.

我今天晚上想要跟你見面。

I want to see you tonight.

我今天晚上要跟你見面。

## 發音提示　Pronunciation

| ❶ [ æ ] | Dad [ dæd ] | at [ æt ] |
|---|---|---|
| | ask [ æsk ] | back [ bæk ] |
| | Sally [ ˈsælɪ ] | |

| | | |
|---|---|---|
| **❷ [n]**<br>（置於母音前） | Nick [ nɪk ] | next [ nɛkst ] |
| | know [ no ] | nice [ naɪs ] |
| | need [ nid ] | night [ naɪt ] |
| | money [ ˋmʌnɪ ] | |

## 朗讀短文　Read aloud the text

🔑 請特別注意 [ æ ]、[ n ]（置於母音前）的發音。

Hi, Dad, it's Nick. I know I said I wouldn't ask again, but I need to borrow some money! It's Sally's birthday next week. I'd like to book a table at a nice restaurant for the night, but I spent the rest of my money on new clothes. I will pay you back this time; I promise! Hope Mom is well. Love you!

## 換句話說　Retell

🔑 Retell the text with the help of the words and expressions below.

book, spend, the rest of, pay, promise, well

## 討論題目　Free Talk

🔑 Talk on the following topic:

◆ Have you ever borrowed money from your parents? What did you spend the money on?

107

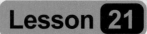

# Lesson 21

# What's Wrong?
## 怎麼了？

---

**搭配筆記聆聽會話** **Listen to the text with the help of the notes given**

| | |
|---|---|
| Don't worry. | 別擔心。 |
| obviously | 顯然地 |
| beer | 啤酒 |
| taste | 嚐起來 |
| awful | 很差的 |
| I wish I hadn't asked. | 真希望我沒問就好了。 |

---

**再次聆聽並回答問題** **Listen again and answer the questions below**

🎙 Questions for discussion:

1 What is the man drinking?

2 What does the man say about the weather?

3 What does the man say about the beer?

Ⓐ What's wrong?

Ⓑ Nothing's wrong. Don't worry.

Ⓐ Something is obviously wrong. You haven't drunk your beer. Just tell me.

Ⓑ Oh, everything's wrong! It's always raining. I don't have any money. My back hurts. I'm getting old. This beer tastes awful.

Ⓐ I wish I hadn't asked.


Ⓐ 怎麼了？

Ⓑ 沒事。別擔心。

Ⓐ 很顯然有事情不對勁。你還沒喝你的啤酒。就告訴我吧。

Ⓑ 喔，所有事都出錯了！總是在下雨。我沒有任何錢。我背痛。我愈來愈老了。這啤酒很難喝。

Ⓐ 真希望我沒問就好了。

**❶ obviously** [ ˋɑbvɪəslɪ ] *adv.* 顯然地
= clearly [ ˋklɪrlɪ ]
= evidently [ ˋɛvədəntlɪ ]

It was obviously Ryan's fault.
= It was clearly Ryan's fault.
= It was evidently Ryan's fault.
這很顯然是萊恩的錯。

**❷ drink** [ drɪŋk ] *vt. & vi.* 喝
（三態為：drink, drank [ dræŋk ], drunk [ drʌŋk ]）

You need to drink plenty of water.
你需要喝大量的水。

**❸ beer** [ bɪr ] *n.* 啤酒

**❹ money** [ ˋmʌnɪ ] *n.* 金錢（不可數）

 **Notes**

money 為不可數名詞，故不能用 one money、two moneys 來表示「一塊錢」、「兩塊錢」。若要表示金錢數量則要用 dollar（美元）、euro（歐元）、dime（十分錢）、cent（一分錢）等表示金錢單位的單字。

**❺ back** [ bæk ] *n.* 背部

**❻ hurt** [ hɝt ] *vi.* 疼痛 & *vt.* 弄傷（三態同形）

My head hurts a lot.
我的頭很痛。

Henry hurt his ankle when playing soccer.
亨利踢足球的時候弄傷了腳踝。

**❼ old** [ old ] *a.* 老的；舊的

**❽ taste** [ test ] *vi.* 嚐起來 & *n.* 味道
taste + 形容詞　　嚐起來……
taste like + 名詞　　嚐起來像……

The soup tastes great.
這碗湯喝起來真棒。

This cake tastes like pumpkin.
這塊蛋糕吃起來像南瓜。

**❾ awful** [ ˈɔfl̩ ] *a.* 很差的；可怕的
= **horrible** [ ˈhɔrəbl̩ ]
= **terrible** [ ˈtɛrəbl̩ ]

**❿ wish** [ wɪʃ ] *vt.* 希望；祝福 & *n.* 願望
I wish you a happy birthday.
我祝你生日快樂。

## 口語新技能　New Skills

**❶** 詢問「怎麼了？」的說法

| | |
|---|---|
| What's wrong? | 怎麼了？ |
| What is it? | 怎麼了？ |
| What's the problem? | 有什麼問題嗎？ |
| What's the matter? | 有什麼問題嗎？ |
| What happened? | 發生什麼事了？ |
| Is (there) something / anything wrong? | 有什麼問題嗎？ |

### 🎣 Notes

"What's wrong?" 勿與下列句子搞混：

**What's wrong with you?** 你有什麼毛病？

此句並非關心別人的問句，而是質疑他人或表示對他人感到不耐煩時使用的
問句。

## 2 與 worry 相關的常見說法

| | |
|---|---|
| Don't worry. | 別擔心。 |
| Nothing to worry about. | 沒有什麼好擔心的。 |
| Not to worry. | 別擔心。 |
| No worries. | 沒事。 |

上述句子可使用於下列兩種場合：

**a 回覆他人詢問怎麼了**

- **A** You look stressed. What's wrong?
- **B** Nothing to worry about. I just have to deal with some clients.
- **A** 你看起來焦躁。怎麼了嗎？
- **B** 沒什麼好擔心的。我只是需要應付一些客戶而已。

**b 回覆他人道歉**

- **A** I'm sorry. It was my fault.
- **B** Don't worry. It's no big deal.
- **A** 抱歉。那是我的錯。
- **B** 別擔心。不是什麼大事。

---

### 簡短對答 Quick Response

◆ Make quick responses to the sentences you hear.

---

### 討論題目 Free Talk

Talk on the following topic:

◆ What do you usually worry about?

112

# Lesson 22

# I Was on Top of the World
## 我開心極了

朗讀 ▶ Lesson 22

## 搭配筆記聆聽短文 Listen to the text with the help of the notes given

| | |
|---|---|
| a former classmate | 以前的同學 |
| crush | 喜歡的人 |
| She wasn't dating anyone. | 她沒有交往的對象。 |
| again | 再次 |
| I was on top of the world. | 我開心極了。 |

## 再次聆聽並回答問題 Listen again and answer the questions below

🔑 Questions for discussion:

**1** Who did the speaker meet?

**2** Did the speaker think the woman like him in high school?

**3** Is the woman single?

Yesterday, I was at the train station when I met a former classmate. She was my crush in high school. I think I was her crush, too. She told me she wasn't dating anyone, and she wants to see me again. I was on top of the world. I hope she was, too.

我昨天在火車站遇到了以前的同學。她是我高中喜歡的人。我想她對我也有好感。她告訴我她沒有交往的對象，也想要再跟我碰面。我開心極了。我希望她也是。

**❶ station** [ ˈsteʃən ] *n.* 車站
the bus / train / subway station　　公車 / 火車 / 地鐵車站

**❷ former** [ ˈfɔrmɚ ] *a.* 以前的，從前的

**❸ crush** [ krʌʃ ] *n.* 迷戀 (的對象) & *vi.* 迷戀 (與介詞 on 並用)
have a (huge) crush on sb　　(非常) 迷戀某人

We both know that Justin once had a crush on Selena.
= We both know that Justin once crushed on Selena.
我們都知道賈斯汀曾迷戀過賽琳娜。

**❹ date** [ det ] *vt.* 與……談戀愛 & *n.* 約會；約會的對象；日期
go on a date with sb　　與某人約會

Jessie finally went on a date with her Prince Charming.
潔西終於和她的夢中情人約會了。

That lady with curly blonde hair over there is Eric's date.
那邊那位金色捲髮女士是艾瑞克的約會對象。

**❺ top** [ tɑp ] *n.* 頂端
on top of...　　在……的頂端

**❶** 談戀愛相關說法

date 除作名詞表「日期；約會」，亦可作動詞表「與……談戀愛」，故和某人談戀愛 / 約會可以這麼說：
date sb　　和某人談戀愛 / 約會 (date 作動詞)
= be seeing sb
= go out with sb
How long have you been dating Ellen?
= How long have you been seeing Ellen?
= How long have you been going out with Ellen?
你跟艾倫交往多久了？

CH 2
溝通與社交

**2** 表開心的說法

I'm on top of the world!　　我快樂極了！

### Notes

be on top of the world 字面上的意思是在世界的頂端，其實是用以比喻「開心極了，十分快樂」。

下列說法亦可表示開心、快樂：

| | |
|---|---|
| I'm very / so happy! | 我非常開心！ |
| I couldn't be happier! | 我再開心不過了！ |
| I'm on cloud nine! | 我高興極了！ |
| I'm tickled pink! | 我高興極了！ |

## 發音提示　Pronunciation

| | | | |
|---|---|---|---|
| **1** [ ʃ ] | station [ ˈsteʃən ] | | she [ ʃi ] |
| | crush [ krʌʃ ] | | |

| | | | |
|---|---|---|---|
| **2** [ m ]<br>（置於母音前） | met [ mɛt ] | | my [ maɪ ] |
| | classmate [ ˈklæsˌmet ] | | me [ mi ] |

## 朗讀短文　Read aloud the text

請特別注意 [ ʃ ]、[ m ]（置於母音前）的發音。

Yesterday, I was at the train station when I met a former classmate. She was my crush in high school. I think I was her crush, too. She told me she wasn't dating anyone, and she wants to see me again. I was on top of the world. I hope she was, too.

## 換句話說 Retell

📍 Retell the text from the perspective of the woman with the help of the words and expressions below.

**station, former, crush, date, top**

## 討論題目 Free Talk

📍 Talk on the following topic:

◇ Have you ever run into an old friend?

# Where Were You Last Night?
## 你昨晚去哪裡了？

---

**搭配筆記聆聽會話** **Listen to the text with the help of the notes given**

| | |
|---|---|
| last night | 昨晚 |
| chat | 聊天 |
| I stayed at his place. | 我待在他家。 |
| You should've called. | 你應該打通電話的。 |
| answer | 應答 |

**再次聆聽並回答問題** **Listen again and answer the questions below**

🔑 Questions for discussion:

1 Where was the man last night?

2 Did the man call last night?

3 Where was the woman last night?

## 實用會話 Dialogue

CH 2
溝通與社交

Ⓐ Where were you last night?

Ⓑ I was chatting with Mark.

Ⓐ Why didn't you come home?

Ⓑ It got too late, so I stayed at his place.

Ⓐ I was worried. You should've called.

Ⓑ Actually, I did, but there was no answer. Where were you last night?

Ⓐ Err... I was chatting with Becky!

Ⓐ 你昨晚去哪裡了？

Ⓑ 我在跟馬克聊天。

Ⓐ 你為什麼沒回家？

Ⓑ 時間太晚了，所以我就待在他家。

Ⓐ 我很擔心。你應該打通電話的。

Ⓑ 事實上我有打，但沒有人接。你昨晚去哪裡了？

Ⓐ 呃……。我在跟貝琪聊天！

## 單字片語 Vocabulary and Phrases

**❶ chat** [ tʃæt ] *vi.* & *n.* 聊天，閒談
（三態為：chat, chatted [ ˋtʃætɪd ], chatted）
chat with sb　　與某人聊天
= have a chat with sb

I had a good time chatting with John at the party.
我在派對上與約翰聊得很愉快。

**❷ late** [ let ] *a.* (時間) 晚的

It's late, so I suppose you must go home.
時間很晚了，所以我想你必須回家。

**❸ stay** [ ste ] *vi.* 停留，留下
stay (at) home　　待在家裡

**❹ place** [ ples ] *n.* 家，住處
sb's place　　某人的家

**❺ worried** [ ˋwɜɪd ] *a.* 擔心的

Michael isn't worried about the situation.
麥可並不擔心這個狀況。

**❻ answer** [ ˋænsɚ ] *n.* (電話的) 應答，接聽 & *vt.* 回應 (電話)
answer the phone　　接電話

## 口語新技能 New Skills

🎤 表示「本應該……」的說法

should have + 過去分詞　　本應該……
was to have + 過去分詞　　本應該……

You <u>should have</u> handed in your report on time.
= You were to have handed in your report on time.
你本應該準時繳交你的報告。（實際上你並沒有準時交報告。）

比較

ⓐ would have + 過去分詞　　本來想……
I would have gotten there on time, but my car broke down.
我本來想準時抵達，但是我的車拋錨了。

ⓑ could have + 過去分詞　　本來可以……
If you were more careful, these mistakes could have been avoided.
如果你更細心的話就可以避免這些錯誤了。

## 簡短對答 Quick Response

◆ Make quick responses to the sentences you hear.

## 討論題目 Free Talk

🎤 Talk on the following topic:

◆ Do you often stay out late with your friends?

# Lesson 24

# Hobbies Vary
# from Person to Person
## 每個人嗜好不同

**搭配筆記聆聽短文** **Listen to the text with the help of the notes given**

| | |
|---|---|
| completely | 完全地 |
| hobbies and interests | 嗜好與興趣 |
| be scared of heights | 有懼高症 |
| teetotal | 滴酒不沾 |
| force | 逼，強迫 |
| plan activities | 計劃活動 |

**再次聆聽並回答問題** **Listen again and answer the questions below**

Questions for discussion:

1 Do the speaker's friends have the same hobby?

2 Does the speaker have a friend who doesn't drink?

3 Is it easy for the speaker to plan activities?

短文聽讀 **Text**

My friends all have completely different hobbies and interests. One loves rock climbing, while another is scared of heights. One likes to play soccer, but another will only watch it on TV. One goes drinking every weekend, but another is teetotal. And one loves to go running, but another has to be forced just to walk anywhere! This makes planning activities very difficult!

我所有的朋友都有完全不一樣的嗜好與興趣。一個是熱愛攀岩,而另一個是有懼高症。一個喜歡踢足球,但另一個只喜歡看電視的足球比賽。一個是每個週末都會去喝上一杯,另外一個卻滴酒不沾。一個是超愛跑步,另一個則必須得逼他動才會上路!這麼一來要計劃活動就會變得很困難!

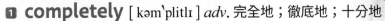

**1** **completely** [ kəmˈplitlɪ ] *adv.* 完全地；徹底地；十分地
= **totally** [ ˈtotl̩ɪ ]
= **utterly** [ ˈʌtəlɪ ]

I'm sorry, but the mistake was completely accidental.
很抱歉，這個錯誤完全是無心之過。

**2** **hobby** [ ˈhɑbɪ ] *n.* 嗜好

**3** **rock climbing**　　　攀岩
go rock climbing　　去攀岩

**4** **be scared of...**　　害怕……(= be afraid of...)
**scared** [ skɛrd ] *a.* 感到害怕的 (= afraid [ əˈfred ])

When I was very young, I was scared of dogs.
我小的時候很怕狗。

**5** **height** [ haɪt ] *n.* 高度；極度；頂點

One of Johnny's weaknesses is that he is afraid of heights.
強尼的弱點之一就是懼高。

**6** **teetotal** [ ˌtiˈtotl̩ / ˈtiˌtotl̩ ] *a.* 滴酒不沾的

Gina married an ideal husband because, like her, he is teetotal.
吉娜嫁給一個理想的老公，因為他跟她一樣滴酒不沾。

**7** **force** [ fɔrs ] *vt.* 強迫；施壓 & *n.* 武力；暴力；力

Don't force me to do anything I don't want to do.
不要強迫我做任何我不想做的事。

**8** **anywhere** [ ˈɛnɪˌ(h)wɛr ] *adv.* 任何地方 (= anyplace)

Stop asking. I didn't go anywhere last night.
別問了。昨天晚上我什麼地方都沒去。

**9** **activity** [ ækˈtɪvətɪ ] *n.* 活動

## 實用詞句　**Useful Expressions**

**1** 表示「一個……，另一個……」的說法

**a** 用於限定的兩者：

one... the other...　一個……，另一個……

使用本結構時，通常前面常置「two + 複數名詞」。換言之，在「two + 複數名詞」之後，才用此結構。

I have two uncles. One is a musician, and / while the other is a teacher.

我有兩個叔叔。一個是音樂家，另一個是老師。

**b** 用於非限定的三者以上：

one... another...　一個……，另一個……

Hobbies vary with people. One may enjoy collecting records, while another may like taking pictures.

嗜好因人而異。一個可能喜歡蒐集唱片，另一個卻喜歡攝影。

**c** 用於限定的三者以上：

one... the others...　一個……，其餘……

There are twenty students in our class. Only one doesn't need glasses, and the others (= the rest) all wear glasses.

我們班有二十個學生。只有一個不戴眼鏡，其餘的都戴眼鏡。

**d** 用於限定的三者：

one... another... the other...　一個……，一個……，另一個……

本結構常用在「three + 複數名詞」之後。

Gina has three younger sisters. One is a dancer, another is a singer, and / while the other is an actress.

吉娜有三個妹妹。一個是舞者，一個是歌手，另一個則是演員。

**e** 用於非限定的兩群：

some... others...　一些……，另一些……

Interests vary with people. Some may enjoy swimming, while others may love reading.

興趣因人而異。有些人可能喜歡游泳，有些人則可能喜歡閱讀。

CH 2
溝通與社交

125

**f** 用於限定的群體：

some... the others...　　一些……，其餘……

Of the fourteen classmates of mine, some
have their own businesses, and the others (= the rest)
are all office workers.

我的十四個同學中，有些擁有自己的事業，其餘的都是上班族。

**2** 使役動詞 make 的用法

make 表「使……成為……」時，為不完全及物動詞，其後不可用不定詞片語
作受詞。此外，make 之後的受詞，要用形容詞或名詞作補語，句型如下：

主詞 + make + 受詞 + N/Adj.

Jimmy's teacher made him (into) a good student.

吉米的老師使他成為好學生。

The trip to Paris made Jill happy.

那次的巴黎之旅使吉兒很快樂。

## 發音提示　Pronunciation

| ❶ [ aɪ ] | my [ maɪ ] | height [ haɪt ] |
|---|---|---|
| | climb [ klaɪm ] | like [ laɪk ] |
| | while [ (h)waɪl ] | |

| ❷ [ ʌ ] | one [ wʌn ] | but [ bʌt ] |
|---|---|---|
| | love [ lʌv ] | run [ rʌn ] |
| | another [ əˈnʌðɚ ] | just [ dʒʌst ] |

## 朗讀短文 Read aloud the text

請特別注意 [ aɪ ]、[ ʌ ] 的發音。

My friends all have completely different hobbies and interests. One loves rock climbing, while another is scared of heights. One likes to play soccer, but another will only watch it on TV. One goes drinking every weekend, but another is teetotal. And one loves to go running, but another has to be forced just to walk anywhere! This makes planning activities very difficult!

## 換句話說 Retell

Retell the text with the help of the words and expressions below.

completely, hobby, rock climbing, be scared of, height, teetotal, force, anywhere, activity

## 討論題目 Free Talk

Talk on the following topic:

◆ What are your friends' hobbies?

# Plans for the New Year
## 新年的計畫

**搭配筆記聆聽會話** **Listen to the text with the help of the notes given**

| | |
|---|---|
| the New Year | 新年 |
| watch the fireworks | 看煙火 |
| buddy | 好朋友 |
| sunrise | 日出 |
| cool | 很酷的 |
| Sounds good! | 聽起來不錯！ |

**再次聆聽並回答問題** **Listen again and answer the questions below**

📍 Questions for discussion:

1 Who does the woman plan to visit?

2 Who will the man watch the fireworks with?

3 Where might the woman go after she visits her grandparents?

**實用會話 Dialogue**

A Do you have any plans for the New Year?

B I would like to visit my grandparents. I miss them a lot. How about you?

A I would like to watch the fireworks at midnight with my buddies. And to see the sunrise at dawn would also be cool.

B Maybe I could come meet you after I visit my grandparents.

A Sounds good!

A 對於過新年你有什麼計畫嗎？

B 我想要去看我的爺爺奶奶。我非常想念他們。那你呢？

A 我想要跟我的好朋友一起看午夜的煙火。然後破曉時去看日出也很酷。

B 也許我可以在去我爺爺奶奶家之後來跟你碰面。

A 聽起來不錯！

**❶ fireworks** [ ˈfaɪrˌwɝks ] *n.* 煙火 (恆用複數)
set off fireworks　　放煙火

Fireworks lit up the night sky over New York City.
煙火照亮了紐約市的夜空。

**❷ midnight** [ ˈmɪdˌnaɪt ] *n.* 午夜
midday [ ˈmɪdˌde ] *n.* 正午

An earthquake happened at midnight last night.
昨天午夜發生了地震。

**❸ buddy** [ ˈbʌdɪ ] *n.* 好朋友；夥伴

Scott found that his upstairs neighbor was his old college buddy.
史考特發現他的樓上鄰居竟然是他大學時代的好朋友。

**❹ sunrise** [ ˈsʌnˌraɪz ] *n.* 日出

The farmers are used to getting up at sunrise.
那些農夫習慣在日出時分起床。

**❺ dawn** [ dɔn ] *n.* 黎明 (= daybreak [ ˈdeˌbrek ])

Norman and his buddies got up at dawn to watch the sunrise together.
諾曼和他的好朋友黎明即起，一起欣賞日出。

**❻ cool** [ kul ] *a.* 酷的；涼爽的；冷靜的

Wow! That T-shirt is really cool. Where did you get it?
哇塞！那件上衣真酷。你是在哪裡買的？

## 口語新技能　New Skills

📍 「介詞 at + 時間名詞」形成的時間副詞

◆ 介詞 at 常與下列時間名詞並用，形成時間副詞：

| at | | |
|---|---|---|
| | midnight | 在午夜時分 |
| | midday / noon | 在正午時分 |
| | dawn | 在黎明時分 |
| | daybreak | 在破曉時分 |
| | dusk / twilight | 在黃昏時分 |
| | sunrise | 在日出時分 |
| | sunset | 在日落時分 |

The pregnant woman's water broke at midnight and was rushed to the hospital.

那位懷孕婦女的羊水在半夜破了而被送往醫院。

In the old days, farmers would get up at sunrise and rest at sunset.

在以前的年代，農夫會日出而作，日入而息。

## 簡短對答　Quick Response

◆ Make quick responses to the sentences you hear.

## 討論題目　Free Talk

📍 Talk on the following topic:

◆ What did you do for New Year's Eve last year?

# Skipping a Meal
## 不吃飯

**搭配筆記聆聽短文** Listen to the text with the help of the notes given

| | |
|---|---|
| meal | 一餐 |
| a bright idea | 聰明絕頂的想法 |
| lose weight | 減重 |
| article | 文章 |
| overeat | 暴飲暴食 |

**再次聆聽並回答問題** Listen again and answer the questions below

Questions for discussion:

1. What does Graham think is a bright idea?
2. Why does Graham want to eat less?
3. According to the article, what might happen if you skip a meal?

My friend, Graham, thinks skipping meals is a bright idea. He wants to lose weight quickly; therefore, he says eating less would be the best way to do so. However, I read an article that says skipping meals could come with health problems. Moreover, you're likely to overeat at the next meal, as you're so hungry. I'll have to tell him about this the next time I see him!

葛萊翰是我的朋友，他覺得不吃飯是個聰明絕頂的想法。他想要快速減重，因此，他說少吃一點會是最好的方法。不過，我讀了一篇文章，它說不吃飯會引發健康問題。此外，你很有可能因為太餓了，所以下一餐會暴飲暴食。下一次我見到他時，我得告訴他這件事情！

**1** **skip** [ skɪp ] *vt. & vi.* 略過，跳過
（三態為：skip, skipped [ skɪpt ], skipped）
skip breakfast / lunch / dinner　　不吃早餐 / 午餐 / 晚餐
skip class　　翹課

Tom skipped lunch in order to get his work done.
湯姆略過午餐沒吃以把工作做完。

**2** **bright** [ braɪt ] *a.* 聰明的，聰穎的；明亮的

**3** **lose weight** [ wet ]　　減重
gain [ gen ] weight　　增重

**4** **article** [ ˋɑrtɪkḷ ] *n.* 文章

**5** **likely** [ ˋlaɪklɪ ] *a.* 可能的
be likely to V　　很可能……

The baseball team is likely to win the game.
這支棒球隊很可能會贏得這場比賽。

**6** **overeat** [ ͵ovəˋit ] *vi.* 暴食
（三態為：overeat, overate [ ͵ovəˋet ], overeaten [ ͵ovəˋitn̩ ]）

I tend to overeat when I am under stress.
處於壓力下時，我很容易飲食過量。

**7** **hungry** [ ˋhʌŋgrɪ ] *a.* 饑餓的

🔑 介紹常見的副詞連接詞

**a** **副詞連接詞的功能**

副詞連接詞顧名思義就是具有連接詞意味的副詞，但此類副詞並不具有連接詞的功用。在兩句中出現時，該副詞前須使用分號，以連接兩句，並通常於其後置逗點，此類副詞亦可置句首。

**b** 副詞連接詞的種類

1) **therefore、thus、hence** 表「因此」：

The desserts were tasty; | therefore, | I ate a lot.
| thus |
| hence, |

= The desserts were tasty. | Therefore, | I ate a lot.
| Thus |
| Hence, |

= The desserts were tasty, so I ate a lot.

= The desserts were tasty, and thus I ate a lot.

甜點很可口，因此我吃了很多。

🔖 **Notes**

therefore 與 hence 後通常要加逗點，thus 則可不用。

2) **however、nevertheless、nonetheless** 表「不過，然而」：

The cake was nice; | however, | I didn't eat much.
| nevertheless, |
| nonetheless, |

= The cake was nice. | However, | I didn't eat much.
| Nevertheless, |
| Nonetheless, |

= The cake was nice, but I didn't eat much.

蛋糕還不錯，不過我沒有吃很多。

3) **moreover、furthermore、in addition** 表「除此之外」：

The rent is cheap; | moreover, | the location is perfect.
| furthermore, |
| in addition, |

= The rent is cheap. | Moreover, | the location is perfect.
| Furthermore, |
| In addition, |

= The rent is cheap, and the location is perfect.

房租便宜，除此之外，地點更是棒得沒話講。

CH 2 溝通與社交

**c** therefore 和 however 亦可插入句中，
此時應於該詞的兩旁各置逗點，習慣的用法如下：

1) 置於主詞與動詞之間

   The desserts were tasty. I, therefore, ate a lot.
   甜點很可口，因此我吃了很多。

2) 置於主詞與助動詞之間

   The cake was nice. I, however, didn't eat much.
   蛋糕還不錯，不過我沒有吃很多。

3) 置於助動詞與動詞之間

   Your idea is nice. There may, however, be a problem with it.
   你的點子很好。但是它可能會有個問題。

## 發音提示　**Pronunciation**

| **❶** [ U ] | would [ wʊd ] | could [ kʊd ] |
|---|---|---|

| | want [ wɑnt ] | way [ we ] |
|---|---|---|
| **❷** [ W ] | weight [ wet ] | with [ wɪð ] |
| | would [ wʊd ] | |

## 朗讀短文　**Read aloud the text**

請特別注意 [ U ]、[ W ] 的發音。

My friend, Graham, thinks skipping meals is a bright idea. He wants to lose weight quickly; therefore, he says eating less would be the best way to do so. However, I read an article that says skipping meals could come with health problems. Moreover, you're likely to overeat at the next meal, as you're so hungry. I'll have to tell him about this the next time I see him!

## 換句話說 `Retell`

📌 Retell the text with the help of the words and expressions below.

**skip, bright, lose weight, article, likely, overeat, hungry**

## 討論題目 `Free Talk`

📌 Talk on the following topic:

◆ What methods have you tried when trying to lose weight?

# Keeping the Love Alive
## 保持熱戀

**搭配筆記聆聽會話** Listen to the text with the help of the notes given

| | |
|---|---|
| fall in love | 墜入愛河 |
| secret | 祕訣；祕密 |
| at least | 至少 |
| go away | 外出度假 |
| spark | 火花 |

**再次聆聽並回答問題** Listen again and answer the questions below

 Questions for discussion:

**1** Is the woman married?

**2** What does the woman do to keep the love alive?

**3** Does the man think it's a good idea?

🅐 Since we got married, my husband and I have fallen deeper in love.

🅑 Wow, what's your secret? How do you keep the love alive?

🅐 At least once a month, we go away together. Even if it's just for one night, it helps bring the spark back to our relationship.

🅑 Aww... How lovely! I'm going to try that.

🅐 自從我和我老公結婚後,我們更深愛彼此了。

🅑 哇,你們的祕訣是什麼?你們怎麼保持熱戀的?

🅐 我們至少一個月會去度假一次。即使只有一個晚上,那也有助於把火花帶回我們的關係中。

🅑 噢……。真好!我也要來試試看。

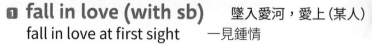

❶ **fall in love (with sb)**　墜入愛河，愛上 (某人)
fall in love at first sight　一見鍾情

Bella and Edward fell in love with each other at first sight.
貝拉和愛德華兩人一見鍾情。

❷ **deep** [ dip ] *a.* 深的

❸ **secret** [ ˈsikrɪt ] *n.* 祕訣，訣竅；祕密

❹ **alive** [ əˈlaɪv ] *a.* 活著的

❺ **go away**　外出 (尤指度假)；走開

The Simpson family usually goes away for the summer.
辛普森一家夏天時通常會去度假。

❻ **spark** [ spɑrk ] *n.* 火花

❼ **relationship** [ rɪˈleʃənˌʃɪp ] *n.* 關係

口語新技能 **New Skills**

❶ 表示「至少」的說法

**at least**　至少
at least 為副詞片語，於句中使用時通常用以修飾數字。
Mindy spent at least two hours doing her homework last night.
明蒂昨晚花了至少兩小時寫作業。
比較
**at most**　最多
It takes at most one hour to get to the airport.
最多只要花一小時就能到機場。

❷ 表示「即使」的說法

**even if...**　即使……；就算……(為連接詞)
Even if you wear a mask, I can still recognize you.
即使你戴了面具，我仍可以認出你。

**比較**

even though... 雖然……（為連接詞）

= although...

= though...

Even though Sandy is poor, she still manages to raise her children.

雖然珊蒂很窮，她仍勉強能夠撫養她的孩子。

**簡短對答** Quick Response

◆ Make quick responses to the sentences you hear.

**討論題目** Free Talk

Talk on the following topic:

◆ When in a relationship, what is a good way to keep the love alive?

# First Time for Everything
## 凡事都有第一次

### 搭配筆記聆聽短文 Listen to the text with the help of the notes given

| | |
|---|---|
| cook | 下廚，烹飪 |
| accordingly | 因此 |
| term | 學期 |
| run out of money | 錢用完，缺錢 |
| on a budget | 預算吃緊 |
| food poisoning | 食物中毒 |

### 再次聆聽並回答問題 Listen again and answer the questions below

📍 Questions for discussion:

1 Has the speaker ever cooked before going to college?

2 Why did the speaker decide to start cooking?

3 Did the speaker's housemates get sick from the food?

I had never cooked before I went to college; accordingly, I spent the first three weeks of the term eating out. I was just enjoying that lifestyle when I started to run out of money. As a result, I began watching videos about cooking on a budget. On the following weekend, I made curry for all my housemates. Thankfully, no one got food poisoning! There's a first time for everything, I guess.

我上大學前從未下廚過,因此我學期的前三週都在外用餐。當我正享受這樣的生活方式時,我的錢就快用完了。因此,我開始看在預算吃緊的情況下做菜的影片。接下來的週末,我做了咖哩給我所有的室友吃。幸好,沒人食物中毒!我想,凡事都有第一次。

## 單字片語 Vocabulary and Phrases

**1 cook** [ kʊk ] *vi.* & *vt.* 烹調 & *n.* 廚師
cook a meal　煮飯
cook lunch / dinner　煮午 / 晚餐

Too many cooks spoil the broth.
太多廚師會壞了羹湯 / 人多手雜。(諺語)

**2 term** [ tɝm ] *n.* 學期

**3 eat out**　在外用餐
= dine out (較正式的用法)
eat in　在家用餐

Eating in is cheaper than eating out.
在家吃飯比在外用餐便宜。

**4 lifestyle** [ ˈlaɪfˌstaɪl ] *n.* 生活方式
a healthy lifestyle　健康的生活方式

**5 run out of...**　用光 (錢、汽油、耐心、精力等)

We're running out of gas, so we have to find a gas station.
我們的汽油快用光了，所以我們得找一間加油站。

I guess I've run out of patience.
我想我已失去耐心了。

**6 following** [ ˈfɑloɪŋ ] *a.* 接著的

**7 curry** [ ˈkɝɪ ] *n.* 咖哩

**8 housemate** [ ˈhaʊsˌmet ] *n.* (住在同一間房子的) 室友
roommate [ ˈrumˌmet ] *n.* (尤指大學同寢室的) 室友

**9 thankfully** [ ˈθæŋkfəlɪ ] *adv.* 幸好，幸虧

There was a car accident this morning. Thankfully, no one was injured.
今早有場車禍。幸好，沒有人受傷。

**10 food poisoning**　食物中毒
poisoning [ ˈpɔɪznɪŋ ] *n.* 中毒

## 實用詞句 Useful Expressions

**1** 介紹表示「因此，所以」的副詞連接詞

**accordingly** [ əˈkɔrdɪŋlɪ ] *adv.* 因此，所以
= **as a result** [ rɪˈzʌlt ]
= **consequently** [ ˈkɑnsəˌkwɛntlɪ ]
= **as a consequence** [ ˈkɑnsəˌkwɛns ]
= **therefore** [ ˈðɛrˌfɔr ]
= **thus** [ ðʌs ]
= **hence** [ hɛns ]
  The cost rose; accordingly, we increased our price.
= The cost rose. Accordingly, we increased our price.
  成本上漲，因此，我們調漲價格。

**2** 介紹與 budget 相關的用語

**budget** [ ˈbʌdʒɪt ] *n.* 預算
on a (tight) budget　　預算吃緊
on / within budget　　在預算內
under budget　　低於預算
over budget　　超出預算
To save money, Jacob lives on a tight budget.
雅各為了存錢過著預算緊繃的生活。
We've completed the project on / within budget.
我們在預算內完成該計畫。
This advertising campaign went over budget.
這項廣告活動的預算超支。

## 發音提示 Pronunciation

| | | |
|---|---|---|
| **1** [ɑ] | college [ ˈkɑlɪdʒ ] | on [ ɑn ] |
| | start [ stɑrt ] | following [ ˈfɑloɪŋ ] |
| | watch [ wɑtʃ ] | got [ gɑt ] |

CH 2 溝通與社交

145

| **2** [ v ] | never [ ˈnɛvɚ ] | everything [ ˈɛvrɪˌθɪŋ ] |
|---|---|---|
| | video [ ˈvɪdɪˌo ] | |

🎙 請特別注意 [ ɑ ]、[ v ] 的發音。

I had **never** cooked before I went to **college**; accordingly, I spent the first three weeks of the term eating out. I was just enjoying that lifestyle when I **started** to run out of money. As a result, I began **watching videos** about cooking on a budget. **On** the **following** weekend, I made curry for all my housemates. Thankfully, no one **got** food poisoning! There's a first time for **everything**, I guess.

## 換句話說 Retell

🎙 Retell the text with the help of the words and expressions below.

cook, term, eat out, lifestyle, run out of, following, curry, housemate, thankfully, food poisoning

## 討論題目 Free Talk

🎙 Talk on the following topic:

◆ Do you consider yourself a good cook?

146

## Lesson 29

# You're Looking Better!
## 你看起來氣色好多了！

**搭配筆記聆聽會話** **Listen to the text with the help of the notes given**

| | |
|---|---|
| a great deal | 非常地，很 |
| I feel much more like myself. | 我感覺好多了。 |
| virus | 病毒 |
| average | 一般的；平均的 |
| snotty | 滿是鼻水的 |

**再次聆聽並回答問題** **Listen again and answer the questions below**

Questions for discussion:

**1** What happened to the woman?

**2** Is the woman feeling better?

**3** Does the woman think the cold was worse than usual?

🅐 Megan, you're looking a great deal better than the last time I saw you!

🅑 Thanks, Brad. Yes, I feel much more like myself.

🅐 That virus really took it out of you.

🅑 Yeah, it was a lot worse than the average cold. I went through far more snotty tissues than normal.

🅐 Too much information!

🅐 梅根,妳比我上次看到妳的時候氣色好很多耶!

🅑 謝謝,布萊德。對,我感覺好多了。

🅐 那病毒真的讓妳筋疲力盡。

🅑 對啊,它比一般感冒還要糟很多。我用了很多紙巾,擦的鼻涕比平常還要多很多。

🅐 妳不必講那麼多!

## 單字片語 Vocabulary and Phrases

**1 virus** [ ˋvaɪrəs ] *n.* 病毒

a computer virus　　電腦病毒

Christy was sent to the hospital because she had a virus.
克莉絲蒂因為被病毒感染了，所以被送到醫院。

**2 take it out of sb**　　使某人筋疲力盡

= tire sb out

tire [ taɪr ] *vt.* & *vi.* 使疲累

This job really took it out of me.

= This job really tired me out.
這份工作真的讓我筋疲力盡。

**3 average** [ ˋævərɪdʒ ] *a.* 一般的；平均的 & *n.* 平均

On average,...　　平均而言，……

An average person sleeps eight hours per day.
一般人每天會睡八小時。

On average, we work 40 hours each week.
平均而言，我們一週工作四十個小時。

**4 cold** [ kold ] *n.* 感冒

catch a cold　　得到感冒

**5 go through...**　　使用……；經歷……

Victoria can go through three cups of coffee a day.
維多莉亞可以每天喝三杯咖啡。

I went through a lot of troubles just to meet you.
我為了見你一面經歷了很多麻煩事。

**6 snotty** [ ˋsnɑtɪ ] *a.* 滿是鼻水的；高傲的，自大的

Keep your snotty handkerchief away from me!
別讓你那滿是鼻水的手帕靠近我！

The snotty boy ignored his father's warning.
自以為是的男孩不理他爸爸的警告。

**7** **tissue** [ `tɪʃʊ] *n.* 紙巾，衛生紙

**8** **information** [ ,ɪnfə`meʃən] *n.* 資訊；消息；
資料 (不可數)

For more information, please visit our website.
想要獲得更多資訊，請至我們的網站查詢。

---

**口語新技能** **New Skills**

📍 表示康復後感到舒服的說法

feel (like) oneself　　感到舒服
= feel well

I'm feeling more like myself after sleeping for the entire day.
= I'm feeling better after sleeping for the entire day.
我睡一整天之後感到舒服多了。

Joan went home because she wasn't feeling quite (like) herself.
= Joan went home because she wasn't feeling well.
瓊安因為不太舒服所以回家了。

---

📍 **Notes**

下列類似的片語亦可表達某人康復後感到舒服多了。

**a** feel like a new person　　感覺好很多
You'll feel like a new person if you get some rest.
你休息一下就會感覺好多了。

**b** feel like a million dollars / bucks　　感覺很健康
The drugs worked wonders! I feel like a million bucks already.
這些藥很有效！我已經感到很健康了。

## 簡短對答 Quick Response

◇ Make quick responses to the sentences you hear.

## 討論題目 Free Talk

🔑 Talk on the following topic:

◇ When was the last time you had a cold?

# Saving Money
## 存錢

---

**搭配筆記聆聽短文** **Listen to the text with the help of the notes given**

| | |
|---|---|
| by the end of the year | 今年年底前 |
| put aside | 存（錢） |
| engagement | 訂婚 |
| propose | 求婚 |
| a candlelit dinner | 燭光晚餐 |

**再次聆聽並回答問題** **Listen again and answer the questions below**

🔑 Questions for discussion:

1 How much will Jonas save by the end of the year?

2 What does Jonas plan to buy with the money?

3 What city does Jonas plan to go to?

Jonas will have saved $5,000 by the end of the year. He will have put aside enough money to buy his girlfriend a beautiful engagement ring. He plans to take her to Paris on a weekend and propose under the Eiffel Tower. He then plans to take her for a candlelit dinner on a cruise on the Seine. Jonas is such a romantic!

到今年年底前，喬納斯就會存好五千美元。他將存到足夠的錢買一隻漂亮的訂婚戒指給他女友。他計劃在一個週末要帶她去巴黎，並在艾菲爾鐵塔下求婚。他接著計劃要帶她到塞納河的遊船上享用燭光晚餐。喬納斯真是個浪漫的人！

**❶ save** [ sev ] *vt.* & *vi.* 存錢，儲蓄
save up (for sth) （為某事物）存錢
John saves $50 each week.
約翰每週存五十美元。
Vicky is saving (up) for a new cellphone.
薇琪正在存錢買新手機。

**❷ put aside sth / put sth aside** 存（錢）；留出（時間）
The couple puts aside $1,000 a month for their wedding.
這對情侶每個月存一千美元用以籌備他們的婚禮。
Let's put aside at least two hours to visit the museum.
咱們至少留兩小時來參觀這座博物館吧。

**❸ an engagement ring** 訂婚戒指
engagement [ ɪnˋgedʒmənt ] *n.* 訂婚

**❹ plan** [ plæn ] *vi.* & *vt.* 計劃 & *n.* 計畫
（三態為：plan, planned [ plænd ], planned）
plan to V 計劃做……
Bella plans to travel around the world.
貝拉計劃環遊世界。
The travel agency helped us plan the trip to Morocco.
旅行社協助我們籌劃去摩洛哥的旅行。

**❺ propose** [ prəˋpoz ] *vi.* 求婚
propose to sb 向某人求婚
Peter proposed to his girlfriend last night.
彼得昨晚向他女友求婚了。

**❻ the Eiffel Tower** [ ˋaɪfḷ ˏtauɚ ] 艾菲爾鐵塔

**❼ a candlelit dinner** 燭光晚餐
candlelit [ ˋkændḷˏlɪt ] *a.* 燭光的
candlelight [ ˋkændḷˏlaɪt ] *n.* 燭光

**8** **cruise** [ kruz ] *n.* 乘船遊覽 & *vi.* & *vt.* 航遊
a round-the-world cruise　　航遊全世界

Let's spend our evening cruising down the Seine.
咱們傍晚來乘船遊覽塞納河吧。

**9** **the Seine** [ sen ]　　塞納河

**10** **romantic** [ roˋmæntɪk ] *n.* 浪漫的人 & *a.* 浪漫的

### 實用詞句　Useful Expressions

**1** 表示「在⋯⋯之前」的說法

by + 時間　　在某時間之前

We have to arrive there by 3 p.m.
= We have to arrive there no later than 3 p.m.
我們下午三點前要抵達那裡。

The students should hand in their reports by this Friday.
= The students should hand in their reports no later than this Friday.
學生們應在本週五以前繳交報告。

比較

by the time...　　等到⋯⋯的時候

> 🔑 **Notes**
>
> by the time 可引導副詞子句，修飾主句，但須注意句子時態的變化。

By the time I arrived, the plane had already taken off.
等到我抵達時，飛機已經起飛了。

By the time you come home, I will have prepared dinner.
等你回到家時，我將已弄好晚餐了。

**2** 表示「如此，這樣」的說法

◆ such + a(n) (+ 形容詞) + 單數名詞　　　如此……

Luke is such a considerate young man.

路克真是個體貼的年輕人。

It's such a sunny day today.

今天真是個晴朗的日子。

◆ such (+ 形容詞) + 複數名詞 / 不可數名詞　　　如此……

They're such lovely kids.

他們是如此可愛的小孩。

I believe everyone will enjoy such nice music.

我相信大家都會享受如此棒的音樂。

---

## 發音提示　Pronunciation

| **❶ [ o ]** | Jonas [ ˈdʒonəs ] | romantic [ roˈmæntɪk ] |
| | propose [ prəˈpoz ] | |

| **❷ [ dʒ ]** | Jonas [ ˈdʒonəs ] | engagement [ ɪnˈgedʒmənt ] |

---

## 朗讀短文　Read aloud the text

🎤 請特別注意 [ o ]、[ dʒ ] 的發音。

Jonas will have saved $5,000 by the end of the year. He will have put aside enough money to buy his girlfriend a beautiful engagement ring. He plans to take her to Paris on a weekend and propose under the Eiffel Tower. He then plans to take her for a candlelit dinner on a cruise on the Seine. Jonas is such a romantic!

## 換句話說 Retell

📌 Retell the text with the help of the words and expressions below.

save, put aside sth, engagement ring, plan, propose, the Eiffel Tower, candlelit dinner, cruise, the Seine, romantic

## 討論題目 Free Talk

📌 Talk on the following topic:

◇ Have you ever saved money in order to buy something expensive?

# My Pet Dog
## 我的寵物狗

**搭配筆記聆聽會話** Listen to the text with the help of the notes given

| neighborhood | 社區 |
|---|---|
| feed | 餵食 |
| at least | 至少 |
| wonder | 想知道 |
| postman | 郵差 |

**再次聆聽並回答問題** Listen again and answer the questions below

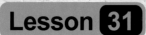 Questions for discussion:

**1** Why is the man's dog fat and slow?

**2** Is the woman's dog friendly?

**3** Is the postman scared of the woman's dog?

🅐 My dog is smarter than any other dog in the neighborhood.

🅑 Yes, but you feed it too much, so it's also fatter and slower than any other dog in the neighborhood.

🅐 Well, at least mine's friendlier than yours!

🅑 What do you mean?

🅐 Ever wondered why the postman doesn't come to your house anymore?

🅐 我的狗比這社區裡的其他狗聰明。

🅑 沒錯，可是你餵牠吃太多東西了，所以牠也比這社區裡的其他狗都還要胖，動作也比較慢。

🅐 嗯，至少我的狗比你的友善！

🅑 你這是什麼意思？

🅐 有沒有想過郵差為什麼都不再靠近你的家？

159

❶ **neighborhood** [ ˋnebɚ͵hʊd ] *n.* 社區
neighbor [ ˋnebɚ ] *n.* 鄰居

Do you live in this neighborhood?
你住在這個社區嗎？

❷ **at least...** 至少⋯⋯
at least + 數字 至少有若干⋯⋯

At least you told the truth.
至少你講出真相了。

You could at least tell me your secret formula!
你至少可以告訴我你的祕方吧！

At least five hundred people came to my concert.
至少有五百人來聽我的音樂會。

❸ **wonder** [ ˋwʌndɚ ] *vt.* 想知道
wonder + 疑問詞 (如 why、what、when 等) 引導的名詞子句
想知道⋯⋯

I wonder why Sally was mad at me.
我想知道莎莉為什麼生我的氣。

Linda wonders what her parents have got her for her birthday.
琳達想知道她爸媽買什麼生日禮物給她。

❹ **postman** [ ˋpostmən ] *n.* 郵差 (英式用法)
= mailman [ ˋmel͵mæn ] (美式用法)

❺ **anymore** [ ˋɛnɪ͵mor ] *adv.* 不再，再也不
anymore 須與否定詞 not 並用，形成下列固定搭配：
not... anymore 不再⋯⋯
= not... any longer
= no longer
= no more (多置句尾，較少用)

John does not love Shelly anymore.
= John does not love Shelly any longer.

= John no longer loves Shelly.
= John loves Shelly no more. (較少用)
約翰不再愛雪莉了。

## 口語新技能 New Skills

📍 表示「你是什麼意思？」的說法

**What do you mean?** 你這是什麼意思？
= What do you mean by that?
= What does that mean?
= What is the meaning of that?

### 📍 Notes

本句有時會用於某人被對方說的言詞冒犯到而反問對方的情況。如下：

🅐 Our team would be more efficient if some people weren't slacking off.

🅑 What do you mean?

🅐 我們團隊如果有些人沒有懈怠的話會更有效率。

🅑 你說這話是什麼意思？

## 簡短對答 Quick Response

◆ Make quick responses to the sentences you hear.

## 討論題目 Free Talk

📍 Talk on the following topic:

◆ What animal would you like to keep as a pet? Why?

161

# Actions Speak Louder Than Words

## 坐而言不如起而行

朗讀 ▶
Lesson 32

---

**搭配筆記聆聽短文** **Listen to the text with the help of the notes given**

| | |
|---|---|
| apart | 分開的 |
| study abroad | 國外留學 |
| move away | 搬走 |
| drift apart | 逐漸疏離 |
| surprise | 使驚喜 |

**再次聆聽並回答問題** **Listen again and answer the questions below**

Questions for discussion:

**1** How long have the speaker and her boyfriend been apart?

**2** Why did the speaker's boyfriend move away?

**3** What will the speaker do?

### 短文聽讀 Text

My boyfriend and I have been apart for more than three months. He went to study abroad, while I stayed here to work. When he first moved away, we spoke on the phone at least twice a day. Now, it's less than three times a week. I can't help but feel like we're drifting apart. So, I'm going to jump on a plane and surprise him. Actions speak louder than words!

我男友和我已經分隔兩地三個多月了。他到國外留學,而我留在本地工作。他剛搬走時,我們至少一天會通兩次電話。但現在一個禮拜還通不到三次電話。我不禁覺得我們的關係正逐漸疏離。所以,我決定去搭飛機並給他一個驚喜。坐而言不如起而行!

163

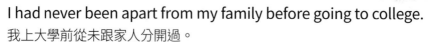

❶ **apart** [ ə`pɑrt ] *a.* & *adv.* 不住在一起 (的)；
(關係) 分開 (的)

I had never been apart from my family before going to college.
我上大學前從未跟家人分開過。

❷ **stay** [ ste ] *vi.* 停留，留下

It's pouring now, so I'm going to stay at my friend's place for a while.
現在正在下大雨，所以我會在我朋友家待一陣子。

❸ **move away**　　搬走
move in / out　　搬進新居 / 搬出去

Ever since Anthony moved away, I've lost contact with him.
自從安東尼搬走後，我便和他失去了聯繫。

We're going to move out of this town this summer.
今年夏天我們將搬離這個小鎮。

❹ **drift apart**　　(關係) 逐漸疏離，漸漸疏遠
drift [ drɪft ] *vi.* 漂移

After a few years, the two friends gradually drifted apart.
幾年後，那一對好友漸行漸遠。

❺ **jump on...**　　搭上 (飛機、火車、公車等大型公共交通工具)

Let's jump on a plane and take a trip to Madrid!
咱們搭上飛機，來趟馬德里之旅吧！

❻ **surprise** [ sə`praɪz ] *vt.* 使驚喜，使感到意外

Tony decided to surprise his wife with a bouquet of roses.
東尼決定用一束玫瑰花給他老婆一個驚喜。

❼ **Actions speak louder than words!**
坐而言不如起而行！(諺語)

## 實用詞句 **Useful Expressions**

 表示「不禁……」的說法

can't help but V　　不禁……，忍不住……
= can't help + V-ing
= can't resist + V-ing
　　When I heard the joke, I couldn't help but laugh.
= When I heard the joke, I couldn't help laughing.
= When I heard the joke, I couldn't resist laughing.
　　當我聽到這則笑話時，我忍不住笑了出來。
　　Chris can't help but feel happy whenever he gazes at his wife.
= Chris can't help feeling happy whenever he gazes at his wife.
= Chris can't resist feeling happy whenever he gazes at his wife.
　　每當克里斯注視著他老婆時，都會不由自主地感到幸福。

CH 2 溝通與社交

## 發音提示 **Pronunciation**

| ❶ [ i ] | three [ θri ] | feel [ fil ] |
|---|---|---|
| | least [ list ] | speak [ spik ] |
| | week [ wik ] | |

| ❷ [ ŋ ] | drifting [ ˈdrɪftɪŋ ] | going [ ˈɡoɪŋ ] |
|---|---|---|

🔖 請特別注意 [ i ]、[ ŋ] 的發音。

My boyfriend and I have been apart for more than three months. He went to study abroad, while I stayed here to work. When he first moved away, we spoke on the phone at least twice a day. Now, it's less than three times a week. I can't help but feel like we're drifting apart. So, I'm going to jump on a plane and surprise him. Actions speak louder than words!

## 換句話說 Retell

🔖 Retell the text with the help of the words and expressions below.

apart, stay, move away, drift apart, jump on, surprise, Actions speak louder than words!

## 討論題目 Free Talk

🔖 Talk on the following topic:

◆ Have you ever been in a long-distance relationship?

166

# Chapter 3

## 休閒娛樂

Leisure Activities

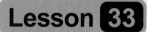

## Lesson 33

# I Want to Go to the Movies
## 我想去看電影

---

**搭配筆記聆聽會話** **Listen to the text with the help of the notes given**

| | |
|---|---|
| cinema | 電影院 |
| from the looks of its trailer | 依據它的預告片看來 |
| cheesy | 庸俗的 |
| boring | 無聊的 |
| get sth over with | (不情願地) 把某事完成 |

**再次聆聽並回答問題** **Listen again and answer the questions below**

📍 Questions for discussion:

1️⃣ Does the man want to watch *I Cannot Love You*?

2️⃣ What does the man say about *I Cannot Love You*?

3️⃣ Does the woman like *Monster Trucks*?

## 實用會話 Dialogue

🅐 Hey, Jim! I want to go to the movies. *I Cannot Love You* is playing at the cinema.

🅑 I do not want to watch that movie. From the looks of its trailer, that movie seems cheesy and boring.

🅐 I watched *Monster Trucks* with you last week. It does not even have a story!

🅑 Fine! Let's go to the movies and get this over with.

🅐 嘿，吉姆！我想去看電影。《我無法愛你》在電影院上映中。

🅑 我不想看那部電影。依據它的預告片看來，那部電影似乎庸俗又無聊。

🅐 我上週跟你去看了《怪獸卡車》。它連劇情都沒有！

🅑 好啦！咱們去電影院把它看完吧。

**❶ trailer** [ ˋtrelɚ ] *n.* 預告片；拖車
a movie trailer　　電影預告片

**❷ cheesy** [ ˋtʃizɪ ] *a.* 庸俗的；劣質的

**❸ boring** [ ˋborɪŋ ] *a.* 無聊的
= dull [ dʌl ]
bored [ bord ] *a.* 感到無聊的

This book is too boring for Irene.
= This book is too dull for Irene.
這本書對愛琳來說太無聊了。

Sammy tends to bite his nails when he gets bored.
山米無聊時會咬他的指甲。

**❹ monster** [ ˋmɑnstɚ ] *n.* 怪獸，怪物

**❺ truck** [ trʌk ] *n.* 卡車，貨車

**❻ last week**　　上週
last month　　上個月
last year　　去年

---

📌 **Notes**

last 在此處為形容詞，表「前一個的，上一個的」。表示「昨天」要說 yesterday [ ˋjɛstɚde ]，而非 last day。英語中，the last day 指的是「最後一天」，此處的 last 則表「最後的」。

---

**❼ story** [ ˋstorɪ ] *n.* 劇情，情節 (= plot [ plɑt ])；故事

**❽ get sth over with**　　(不情願地) 做完某事；熬過某事
比較
get over sth　　從某事中恢復過來
= recover from sth
＊ recover [ rɪˋkʌvɚ ] *vi.* 恢復

I'm glad we can finally get these exams over with.
我很開心我們終於熬過這些考試。

Hurry up and get this over with.
動作快點，趕快做完這件事。

It took me a while to get over the shock.
= It took me a while to recover from the shock.
我花了一些時間才從驚嚇中恢復過來。

## 口語新技能 New Skills

**1** 看電影的說法

◆ 表示「去電影院看電影」，可以這樣說：
go to the movies（movies 恆為複數）
go to the movie theater
go to the cinema（cinema [ ˈsɪnəmə ] 為英式用語）

◆ 若要表示「去看一場電影」，可以這樣說：
go see / catch a movie
see / watch a movie
take in a movie
go to a movie

**2** 電影類型的說法

◆ 詢問對方喜歡看什麼類型的電影，可以這樣說：
What kind of movie do you like (to watch)?
你喜歡看哪種電影？
What is your favorite movie genre?
你最喜歡的電影類型是什麼？
＊ genre [ ˈʒɑnrə ] *n.* 類型

◆ 你可以這樣回答：
I like action movies / films.　　我喜歡動作片。

171

◆ 替換看看：

| comedy　喜劇片 | horror　恐怖片 |
|---|---|
| drama　戲劇片 | romance　愛情片 |
| fantasy　奇幻片 | thriller　驚悚片 |

**❸** From the looks of its trailer,...　依據它的預告片看來，……。

from / by the look(s) of...　依據……判斷 (非正式用語)

= judging from / by...

\* judge [ dʒʌdʒ ] *vi.* & *vt.* 判斷；評價

From the looks of this traffic, we won't arrive until midnight.

= By the looks of this traffic, we won't arrive until midnight.

= Judging from / by this traffic, we won't arrive until midnight.

依據這車流量判斷，我們直到半夜才會抵達。

## 簡短對答 Quick Response

◆ Make quick responses to the sentences you hear.

## 討論題目 Free Talk

🎙 Talk on the following topic:

◆ Do you like to watch movies? What is your favorite movie?

# Lesson 34

# None of My Friends Like Concerts

## 我的朋友沒有一個喜歡演唱會

**搭配筆記聆聽會話** **Listen to the text with the help of the notes given**

| | |
|---|---|
| see a concert | 聽演唱會 |
| county | 縣；郡 |
| for free | 免費 |
| interest | 使……感興趣 |
| That's strange. | 很奇怪。 |

**再次聆聽並回答問題** **Listen again and answer the questions below**

🔖 Questions for discussion:

**1** Where is the man going tonight?

**2** Does the woman like concerts?

**3** What is the woman going to do?

實用會話 **Dialogue**

🅐 Do you want to see a concert tonight? Some of the county's best singers are performing for free.

🅑 Hmm, I don't like concerts. And none of those singers really interest me.

🅐 That's strange. None of my friends like concerts, either.

🅑 Some of my friends do. Let me make a few calls. Someone will go with you!

🅐 你今天晚上要聽演唱會嗎？一些本縣的最佳歌手將要免費表演。

🅑 嗯，我不喜歡聽演唱會。而且那些歌手當中沒有一個能真正引起我的興趣。

🅐 很奇怪。我的朋友也沒有一個喜歡演唱會。

🅑 我有一些朋友喜歡演唱會。我來打幾通電話。總會有人跟你一起去聽演唱會的！

## 單字片語 Vocabulary and Phrases

**❶ county** [ ˋkaʊntɪ ] *n.* 縣；郡

Through hard work, Karen eventually attained her goal of becoming the best singer in her county.

凱倫透過努力，終於達到目標，成為縣裡的最佳歌手。

**❷ singer** [ ˋsɪŋɚ ] *n.* 歌手

The singer has many fans, ranging from children to grandparents.

這名歌手有許多粉絲，從小孩子到爺爺奶奶都有。

**❸ perform** [ pɚˋfɔrm ] *vi.* 表演；表現 & *vt.* 執行；履行

Mary loves being on stage and performs in plays whenever she can.

瑪麗喜歡在臺上表演，只要有機會就在戲裡軋一角。

**❹ for free**　　免費 (= free [ fri ])

= free of charge

This coupon admits two people for free.

這張優惠券可供兩人免費使用。

＊coupon [ ˋkupɑn ] *n.* 優惠券；折價券
　admit [ ədˋmɪt ] *vt.* 准許入場

**❺ interest** [ ˋɪnt(ə)rɪst ] *vt.* 使……感興趣 & *n.* 興趣

The novel interested me a lot. I want to read it again.

那本小說引起我極大的興趣。我想要再讀一遍。

**❻ make a call**　　打電話

make a call to sb　　打電話給某人

Rudy made a call to Lucy inviting her to see a concert.

魯迪打電話給露西邀她去聽演唱會。

**❼ go with...**　　和……一起去；伴隨……

I have two tickets for the concert. Would you like to go with me?

我有兩張演唱會的票，你要和我一起去嗎？

CH
3
休閒娛樂

175

**1** 代名詞 none 的用法

none [ nʌn ] *pron.* 沒有一個；無一人；無一物

none 是代名詞，可用來代替人或物，指三個或三個以上的人或東西當中「沒有一個」，用法如下：

none of the（或 these、those、my、your、his...）+ 複數名詞 + 複數（或單數）動詞

None of his classmates like(s) music.
他的同學當中沒有一個喜歡音樂。

None of those novels are / is interesting.
那些小說當中沒有一本是有趣的。

比較

none of + 數量有三個或三個以上的名詞或代名詞　　都不……

neither of + 數量只有兩個的名詞或代名詞　　都不……

None of my parents smokes.（×）

→ Neither of my parents smokes.（○）
我爸媽都不抽菸。

**2** 副詞 either 的用法

either [ ˈiðɚ / ˈaɪðɚ ] *adv.* 也（不）（與 not 並用）

副詞 either 專用於否定的簡應句中，用法如下：

**a** 與 be 動詞並用：

Jimmy wasn't going home, and Jenny wasn't, either.
吉米不回家，珍妮也不回家。

**b** 與助動詞並用：

Jimmy won't come, and Jenny won't, either.
吉米不來，珍妮也不來。

**c** 與一般動詞並用：

Jimmy has no money, and Jenny doesn't, either.
吉米沒有錢，珍妮也沒有。

## 簡短對答 Quick Response

◆ Make quick responses to the sentences you hear.

## 討論題目 Free Talk

Talk on the following topic:

◆ What was the last concert you went to?

CH
3
休
閒
娛
樂

# Lesson 35

# In a Restaurant
## 在餐廳

**搭配筆記聆聽短文** **Listen to the text with the help of the notes given**

| waiter | 服務員 |
| --- | --- |
| Her pizza is also to die for! | 她做的披薩也棒極了！ |
| menu | 菜單 |
| on the left | 左邊 |
| on the right | 右邊 |
| recommend | 推薦 |

**再次聆聽並回答問題** **Listen again and answer the questions below**

Questions for discussion:

1 What is the name of the restaurant?

2 Does the waiter think the chef's pizza is good?

3 What does the waiter recommend for drinks?

Welcome to Albert's Restaurant. I'm your waiter, Ken. Today, the chef is Leah Roberts. She makes the best soup in town. Her pizza is also to die for! Here is your menu. The food is on the left, and the drinks are on the right. For drinks, I recommend our red wine. It goes well with any of our dishes.

歡迎光臨亞伯特餐廳。我是您的服務員肯恩。今天的主廚是莉雅・羅伯茲。她做出來的湯是本地最好的湯品。她做的披薩也棒極了！這是您的菜單。左邊列的是食物，而飲料則列在右邊。以飲料來說，我推薦本餐廳的紅酒。它跟我們餐廳的任何一道菜都很搭。

**❶ chef** [ ʃɛf ] *n.* 廚師；大廚

**❷ soup** [ sup ] *n.* 湯
eat / have soup　　喝湯

### 🔖 Notes

soup 在西方人眼中是一道菜，故與動詞 eat 或 have 並用，無 drink soup 的用法。

I need a spoon to eat my soup.
我需要一支湯匙來喝湯。

**❸ menu** [ ˋmɛnju ] *n.* 菜單
Can I have the menu, please?
= Can I see the menu, please?
請給我看一下菜單好嗎？

**❹ drink** [ drɪŋk ] *n.* 飲料
a soft drink　　不含酒精的飲料
= a non-alcoholic drink
a sports drink　　運動飲料

**❺ recommend** [ ˏrɛkəˋmɛnd ] *vt.* 推薦；介紹；建議；勸告
I believe Johnny is a competent young man, so I recommend him to you without reservation.
我相信強尼是個能幹的年輕人，所以我毫不保留地把他推薦給您。
＊ without reservation [ ˏrɛzəˋveʃən ]　　毫不保留

**❻ go with...**　　搭配……(= match...)
We had some red wine to go with our turkey dinner.
我們喝紅酒來配火雞晚餐。

**❼ dish** [ dɪʃ ] *n.* 菜餚；碗盤

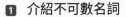
**1** 介紹不可數名詞

**a** 本課提到 soup、pizza、food、drink、wine 這些物質名詞。其中 soup、pizza、wine 是不可數名詞，前面通常不加不定冠詞 a 或 an，也不加數字，但可用下列方式表達：

數詞 + 單位名詞 + of

a bowl of soup 一碗湯
a slice of pizza 一片披薩
a glass of wine 一杯葡萄酒

**b** 除了 of 詞組之外，物質名詞前面可以加 any、little、some、much、a lot of、a great deal of 這些不定數量形容詞來表數量。

Peter doesn't eat much cake.
彼得不太吃蛋糕。

I have a great deal of work to do this afternoon.
今天下午我有很多工作要做。

**c** 某些不可數物質名詞在表示「不同種類」時，可以作可數名詞，此時通常用複數形，像是 food、fruit、fish、wine、tea。

Vending machines offer a wide variety of foods, ranging from cookies to chips.
販賣機賣各式各樣的食物，從餅乾到洋芋片都有。

**2** 表示「非常棒的」的說法

to die for 特別棒的；非常好的
The chef's specialty is Peking duck and it is to die for.
這位大廚的專長是北京烤鴨，而且好吃得不得了。
My grandma's chocolate cake is to die for.
我奶奶做的巧克力蛋糕好吃得不得了。

CH
3

休閒娛樂

181

| **1** [ ʃ ] | chef [ ʃɛf ] | dish [ dɪʃ ] |
| **2** [ i ] | Leah [ ˈliə ] | pizza [ ˈpitsə ] |

## 朗讀短文 **Read aloud the text**

🔖 請特別注意 [ ʃ ]、[ i ] 的發音。

Welcome to Albert's Restaurant. I'm your waiter, Ken. Today, the chef is Leah Roberts. She makes the best soup in town. Her pizza is also to die for! Here is your menu. The food is on the left, and the drinks are on the right. For drinks, I recommend our red wine. It goes well with any of our dishes.

## 換句話說 **Retell**

🔖 Retell the text from the perspective of the chef with the help of the words and expressions below.

**chef, soup, menu, drink, recommend, go with, dish**

## 討論題目 **Free Talk**

🔖 Talk on the following topic:

◆ Do you have a favorite restaurant?
What is your favorite dish?

## Lesson 36

# What Are You Up to?
## 你在幹嘛？

**搭配筆記聆聽會話** **Listen to the text with the help of the notes given**

| | |
|---|---|
| a basketball game | 籃球比賽 |
| at my place | 在我家 |
| a bottle of wine | 一瓶葡萄酒 |
| Shall I bring it over? | 我要帶過去嗎？ |
| alcohol | 酒 |

**再次聆聽並回答問題** **Listen again and answer the questions below**

Questions for discussion:

1 What is the woman doing?

2 What is the man doing?

3 Why doesn't the man want to drink wine?

Ⓐ Hey, Marcy! What are you up to?

Ⓑ I'm watching a basketball game on TV.

Ⓐ I'm cooking dinner at my place. Come over and join me!

Ⓑ Sure! I'm drinking a bottle of wine. It's delicious! Shall I bring it over?

Ⓐ Not for me, thanks. I'm quitting alcohol.

Ⓐ 嘿，瑪希！妳在幹嘛？

Ⓑ 我在看電視上的籃球比賽。

Ⓐ 我正在我家煮晚餐。過來加入我吧！

Ⓑ 好啊！我正在喝葡萄酒。它很美味！我要帶過去嗎？

Ⓐ 我不用了，謝謝。我在戒酒。

**❶ basketball** [ ˋbæskɪtˏbɔl ] *n.* 籃球
play basketball　　打籃球

**❷ game** [ gem ] *n.* 比賽；遊戲
a basketball / baseball game　　籃球 / 棒球比賽
watch / see a game　　看比賽

**❸ cook** [ kʊk ] *vt.* & *vi.* 煮；烹飪 & *n.* 廚師
Mom is cooking curry for us.
= Mom is making curry for us.
老媽在煮咖哩給我們吃。

**❹ bottle** [ ˋbɑtl ] *n.* 瓶子
a bottle of water　　一瓶水
a wine / beer bottle　　一個葡萄酒瓶 / 啤酒瓶

**❺ bring** [ brɪŋ ] *vt.* 帶來 (三態為：bring, brought [ brɔt ], brought)
bring sth over　　帶某物過來

Holly brought some homemade food over.
荷莉帶了一些自己做的食物過來。

**❻ quit** [ kwɪt ] *vt.* & *vi.* 戒除；停止；辭職 (三態同形)
quit + N/V-ing　　戒掉……；停止……

The old man finally quit smoking.
= The old man finally gave up smoking.
這位老先生終於戒菸了。

**❼ alcohol** [ ˋælkəˏhɔl ] *n.* 酒；酒精 (不可數)
alcoholic [ ˏælkəˋhɔlɪk ] *a.* 含酒精的 & *n.* 酗酒者

CH
3
休
閒
娛
樂

**❶** 詢問「你在幹嘛？」的說法

**What are you up to?**　　你在幹嘛？
= What are you doing?

185

sb is up to sth 除了用來單純表示「某人在做某事」之外，亦可用來表示「某人在策劃某事」，通常帶有負面的意思。

**The boys are up to no good.**
那些男孩們要做壞事。

**2** 表示從事球類運動的說法

◆ 表示從事某球類運動要用「play + 球類運動」，中間不能加定冠詞 the。
I'm playing <u>basketball</u>. 我在打籃球。

◆ 替換看看：

| | |
|---|---|
| volleyball 排球 | baseball 棒球 |
| badminton 羽球 | tennis 網球 |
| ping-pong 桌球 | football 美式橄欖球；足球(英式) |
| soccer 足球 (美式) | |

## 簡短對答 Quick Response

◆ Make quick responses to the sentences you hear.

## 討論題目 Free Talk

Talk on the following topic:

◆ What are you up to today?

# The Train Will Depart Soon
## 火車快要開了

**搭配筆記聆聽會話** **Listen to the text with the help of the notes given**

| | |
|---|---|
| I have no idea. | 我不知道。 |
| show up | 出現 |
| unbelievable | 難以置信的 |
| depart | 出發 |
| He needs to be taught a lesson. | 他得記取教訓。 |

**再次聆聽並回答問題** **Listen again and answer the questions below**

Questions for discussion:

**1** Does the woman know where Andy is?

**2** What type of transportation will they take?

**3** What does the woman want to do?

## 實用會話 Dialogue

Ⓐ Where is Andy?

Ⓑ I have no idea. He hasn't shown up yet.

Ⓐ Unbelievable! The train will depart soon. He is going to be late.

Ⓑ We will have to leave without him.

Ⓐ But he will be mad at us.

Ⓑ That's his problem. He needs to be taught a lesson.

Ⓐ OK. You are the boss.


Ⓐ 安迪在哪裡？

Ⓑ 我不知道。他還沒出現。

Ⓐ 真不敢相信！火車快要開了。他會遲到的。

Ⓑ 我們得留下他先離開。

Ⓐ 但是他會對我們很生氣。

Ⓑ 那是他的問題。他得記取教訓。

Ⓐ 好吧。你說了算。

## 單字片語 Vocabulary and Phrases

**❶ show up** 出現

= turn up

= appear

Marcus didn't show up at the party last night.

= Marcus didn't turn up at the party last night.

= Marcus didn't appear at the party last night.
馬克斯昨晚沒有在派對上出現。

**❷ unbelievable** [ ˌʌnbɪˈlivəbl̩ ] *a.* 令人難以置信的

**❸ depart** [ dɪˈpɑrt ] *vi.* 出發，啟程
depart for + 地點　　出發前往某地

We need to wake up early tomorrow. Our plane departs at 7 a.m.
我們明天要早起。班機在早上七點起飛。

Angela departed for New York last week.
安琪拉上週已前往紐約。

**❹ teach sb a lesson** 使某人記取教訓

Johnson is always late to work. I'm going to teach him a lesson!
強森上班總是遲到。我要去教訓他一頓！

**❺ You are the boss.** 你說了算。（此為口語用法）
boss [ bɔs ] *n.* 老闆，上司

📌 表示「我不知道」的說法

表示「我不知道」除了 "I don't know." 之外，也可以這樣說：

I have no idea.

I have no clue.

Haven't got a clue.

I haven't (got) the faintest idea.

I haven't (got) the slightest idea.

It beats me.

Beats me.

＊ beat [ bit ] *vt.* 擊敗 (三態為：beat, beat, beat / beaten [ ˋbitn̩ ])

📌 **Notes**

在美式英語的口語會話中，don't know 常被念作 dunno [ ˋdʌnə ]，為非正式用法。

簡短對答 **Quick Response**

◆ Make quick responses to the sentences you hear.

討論題目 **Free Talk**

📌 Talk on the following topic:

◆ What would you do if your friend were late? Would you wait for your friend?

## Lesson 38

# A Road Trip
## 公路旅行

---

**搭配筆記聆聽短文** **Listen to the text with the help of the notes given**

| | |
|---|---|
| go on a road trip | 去公路旅行 |
| the trip of a lifetime | 畢生難忘的旅行 |
| share | 分攤 |
| cost | 花費 |
| It will be worth it. | 這一切都值得。 |

---

**再次聆聽並回答問題** **Listen again and answer the questions below**

Questions for discussion:

1 Who will the speaker go on a road trip with?

2 What is the final destination of their road trip?

3 What did the speaker say will be expensive?

191

I will go on a road trip next week with my best friend, Tom. We are going to drive from LA to Chicago, and it will be the trip of a lifetime! Tom and I will share the driving, so we won't get too tired. We will also share the cost, as the gas will be really expensive. But it will be worth it!

我下週將會和我最好的朋友湯姆去公路旅行。我們要從洛杉磯開到芝加哥,這將會是畢生難忘的旅行!湯姆和我會輪流開車,所以我們不會太累。我們也會分攤費用,因為油錢真的很貴。但這一切都值得!

**❶ go on a trip** 去旅行
= take a trip

**❷ a road trip** 公路旅行
trip [ trɪp ] *n.* 旅行
a business trip 出差
a school trip 學校旅行，校外教學

**❸ drive** [ draɪv ] *vi.* & *vt.* 駕駛，開車 & *n.* 駕車兜風
(三態為：drive, drove [ drov ], driven [ ˋdrɪvən ])
go for a drive 開車兜風

I saw Peter driving his car yesterday.
我昨天看見彼得在開車。
Do you want to go for a drive?
你想要開車去兜風嗎？

**❹ lifetime** [ ˋlaɪfˏtaɪm ] *n.* 一生
the trip / chance of a lifetime 一生難得的旅行 / 機會
once in a lifetime 一生一次地，千載難逢地

**❺ share** [ ʃɛr ] *vt.* 分攤 (費用)；分擔 (責任)；分享
Let's share the cost.
咱們平分費用吧。

**❻ driving** [ ˋdraɪvɪŋ ] *n.* 駕駛，開車 (不可數)
share the driving 輪流開車

**❼ cost** [ kɔst ] *n.* 費用 & *vt.* 花費 (三態同形)

**❽ gas** [ gæs ] *n.* 汽油 (= gasoline [ ˋgæsəˏlin ])

**❾ expensive** [ ɪkˋspɛnsɪv ] *a.* 昂貴的

**❶ 介詞 worth 的用法**

　　介詞 worth 使用時須置 be 動詞後，其後接動名詞或名詞作受詞，相關用法
如下：

CH
3
休閒娛樂

worth [ wɝθ ] *prep.* 值得
be worth + N/V-ing　　值得……
be (not) worth it　　是 (不) 值得的
= be (not) worthwhile
The novel is worth reading.
這本小說值得一看。

比較

**ⓐ** worthy [ ˈwɝðɪ ] *a.* 值得的
be worthy of + N/V-ing　　值得……
The novel is worthy of reading.
這本小說值得一看。

**ⓑ** worthwhile [ ˌwɝθˈwaɪl ] *a.* 值得做的
It's worthwhile to read this novel.
= It's worth it to read this novel.
這本小說值得一看。

**2** 表示旅行的說法

**ⓐ** trip [ trɪp ] *n.* 旅行，行程
trip 通常指短途旅行，所花費的時間較短，除了 a road trip (公路旅行)
之外，亦有下列常見的搭配：
a day trip　　　　　　一日遊
a round trip　　　　　往返旅程
a business trip　　　　出差
a school / field trip　　校外教學

**ⓑ** journey [ ˈdʒɝnɪ ] *n.* 旅行，旅程
journey 尤指長途、時間較長的旅行。除了用來表示真實的出遊之外，
亦可用以表示心靈層面的旅行，如：
a spiritual journey　　心靈之旅

**ⓒ** travel [ ˈtrævl̩ ] *n.* 旅行
travel 可作不可數名詞，泛指一般旅遊活動。若表示一系列或多次的旅
遊，則必須恆用複數。常見的搭配字詞如下：
air travel　　　　　　　航空旅行
space travel　　　　　　太空旅行
a record of one's travels　某人遊歷的記錄

## 發音提示 Pronunciation

| ❶ [ i ] | week [ wik ] | we [ wi ] |
|---------|--------------|-----------|

| ❷ [ g ] | go [ go ] | get [ gɛt ] |
|---------|-----------|-------------|
| | Chicago [ ʃəˈkɑgo ] | gas [ gæs ] |

## 朗讀短文 Read aloud the text

🎤 請特別注意 [ i ]、[ g ] 的發音。

I will go on a road trip next week with my best friend, Tom. We are going to drive from LA to Chicago, and it will be the trip of a lifetime! Tom and I will share the driving, so we won't get too tired. We will also share the cost, as the gas will be really expensive. But it will be worth it!

## 換句話說 Retell

🎤 Retell the text with the help of the words and expressions below.

go on a trip, a road trip, drive, lifetime, share, driving, cost, gas, expensive

## 討論題目 Free Talk

🎤 Talk on the following topic:

◆ Have you ever been on a road trip before?

# When Will You Be Visiting?
## 你什麼時候要來拜訪？

搭配筆記聆聽會話 **Listen to the text with the help of the notes given**

| | |
|---|---|
| Mexico | 墨西哥 |
| I can't wait to see you. | 我迫不及待見到你。 |
| surprise | 驚喜 |
| That's wonderful! | 太棒了！ |
| fantastic | 很棒的 |

再次聆聽並回答問題 **Listen again and answer the questions below**

🔍 Questions for discussion:

**1** Is the woman in Mexico?

**2** When will the woman fly to Mexico?

**3** Who will go with the woman to Mexico?

## 實用會話 Dialogue

Ⓐ Hi, Grandpa. It's Rosie.

Ⓑ Hi, Rosie. Are you here in Mexico?

Ⓐ No, I'll be flying to Mexico on Monday.

Ⓑ Great! I can't wait to see you again.

Ⓐ I have a surprise. Mom and Dad will be coming with me.

Ⓑ Oh, that's wonderful! We will have a fantastic time together!

Ⓐ 嗨，爺爺。我是蘿西。

Ⓑ 嗨，蘿西。妳人在墨西哥嗎？

Ⓐ 沒有，我星期一才會搭飛機到墨西哥。

Ⓑ 太棒了！我迫不及待再看到妳。

Ⓐ 我有個驚喜。老媽和老爸也會和我一起去。

Ⓑ 喔，那真是太好了！我們會有個超棒的相聚時光！

**❶ fly** [ flaɪ ] *vi.* 乘飛機；飛 & *vt.* 搭乘 (某航空公司)
(三態為：fly, flew [ flu ], flown [ flon ])

fly from A to B　　(航班或乘客)從 A 地飛，B 地降落

This plane will fly from Seoul to New York.
這班飛機將從首爾飛往紐約。

Erin flew to California yesterday.
愛琳昨天搭飛機到加州。

**❷ can't wait to V**　　等不及要做……

wait [ wet ] *vi.* 等候，等待

I can't wait to go camping with my family this weekend.
我等不及這週末要和家人一起去露營了。

**❸ surprise** [ sɚˋpraɪz ] *n.* 意想不到的事；驚訝 & *vt.* 使驚訝

**❹ wonderful** [ ˋwʌndɚfl̩ ] *a.* 令人高興的

**❺ fantastic** [ fænˋtæstɪk ] *a.* 很棒的

**❶** 介詞 in 搭配地方名詞的用法

介詞 in 搭配地方名詞使用時須接「大地方」，如城市、國家：

| in + 地方名詞 (如城市、國家等) | 在…… |
|---|---|
| in my hometown | 在我的故鄉 |
| in the city | 在城市 |
| in Tokyo / Paris / London | 在東京 / 巴黎 / 倫敦 |
| in Spain / Italy / Germany | 在西班牙 / 義大利 / 德國 |
| in Asia / Europe | 在亞洲 / 歐洲 |

比較

介詞 at 與 on 後亦可接地方名詞，惟 at 通常與表「小地點、場所」的地方名詞並用，如某建築物、車站、公園等，而 on 則是與表「街道或平地」等地方名詞並用，如以下：

**ⓐ** at + 地方名詞 (如某建築物、車站、公園等)
　在……

| | |
|---|---|
| at the department store | 在百貨公司 |
| at the post office | 在郵局 |
| at the train station | 在火車站 |
| at the park | 在公園 |

**ⓑ** on + 地方名詞 (如街道、路、有平地的地方等)　　在……

| | |
|---|---|
| on the street | 在街上 |
| on Fifth Avenue | 在第五大道 |
| on campus | 在校園 |
| on the farm / ranch | 在農場 / 牧場上 |

**2** 介詞 on 搭配時間名詞的用法

◆ 介詞 on 可與表「星期與日期」的時間名詞並用，如：

on + 時間名詞 (如星期、日期)　　在……

| | |
|---|---|
| on June 8 | 在六月八日 |
| on September 14 | 在九月十四日 |
| on Monday | 在星期一 |

◆ 替換看看：

| Tuesday | 星期二 | Friday | 星期五 |
|---|---|---|---|
| Wednesday | 星期三 | Saturday | 星期六 |
| Thursday | 星期四 | Sunday | 星期日 |

## 簡短對答 Quick Response

◆ Make quick responses to the sentences you hear.

## 討論題目 Free Talk

🔑 Talk on the following topic:

◆ Have you ever traveled abroad before?

# A Dinner Party
## 晚宴派對

| | |
|---|---|
| late | 晚的，遲到的 |
| overtime | 加班 |
| That's too bad. | 那真糟糕。 |
| save | 保留 |
| spaghetti | 義大利麵 |

Questions for discussion:

1 When is the dinner party?

2 Will the woman be there on time?

3 What will the man save for the woman?

🅐 Are you going to come to my dinner party on Friday night?

🅑 Yes, I'll be there, but I will be late.

🅐 Why are you going to be late?

🅑 I'm going to be working overtime.

🅐 That's too bad. I'll save you some spaghetti and pudding.


🅐 你週五晚上會來參加我的晚宴派對嗎？

🅑 會，我會去，但我會晚點到。

🅐 為什麼你會晚點到？

🅑 我要加班。

🅐 那真糟糕。我會幫你留一些義大利麵和布丁。

**❶ dinner** [ ˈdɪnɚ ] *n.* 晚餐
have dinner　　吃晚餐
have sth for dinner　　晚餐吃某物

**❷ party** [ ˈpɑrtɪ ] *n.* 派對；聚會
a dinner / birthday / farewell party　　晚宴 / 生日 / 歡送派對

**❸ work overtime**　　加班工作
overtime [ ˈovɚˌtaɪm ] *adv. & n.* 加班

**❹ save** [ sev ] *vt.* 保留
save sb sth　　幫某人留某物
= save sth for sb
save me a seat　　幫我留個位子
= save a seat for me

**❺ spaghetti** [ spəˈɡɛtɪ ] *n.* 義大利麵

**❻ pudding** [ ˈpʊdɪŋ ] *n.* 布丁

**❶** 未來式的句構

◆ 未來式除了用助動詞 will 來表示未來發生的動作或狀態，在口語會話中
也常替換為 be going to，句構如下：
主詞 + will + 原形動詞 (+ 表未來的時間副詞)
= 主詞 + be going to + 原形動詞 (+ 表未來的時間副詞)

◆ 根據上述，本課句子可改寫如下：
Are you going to come to my dinner party on Friday night?
→ Will you come to my dinner party on Friday night?
你週五晚上會來參加我的晚宴派對嗎？
I will be late.
→ I'm going to be late.
我會晚點到。

202

**2** 表示同情或可惜的說法

| | |
|---|---|
| That's too bad. | 那真糟糕。 |
| That sucks. | 那真糟糕。（非正式說法） |
| What a shame. | 真可惜。 |
| What a pity! | 真可惜！ |
| Poor you! | 你真可憐！（非正式說法） |
| I'm sorry to hear that. | 很遺憾聽到這消息。 |
| I feel bad for you. | 我為你感到遺憾。 |

**A** I can't go to your party tomorrow. I have to work on a project.

**B** That's too bad.

**A** 我明天無法參加你的派對。我得要弄一份專案。

**B** 那真糟糕。

## 簡短對答 **Quick Response**

◆ Make quick responses to the sentences you hear.

## 討論題目 **Free Talk**

🔑 Talk on the following topic:

◆ Have you ever hosted a dinner party?

# A Great Place to Visit
## 值得一遊的好地方

**搭配筆記聆聽短文** **Listen to the text with the help of the notes given**

| | |
|---|---|
| overlook | 俯瞰 |
| tram | 電車 |
| drift | 漂流 |
| seafood | 海鮮 |
| the friendly locals | 友善的當地人 |
| before you know it | 很快地 |

**再次聆聽並回答問題** **Listen again and answer the questions below**

📍 Questions for discussion:

❶ According to the speaker, is Lisbon a good place to visit?

❷ What transportation can you take in Lisbon?

❸ Are the locals in Lisbon friendly?

Lisbon is a great place to visit. You can see the castle overlooking the city. You can ride the famous tram up into the old town. You can hear the traditional music drifting out of the bars. You can taste the awesome seafood. You can also feel the warmth of the friendly locals. You'll be back in Lisbon again before you know it.

里斯本是一個值得一遊的好地方。你可以看到俯瞰著整個城市的城堡。你可以搭乘聞名於世的電車進入舊城。你可以聽到從酒吧裡飄揚出來的傳統音樂。你可以品嘗超讚的海鮮。你也可以感受到當地人溫馨的友誼。很快地你將會重遊里斯本。

**❶ castle** [ ˋkæsl̩ ] *n.* 城堡

**❷ overlook** [ ˌovɚˋlʊk ] *vt.* 俯瞰；忽略

The small museum is located on a hilltop overlooking the valley.
那間小博物館坐落在山頂上，可以俯瞰山谷。

**❸ tram** [ træm ] *n.* 有軌電車 (英式用法)
= tramcar (英式用法)
= streetcar (美式用法)

**❹ traditional** [ trəˋdɪʃən̩l ] *a.* 傳統的

Paul prefers the traditional music of his homeland to Western music.
保羅喜歡家鄉的傳統音樂甚於西洋音樂。

**❺ drift** [ drɪft ] *vi.* 漂流；遊蕩；漫遊 & *n.* 漂流

The boat drifted slowly down the river because its engine was out of order.
那艘船由於引擎壞了，所以就順著河流慢慢漂流。

**❻ bar** [ bɑr ] *n.* 酒吧；吧台
a lounge [ laʊndʒ ] bar　雅座酒吧

**❼ taste** [ test ] *vt.* 品嚐 & *vi.* 嚐起來 & *n.* 味道

Amy had a strange facial expression when she tasted this dish.
艾咪吃這道菜時臉上有奇怪的表情。

**❽ awesome** [ ˋɔsəm ] *a.* 棒極了 (口語)；很棒的；令人敬畏的

Bill thought the concert was awesome.
比爾認為那場音樂會棒極了。

**❾ seafood** [ ˋsiˌfud ] *n.* 海鮮；海產 (不可數)

**❿ warmth** [ wɔrmθ ] *n.* 溫暖

**⓫ friendly** [ ˋfrɛndlɪ ] *a.* 友善的
be friendly with sb　跟某人很要好

It is just part of Peter's nature to be friendly to / toward(s) people.
待人親切正是彼得的天性之一。

⑫ **local** [ `lokl ] *n.* 當地人；本地人
                    & *a.* 當地的；本地的

A kind-hearted local showed me the way
to the gas station.
一個好心的當地人指引我前往加油站的路。

## 實用詞句 Useful Expressions

**1** 知覺動詞的用法

**ⓐ** 知覺動詞有三類：
看：see、observe、notice、behold、look at、watch（注意看）
聽：hear、listen to（注意聽）
感覺：feel

**ⓑ** 這種表「看」、「聽」、「感覺」的知覺動詞，可作不完全及物動詞，加了受詞之後，可接原形動詞作受詞補語，表已發生的事實，譯成「……了」，句型如下：

知覺動詞 + 受詞 + 原形動詞

I saw James enter the restroom.
我看見詹姆士進了廁所。

I never heard Rick speak English.
我從未聽過瑞克講英語。

I felt the floor shake.
我感覺地面搖動了。

**ⓒ** 表進行狀態時，用現在分詞作補語，譯成「……正在……」，句型如下：

知覺動詞 + 受詞 + 現在分詞

I saw Jack dancing when I walked in.
我走進來時，看見傑克正在跳舞。

As I pushed the door open, I heard Peter singing.
我推開門時，聽見彼得正在唱歌。

I felt his hand touching mine.
我感覺到他的手正在觸碰我的手。

**2** 表示「很快地」的說法

**before you know it** 很快地 / 轉眼間 / 在不知不覺中

= very soon

Time flies. You get married, have children, and before you know it, you are a grandmother.

= Time flies. You get married, have children, and very soon, you are a grandmother.

光陰似箭。結婚、生子，然後不知不覺 / 很快就當上了奶奶。

## 發音提示 Pronunciation

| **❶ [ aʊ ]** | town [ taʊn ] | out [ aʊt ] |
|---|---|---|

| **❷ [ z ]** | Lisbon [ ˈlɪzbən ] | music [ ˈmjuzɪk ] |
|---|---|---|
| | visit [ ˈvɪzɪt ] | |

## 朗讀短文 Read aloud the text

🎙 請特別注意 [ aʊ ]、[ z ] 的發音。

Lisbon is a great place to visit. You can see the castle overlooking the city. You can ride the famous tram up into the old town. You can hear the traditional music drifting out of the bars. You can taste the awesome seafood. You can also feel the warmth of the friendly locals. You'll be back in Lisbon again before you know it.

## 換句話說 Retell

Retell the text with the help of the words and expressions below.

castle, overlook, tram, traditional, drift, bar, taste, awesome, seafood, warmth, friendly, local

## 討論題目 Free Talk

Talk on the following topic:

◇ Is there a city you would like to visit again? Why?

CH
3
休
閒
娛
樂

# Lesson 42

# Cutting Down on Caffeine
## 少喝咖啡

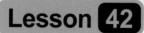

**Lesson 42**

---

**搭配筆記聆聽會話** | **Listen to the text with the help of the notes given**

| | |
|---|---|
| neither | (兩者) 都不要 |
| cut down on... | 減少…… |
| caffeine | 咖啡因 |
| Which would you prefer? | 你比較想要哪一種？ |
| ice | 冰塊；冰 |

**再次聆聽並回答問題** | **Listen again and answer the questions below**

Questions for discussion:

1 Why doesn't the woman want tea or coffee?

2 What does the woman prefer to drink?

3 Does the woman want some ice for her drink?

**實用會話** Dialogue

Ⓐ Would you like tea or coffee?

Ⓑ Neither, thanks. I'm cutting down on caffeine.

Ⓐ What would you like to drink then?

Ⓑ Do you have either water or juice?

Ⓐ I have both. Which would you prefer?

Ⓑ Hmm, just water. Thanks.

Ⓐ No problem. Shall I add some ice?

Ⓑ Sure!

Ⓐ 你要喝茶還是咖啡？

Ⓑ 謝謝，都不要。我正在減少咖啡因的攝取。

Ⓐ 這樣的話你要喝什麼？

**B** 你有水或果汁嗎？

**A** 這兩種我都有。你比較想要哪一種？

**B** 嗯，水就好。謝謝。

**A** 沒問題。要我加點冰塊嗎？

**B** 當然！

## 單字片語　Vocabulary and Phrases

**1** **neither** [ ˈniðɚ / ˈnaɪðɚ ] *pron.* 兩者都不

I watched two movies yesterday, but neither was good.
我昨天看了兩部電影，但兩部都不好看。

**2** **cut down on...** 　　減少……（cut 三態同形）

Peter has been trying to cut down on caffeine.
彼得一直在嘗試要減少攝取咖啡因。

**3** **caffeine** [ kæˈfin ] *n.* 咖啡因
decaffeinated [ dɪˈkæfɪˌnetɪd ] *a.* 去咖啡因的

An overdose of caffeine could be lethal.
咖啡因過量可能致命。

＊ lethal [ ˈliθəl ] *a.* 致命的

**4** **ice** [ aɪs ] *n.* 冰塊；冰（不可數）

I've put the bottle of champagne on ice.
我已經把那瓶香檳拿去冰了。

## 口語新技能　New Skills

**1** 對等連接詞 either A or B 的用法

either A or B　　不是 A 就是 B

"either... or..." 為對等連接詞，可連接對等的單字、片語或子句。此對等連接詞連接兩個主詞時，動詞的單複數須以最靠近的主詞做變化。

Either you or he has borrowed the book.
要不就是你，要不就是他把書借走了。
You can choose to either stay or leave.
你可以選擇留下或是離開。

❷ 動詞 prefer 的用法

prefer [ prɪˋfɝ ] vt. 比較喜歡，偏好
(三態為：prefer, preferred [ prɪˋfɝd ], preferred)
prefer A to B　　喜歡 A 勝於 B
prefer to V rather than V　　喜歡……勝於……
= prefer to V instead of V-ing
I prefer tea to coffee in the morning.
= I prefer to drink tea rather than drink coffee in the morning.
= I prefer to drink tea instead of drinking coffee in the morning.
我早上喜歡喝茶勝於喝咖啡。

## 簡短對答　Quick Response

◇ Make quick responses to the sentences you hear.

## 討論題目　Free Talk

🔑 Talk on the following topic:

◇ Do you like to drink coffee? How do you usually take your coffee?

# It's My Treat
## 我請客

搭配筆記聆聽會話 **Listen to the text with the help of the notes given**

| | |
|---|---|
| check | 帳單 |
| Absolutely not. | 絕對不行。 |
| Let's go Dutch. | 咱們平分吧。 |
| moreover | 除此之外 |
| Deal. | 一言為定。 |

再次聆聽並回答問題 **Listen again and answer the questions below**

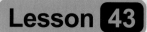 Questions for discussion:

**❶** Where are the man and woman most likely at?

**❷** What did the woman buy for the man?

**❸** Who is paying for the meal?

🅰 Shall we get the check?

🅱 Sure, but it's my treat.

🅰 Absolutely not. Let's go Dutch.

🅱 No, no. You traveled all this way to see me. Moreover, you bought me that expensive watch and that lovely shirt. Therefore, I'm paying for this!

🅰 OK, OK. However, I'm paying tomorrow night!

🅱 Deal.


🅰 咱們要結帳了嗎？

🅱 好呀，但這餐我請客。

🅰 絕對不行。咱們平分吧。

**B** 不，不要。你大老遠跑來看我。除此之外，你還買給我那只昂貴的手錶和那件好看的襯衫。所以，這餐我來付！

**A** 好，好。不過，明晚由我來付！

**B** 一言為定。

## 單字片語 Vocabulary and Phrases

**1 check** [ tʃɛk ] *n.* 帳單
= bill [ bɪl ]
get / have / pay the check / bill　　付帳單，買單

**2 go Dutch (with sb)**　(和某人) 分攤費用，各付各的
= split the check / bill
Dutch [ dʌtʃ ] *a.* 荷蘭的
split [ splɪt ] *vt.* 均分，分配 (三態同形)
Let's go Dutch.
= Let's split the check / bill.
咱們平分費用吧。

> 📍 **Notes**
>
> 現今有愈來愈多母語人士認為 "Let's go Dutch." 是較舊的說法，雖然還是會有部分的人使用，不過大多數的人較常以 "Let's split the check / bill." 來表示。

**3 moreover** [ mɔr`ovɚ ] *adv.* 此外，而且
The rent of my new apartment is cheap. Moreover, the location is perfect.
我新公寓的房租很便宜。此外，地點非常完美。

**4 expensive** [ ɪk`spɛnsɪv ] *a.* 昂貴的
cheap [ tʃip ] *a.* 便宜的

⑤ **lovely** [ ˈlʌvlɪ ] *a.* 美麗的；可愛的；令人愉快的

What a lovely daughter you have!
你女兒真漂亮！

⑥ **pay** [ pe ] *vi. & vt.* 付款（三態為：pay, paid [ ped ], paid）
pay for...　　付……的費用

Let me pay for the meal.
這頓飯讓我來付錢。

The boss pays her secretary $2,000 a month.
這位老闆每個月付給她祕書兩千美元的薪水。

⑦ **deal** [ dil ] *n.* 協定，交易
Deal.　　一言為定／就這麼辦。（常於口語使用）
= It's a deal.

Ⓐ Say, how about we meet at 2 p.m.?

Ⓑ Deal! / It's a deal!

Ⓐ 哎，我們下午兩點碰面怎麼樣呢？

Ⓑ 沒問題！

## 口語新技能　New Skills

① 表示「我請客」的說法

It's my treat.　　我請客。
＊ treat [ trit ] *n.* 款待，招待

其他表示「請客」的說法：
It's on me.
I'll get the check / bill.
I'll pick up the check / bill.
I'll take care of the check / bill.

② 以 absolutely 表示強烈否定或肯定的用法

Absolutely not.　　絕對不行／當然不。（於口語使用，表示強烈否定）
Absolutely.　　正是／當然。（於口語使用，表示強烈肯定）

Ⓐ Did the fish taste good?
Ⓑ Absolutely not!
Ⓐ 魚好吃嗎？
Ⓑ 一點都不！

Ⓐ This film is awesome.
Ⓑ Absolutely!
Ⓐ 這部電影好極了。
Ⓑ 完全同意！

## 簡短對答 Quick Response

◆ Make quick responses to the sentences you hear.

## 討論題目 Free Talk

📌 Talk on the following topic:

◆ Have you ever treated your friends to a meal? What was the occasion?

# Lesson 44

# Spending the Holidays Abroad

## 出國度假

**搭配筆記聆聽短文** **Listen to the text with the help of the notes given**

| | |
|---|---|
| vacation | 假期 |
| awkward | 尷尬的 |
| recently | 最近 |
| become closer and closer | 愈來愈親近 |
| tan | 曬黑 |

**再次聆聽並回答問題** **Listen again and answer the questions below**

📌 Questions for discussion:

**1** Who is the speaker spending the holidays with?

**2** Was the speaker close to her boyfriend's family at first?

**3** What will the speaker do with her boyfriend's dad?

I'm getting more and more excited about the vacation! My boyfriend and I are going to spend the holidays with his family in Bali. I used to feel a bit awkward around his family, but recently we've become closer and closer. In fact, I'm going to play tennis with my boyfriend's brother, go surfing with his dad, and work on my tan with his mom. I can't wait!

我愈來愈期待假期了！我男朋友與我要和他的家人去峇厘島度假。我之前與他家人相處會感到些許尷尬，但最近我們愈來愈親近。事實上，我要與他的弟弟打網球、與他的爸爸一起衝浪，還要與他的媽媽一起做日光浴。我等不及了！

**1 vacation** [ veˈkeʃən ] *n.* 假期
  spend one's / the vacation　度假
  go on vacation　去度假
  be on vacation　度假中
= be on holiday（英式用法）

**2 holiday** [ ˈhɑləˌde ] *n.* 假期；假日
  spend one's / the holiday(s)　度假

> 🎙 **Notes**
>
> the holidays 通常指西方十二月底至一月初的長假，這期間包含耶誕節及新年假期。注意此時 holiday 應用複數形。

**3 bit** [ bɪt ] *n.* 少量；小塊
  a (little) bit...　一點兒……，有點……
= a little...
  a bit of...　一點點的……

  The new student is a little bit shy.
= The new student is a little shy.
  新學生有點害羞。
  I added a bit of salt to the soup.
  我在湯裡加了一點點鹽巴。

**4 awkward** [ ˈɔkwəd ] *a.* 尷尬的；笨拙的

**5 recently** [ ˈrisn̩tlɪ ] *adv.* 最近
= lately [ ˈletlɪ ]

**6 tennis** [ ˈtɛnɪs ] *n.* 網球
  play tennis　打網球

**7 surf** [ sɝf ] *vi.* 衝浪 & *vt.* 瀏覽（網頁）
  go surfing　去衝浪
  surf the internet　上網

**8** **work on sth** 　努力做……；致力於……

I can't go out with you. I need to work on my report.
我不能跟你出去。我需要做報告。

Jason needs to work on his pronunciation.
傑森需要勤加練習發音。

**9** **tan** [ tæn ] *n.* 古銅膚色 (= suntan [ ˈsʌntæn ]) & *vi.* 曬黑
(三態為：tan, tanned, tanned) & *a.* 古銅膚色的 (= tanned [ tænd ])

Samantha got a nice tan at the beach.
珊曼莎在沙灘上曬得一身漂亮的古銅色。

Some people don't tan easily.
有些人不容易曬黑。

Look how tan and healthy-looking her skin is.
= Look how tanned and healthy-looking her skin is.
你看看她一身漂亮的古銅膚色，看起來真健康。

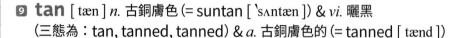

**實用詞句** **Useful Expressions**

🔑 介紹 more and more 的用法

　more and more 通常用於進行式的句子中，可作形容詞或副詞。

**a** 作形容詞時，more and more 可譯為「愈來愈多的……」，其後須接複
數名詞或不可數名詞。

More and more people are gathering at the square.
愈來愈多人在廣場聚集。

I'm making more and more money.
我賺的錢愈來愈多了。

**b** 作副詞時，more and more 可譯為「愈來愈……」，其後須接形容詞或
副詞。

The questions are getting more and more difficult.
問題愈來愈難了。

Selene is getting sick more and more often.
賽琳愈來愈常生病了。

**Notes**

more and more 作副詞時，等同於副詞 increasingly [ ɪnˈkrisɪŋlɪ ]，其後不須接比較級，故上述例句亦可改寫為：

    The questions are getting more and more difficult.

= The questions are getting increasingly difficult.

    Selene is getting sick more and more often.

= Selene is getting sick increasingly often.

**c** 若要以單音節形容詞或副詞表示「愈來愈……」，應使用「比較級 + and + 比較級」的句型，而非 more and more。

    James is getting more and more fat. (×)

→ James is getting fatter and fatter. (○)

    詹姆士愈來愈胖了。

    Wendy's grades are getting more and more good. (×)

→ Wendy's grades are getting better and better. (○)

    溫蒂的成績愈來愈好了。

## 發音提示 Pronunciation

| **①** [e] | vacation [ veˈkeʃən ] | play [ ple ] |
|---|---|---|
| | holiday [ ˈhɑləˌde ] | wait [ wet ] |

| **②** [f] | boyfriend [ ˈbɔɪˌfrɛnd ] | fact [ fækt ] |
|---|---|---|
| | family [ ˈfæməlɪ ] | surf [ sɝf ] |
| | feel [ fil ] | |

CH 3 休閒娛樂

223

📍 請特別注意 [ e ]、[ f ] 的發音。

I'm getting more and more excited about the vacation! My boyfriend and I are going to spend the holidays with his family in Bali. I used to feel a bit awkward around his family, but recently we've become closer and closer. In fact, I'm going to play tennis with my boyfriend's brother, go surfing with his dad, and work on my tan with his mom. I can't wait!

換句話說 **Retell**

📍 Retell the text with the help of the words and expressions below.

vacation, holiday, bit, awkward, recently, tennis, surf, work on sth, tan

討論題目 **Free Talk**

📍 Talk on the following topic:

◆ What would you like to do if you're having a vacation at a summer resort?

# Skydiving
## 跳傘

搭配筆記聆聽會話 **Listen to the text with the help of the notes given**

| amazing | 非常好的 |
| --- | --- |
| skydiving | 跳傘 |
| priority | 優先的事物 |
| promise | 承諾 |

再次聆聽並回答問題 **Listen again and answer the questions below**

🎙 Questions for discussion:

**1** What has the man done during his vacation?

**2** Does the man think skydiving is safe?

**3** What does the woman want the man to do?

🅐 Hi, Mom!

🅑 Hi, Lucas. How's the vacation going?

🅐 It's amazing here, Mom. There's so much to do. I've already gone skydiving twice!

🅑 Oh, I hope you're being careful!

🅐 Don't worry, Mom. Safety has always been their top priority.

🅑 Just promise me you'll keep calling every day to let me know you're OK.

🅐 Sure thing.


🅐 嗨，老媽！

🅑 嗨，路卡斯。假期過得怎麼樣呢？

Ⓐ 老媽，這裡真是太棒了。有好多事情可以做。
我已經去跳傘兩次了！

Ⓑ 喔，我希望你有小心一點！

Ⓐ 老媽，別擔心。安全一直是他們的首要之務。

Ⓑ 答應我你會持續每天打電話，好讓我知道你沒事。

Ⓐ 沒問題。

## 單字片語 Vocabulary and Phrases

**1** **amazing** [ əˋmezɪŋ ] *a.* 非常好的；令人驚喜的

**2** **skydiving** [ ˋskaɪˏdaɪvɪŋ ] *n.* 跳傘

**3** **twice** [ twaɪs ] *adv.* 兩次
once [ wʌns ] *adv.* 一次
three / four / five times　　三 / 四 / 五次

**4** **careful** [ ˋkɛrfḷ ] *a.* 小心的，謹慎的
be careful about...　　謹慎處理……

**5** **safety** [ ˋseftɪ ] *n.* 安全

**6** **one's top priority**　　某人最重要的事
priority [ praɪˋɔrətɪ ] *n.* 優先的事物

Our top priority is to improve the quality of our products.
我們的首要任務就是改善商品品質。

**7** **promise** [ ˋprɑmɪs ] *vt.* 承諾 & *n.* 諾言
promise (sb) to V　　承諾（某人）從事……
Abby promised to teach me how to make muffins.
艾比承諾要教我做瑪芬蛋糕。

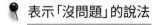
### 表示「沒問題」的說法

此處的「沒問題」是用於答應某請求或要求，常見的說法如下：

Sure thing.

Sure.

No problem.

Absolutely.

Certainly.

Roger (that). 　　遵命／收到。（原為無線電通訊用語）

Ⓐ Please give me a call as soon as you receive the package.

Ⓑ No problem.

Ⓐ 麻煩你一收到包裹就打電話給我。

Ⓑ 沒問題。

### 簡短對答 Quick Response

◆ Make quick responses to the sentences you hear.

### 討論題目 Free Talk

Talk on the following topic:

◆ Have you ever wanted to try an extreme sport? What kind of extreme sport would you like to try?

# Picking Someone Up at the Airport

## 去機場接某人

**搭配筆記聆聽會話** Listen to the text with the help of the notes given

| | |
|---|---|
| schedule | 行程 |
| land | 降落 |
| by noon | 在中午之前 |
| serve | 供應 (餐點) |
| on the way home | 在回家路上 |

**再次聆聽並回答問題** Listen again and answer the questions below

Questions for discussion:

**1** What type of transportation will the man take?

**2** Will the man have breakfast with the woman?

**3** What day will the man and woman meet?

**實用會話 Dialogue**

Ⓐ Hi, Richard. What's the schedule for Saturday?

Ⓑ I will have landed at the airport by noon.

Ⓐ Will you have eaten when I pick you up?

Ⓑ I think they will serve breakfast on the plane.

Ⓐ So, maybe we could get lunch on the way home?

Ⓑ Sounds good.

Ⓐ Cool. See you on Saturday!


Ⓐ 嗨，理查。你星期六的行程是什麼？

Ⓑ 我將於中午之前抵達機場。

Ⓐ 我去接你時，你將已經用過餐了嗎？

Ⓑ 我想他們會在飛機上提供早餐。

Ⓐ 那麼，或許我們可以在回家路上吃午餐？

Ⓑ 聽起來不錯。

Ⓐ 太好了。星期六見！

## 單字片語 Vocabulary and Phrases

❶ **schedule** [ ˋskɛdʒul ] *n.* 行程表；進度表；時刻表

| | |
|---|---|
| a tight schedule | 忙碌的行程 |
| on schedule | 按照進度 |
| behind schedule | 進度落後 |
| ahead of schedule | 進度超前 |
| a bus / train schedule | 公車 / 火車時刻表 |

= a bus / train timetable [ ˋtaɪm͵tebḷ ]

❷ **land** [ lænd ] *vi.* (搭機、船等) 抵達；(飛機) 降落

take off　(飛機) 起飛

We will land at Sydney Airport at 7 a.m. local time.
我們將於當地時間早上七點飛抵雪梨機場。

The plane landed / took off on schedule.
該班飛機按行程計畫降落 / 起飛。

❸ **airport** [ ˋɛr͵pɔrt ] *n.* 機場

❹ **noon** [ nun ] *n.* 中午，正午

= midday [ ˋmɪd͵de ]

❺ **serve** [ sɝv ] *vt.* 供應 (餐點)

serve breakfast / lunch / dinner　供應早餐 / 午餐 / 晚餐

The waiter will serve your food in a few minutes.
幾分鐘後就會有服務生過來為您上菜。

❻ **get lunch**　吃午餐

CH
3
休閒娛樂

表「吃午餐」，動詞「吃」除了可以使用 get 之外，亦可用 have 或 grab，不過 grab 較有因時間緊湊所以匆匆找東西來吃之意。

| have lunch | 吃午餐 |
| --- | --- |
| grab lunch | 趕緊隨便吃個午餐 |

## 口語新技能 New Skills

**1** 表示「(開車) 載某人」的說法

**pick sb up** (開車) 載某人

Will your boyfriend pick you up today?
你男友今天會來接你嗎？

此片語亦可用於表示「抱起某人」，如：

The little girl asked her mom to pick her up.
小女孩叫她媽媽把她抱起來。

**比較**

**pick sth up** 撿起某物；整理 (房間等)

Lisa picked up the pencil and put it on the table.
莉莎把鉛筆撿起來並將它放在桌上。

Your room is such a mess. Go pick up your room!
你的房間真亂。趕緊去整理房間！

**2** 形容詞 cool 在口語會話中的常見用法

cool 一詞作形容詞可表「涼爽的」或「時髦的，酷的」，不過 cool 亦常於口語中使用，用以表示贊同，或可以接受對方所說的事情。

Ⓐ Ryan said he finished the assignment.

Ⓑ Cool!

Ⓐ 萊恩說他完成作業了。

Ⓑ 太好了！

232

**A** How about eating out tonight?

**B** Yeah, cool.

= Yeah, I'm cool with that.

= Yeah, that'd be cool.

**A** 今晚外出用餐怎麼樣啊？

**B** 好呀，沒問題。

## 簡短對答 Quick Response

◇ Make quick responses to the sentences you hear.

## 討論題目 Free Talk

🎙 Talk on the following topic:

◇ When was the last time you traveled by plane?

# You Get What You Pay for
## 一分錢一分貨

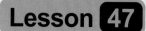

搭配筆記聆聽會話 **Listen to the text with the help of the notes given**

| | |
|---|---|
| storage space | 儲存空間 |
| feature | 功能 |
| difficult | 困難的 |
| cheap | 便宜的 |
| You get what you pay for. | 一分錢一分貨。 |

再次聆聽並回答問題 **Listen again and answer the questions below**

🔑 Questions for discussion:

1 Does the man think his new phone is good?

2 Is the man's new phone easier to use than his old one?

3 Is the man's new phone cheaper than his old one?

🅰 How's your new phone, Sam?

🅱 Not too good. It's got less storage space and fewer features than my old phone.

🅰 Oh, that's a shame.

🅱 It's more difficult to use than my old phone, too.

🅰 But it cost you less money, right?

🅱 Yeah, it was a lot cheaper than my old one.

🅰 Well, you get what you pay for!

🅰 山姆，你的新手機怎麼樣啊？

🅱 不太好。它的存儲空間比我舊手機的還要小，功能也比較少。

🅰 喔，真可惜。

**B** 它也比我的舊手機還難使用。

**A** 但它比較便宜，對嗎？

**B** 是呀，它比我舊的手機還要便宜許多。

**A** 嗯，一分錢一分貨啊！

## 單字片語　Vocabulary and Phrases

**1** **storage space**　(手機、電腦等的) 儲存空間；收納空間
storage [ ˋstɔrɪdʒ ] *n.* 儲存，儲藏
space [ spes ] *n.* 空間

**2** **feature** [ ˋfitʃɚ ] *n.* 特點，特色 & *vt.* 以……為特色
the (main) feature of...　……的 (主要) 特色

This week's talk show features an interview with the famous actor.
本週的談話節目主要是與那位著名演員的訪談。

**3** **That's a shame.**　真可惜 / 真遺憾。
= What a shame.
　**A** Gary, I can't go to your party tomorrow. I have to study.
　**B** That's a shame.
　**A** 蓋瑞，我明天無法參加你的派對。我得讀書。
　**B** 真可惜。

**4** **You get what you pay for!**　一分錢一分貨！

## 口語新技能　New Skills

🎙 介紹可修飾比較級的副詞

下列六個副詞可用以修飾比較級形容詞或副詞，常用來表示「更加」、「甚至」，使用時須置被修飾的形容詞或副詞之前：

| | |
|---|---|
| a lot | a great deal |
| far | still |
| much | even |

(其中以 a lot、far、much 較為常用)

This real leather sofa is <u>far more expensive</u> than that faux leather one.

這個真皮沙發比那個人造皮沙發來得更貴。

＊faux [ fo ] *a.* 人造的

Adam studies <u>much harder</u> than anyone of them.

亞當比他們之中任何一個都用功得多。

## 簡短對答 Quick Response

◇ Make quick responses to the sentences you hear.

## 討論題目 Free Talk

🔑 Talk on the following topic:

◇ What features of your phone do you like or dislike?

# Notes

# Chapter 4

## 職場與教育
### Work and Education

239

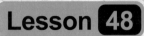

# Lesson 48

朗讀 ▶ Lesson 48

# A Busy Day
## 忙碌的一天

---

**搭配筆記聆聽短文** **Listen to the text with the help of the notes given**

| | |
|---|---|
| a breakfast meeting | 朝會 |
| client | 客戶 |
| supplier | 供應商 |
| colleague | 同事 |
| take me out for dinner | 帶我去吃晚餐 |
| come to think of it | 回想了一下 |

**再次聆聽並回答問題** **Listen again and answer the questions below**

🔑 Questions for discussion:

**1** What time did the speaker have lunch?

**2** Who did the speaker meet at three?

**3** Who is the speaker going out with for dinner?

I'm having such a busy day today. I had a breakfast meeting at 8 o'clock, lunch with a client at twelve, and coffee with a supplier at three. I am going for drinks with colleagues at 6 o'clock, and my boss is taking me out for dinner at 8. Come to think of it, it's just a day of eating and drinking!

我今天很忙碌。我八點開了個朝會,十二點與客戶吃了午餐,三點跟供應商喝了杯咖啡。我六點要跟同事們去小酌幾杯,然後我老闆八點要請我吃晚餐。我回想了一下,今天只不過是又吃又喝的一天!

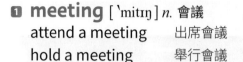

**❶ meeting** [ 'mitɪŋ ] *n.* 會議
attend a meeting　　出席會議
hold a meeting　　舉行會議

Our CEO will also attend the meeting.
本公司執行長也會參加這場會議。

We are holding a meeting to talk about the issue.
我們將舉行會議討論這個問題。

**❷ client** [ 'klaɪənt ] *n.* 客戶

**❸ supplier** [ sə'plaɪɚ ] *n.* 供應商
supply [ sə'plaɪ ] *vt.* 供應 (三態為：supply, supplied [ sə'plaɪd ], supplied)
　　　　　　　　& *n.* 補給品 (恆用複數)

supply sb with sth　　供應某人某物

The store supplied us with everything we need.
那間店提供給我們一切所需。

The hospital is in need of medical supplies.
這間醫院亟需醫療用品。

**❹ drink** [ drɪŋk ] *n.* 飲料 (此處特指酒或酒精飲料)
go for a drink　　去喝一杯 (酒)
have a drink　　喝一杯 (酒)

Rick and his friends went for a drink.
瑞克和他幾個朋友去喝酒了。

Have a drink and relax!
喝杯酒放鬆一下！

**❺ colleague** [ 'kɑlig ] *n.* 同事
= co-worker [ 'ko,wɝkɚ ]

William has trouble getting along with his colleagues.
= William has trouble getting along with his co-workers.
威廉跟同事處不來。

**1** **Come to think of it, it's just a day of eating and drinking!**
我回想了一下，今天只不過是又吃又喝的一天！

---

come to think of it　　這樣一想；突然想到（非正式用語）

Come to think of it, it was probably my fault.

= Now that I think of / about it, it was probably my fault.

= When I think about it, it was probably my fault.
我回想了一下，這可能是我的錯。

Come to think of it, Josephine was there at the party.
我回想了一下，約瑟芬有參加派對。

**2** 介紹「帶某人出去」的說法

---

take sb out for / to...　　帶某人出去……

My boyfriend is taking me out for dinner.
我男朋友要帶我去吃晚餐。

I'm taking my kids out to the amusement park.
我要帶我的孩子們去遊樂園。

🔖 **Notes**

---

下列為容易與 "take sb out for / to..." 混淆的片語：

**ⓐ** **take sb/sth out**　　除掉某人 / 某物（非正式用語）

The soldiers took out the enemy.
士兵們殺掉敵人了。

**ⓑ** **take one's anger out on sb**　　向某人發洩怒氣（非正式用語）

Philip took his anger out on his friends.
菲力浦將怒氣發洩到他朋友身上。

Don't take it out on your family.
別拿你的家人出氣。

| **①** [ tʃ ] | such [ sʌtʃ ] |
| | lunch [ lʌntʃ ] |

| **②** [ ɑ ] | o'clock [ əˈklɑk ] |
| | colleague [ ˈkɑlig ] |

朗讀短文 **Read aloud the text**

🔖 請特別注意 [ tʃ ]、[ ɑ ] 的發音。

I'm having such a busy day today. I had a breakfast meeting at 8 o'clock, lunch with a client at twelve, and coffee with a supplier at three. I am going for drinks with colleagues at 6 o'clock, and my boss is taking me out for dinner at 8. Come to think of it, it's just a day of eating and drinking!

換句話說 **Retell**

🔖 Retell the text with the help of the words and expressions below.

**meeting, client, supplier, drink, colleague**

討論題目 **Free Talk**

🔖 Talk on the following topic:

◆ Describe a day for you at work.
Are you usually busy?

# Studying for a Test
## 準備考試

## 搭配筆記聆聽會話 Listen to the text with the help of the notes given

| | |
|---|---|
| study English | 讀英文 |
| library | 圖書館 |
| quiet | 安靜的 |
| discuss | 討論 |
| cafeteria | 自助餐廳 |
| No way! | 不行！ |
| noisy | 吵雜的 |

## 再次聆聽並回答問題 Listen again and answer the questions below

🔑 Questions for discussion:

1. What are they going to study?
2. Where does the woman want to go?
3. Does the man want to go to the cafeteria?

## 實用會話 Dialogue

Ⓐ Do you want to study English together this afternoon?

Ⓑ OK. Where do you want to go?

Ⓐ To the library. It's a good place to study because it's quiet.

Ⓑ But we can't talk in the library. We might need to discuss things, so let's find another place to study.

Ⓐ How about the cafeteria?

Ⓑ No way! It's always so noisy there.


Ⓐ 今天下午你想要來一起讀英文嗎？

Ⓑ 好。你想要去哪裡讀呢？

Ⓐ 去圖書館。圖書館很安靜，所以是個讀書的好地方。

Ⓑ 可是我們不能在圖書館裡講話。我們可能需要討論一些事情，所以我們找別的地方讀書吧。

Ⓐ 去自助餐廳好不好？

Ⓑ 不行！那裡總是很吵雜。

❶ **afternoon** [ ˌæftɚˋnun ] *n.* 下午
　morning [ ˋmɔrnɪŋ ] *n.* 早上
　evening [ ˋivnɪŋ ] *n.* 傍晚，晚上
　in the morning / afternoon / evening　　在早上 / 下午 / 晚上

❷ **library** [ ˋlaɪˌbrɛrɪ ] *n.* 圖書館

❸ **quiet** [ ˋkwaɪət ] *a.* 安靜的 & *vi.* 安靜下來
　Be quiet, everybody!
= 　Quiet down, everybody!
　各位，安靜！

❹ **discuss** [ dɪˋskʌs ] *vt.* 討論
　discuss 是及物動詞，故不可說：
　discuss about the problem（×）
→ 　discuss the problem（○）
　The professor discussed the case with us.
　那位教授和我們討論這個案例。

❺ **cafeteria** [ ˌkæfəˋtɪrɪə ] *n.* 自助餐廳

❻ **noisy** [ ˋnɔɪzɪ ] *a.* 吵鬧的
　The room was crowded and noisy.
　房間又擠又吵。

口語新技能 **New Skills**

🎙 拒絕他人的說法

　要拒絕他人的請求除了用 "No." 之外，也可使用下列句子以加強語氣表示強烈拒絕：
　No way!　　　　　　　　　不行！
　Impossible!　　　　　　　不可能！
　That's out of the question!　沒得討論！
　I'm not doing that!　　　　我不要！

CH
4
職場與教育

Over my dead body! 死都別想！
Not on your life! 休想！

 Can you lend me some money?

 No way!

 你可以借我一些錢嗎？

 門兒都沒有！

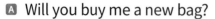

 Will you buy me a new bag?

 Not on your life!

 你會買新包包給我嗎？

 休想！

## 簡短對答　Quick Response

◆ Make quick responses to the sentences you hear.

## 討論題目　Free Talk

🔑 Talk on the following topic:

◆ How do you prepare for a test?

## Lesson 50

# My Internship
## 我的實習

### 搭配筆記聆聽短文 Listen to the text with the help of the notes given

| | |
|---|---|
| intern | 實習生 |
| I was quite disappointed. | 我感到相當失望。 |
| empty | 清空 |
| clock in | 打卡上班 |
| computer skills | 電腦技巧 |

### 再次聆聽並回答問題 Listen again and answer the questions below

Questions for discussion:

1. Where did the speaker have the internship?
2. Was the speaker satisfied with the internship?
3. Did the speaker gain computer skills?

**短文聽讀 Text**

I was an intern at a large technology company last summer. Before the internship started, I was very excited. However, after I started work, I was quite disappointed. I had to empty over fifty trash cans before everyone arrived in the morning. And after they clocked in, I had to make everyone coffee. That's all I did for three months. As for gaining computer skills, don't even ask!

我去年夏天在一間大型科技公司擔任實習生。在實習開始之前，我很興奮。不過，開始工作後我感到相當失望。早上在大家抵達前，我得清空五十多個垃圾桶。他們打卡上班後，我必須為每一個人泡咖啡。那就是我三個月以來所做的事。至於習得電腦技巧，問都別問了！

❶ **intern** [ ˋɪntɝn ] *n.* 實習生；實習醫生

❷ **technology** [ tɛkˋnɑlədʒɪ ] *n.* 科技

❸ **company** [ ˋkʌmpənɪ ] *n.* 公司

❹ **summer** [ ˋsʌmɚ ] *n.* 夏天
其他季節的說法：
spring [ sprɪŋ ] *n.* 春天
fall [ fɔl ] *n.* 秋天
= autumn [ ˋɔtəm ]
winter [ ˋwɪntɚ ] *n.* 冬天

❺ **internship** [ ˋɪntɝnˏʃɪp ] *n.* 實習

❻ **empty** [ ˋɛmptɪ ] *vt.* 使變空；使倒空 & *a.* 空的
（三態為：empty, emptied [ ˋɛmptɪd ], emptied）

Evan emptied the water out of the bottle.
伊凡把瓶子裡的水倒空。

❼ **clock in**　　上班打卡
= punch [ pʌntʃ ] in
clock out　　下班打卡
= punch out

❽ **gain** [ gen ] *vt.* 獲得；贏得

That school policy never gained students' support.
那條校規從未獲得學生的支持。

❾ **skill** [ skɪl ] *n.* 技能，技巧

❶ 副詞 quite 的用法

quite [ kwaɪt ] *adv.* 十分，相當地
= fairly [ ˋfɛrlɪ ]
= pretty [ ˋprɪtɪ ]

CH
4
職場與教育

not quite　　　不完全

quite a bit　　相當多

I'm quite tired after working all day.

= I'm fairly tired after working all day.

= I'm pretty tired after working all day.

工作一整天後我還蠻累的。

What the news report said was not quite true.

新聞報導所說的並不全然是事實。

Ⓐ Are you ready?

Ⓑ No, not quite.

Ⓐ 你準備好了嗎？

Ⓑ 不，還沒。

Frank is not as poor as you think. In fact, he has quite a bit of money.

法蘭克並非你想像的那麼窮。事實上，他有不少錢。

**❷ 表示「至於」的說法**

as for...　　至於……（常置於句首）

As for where to travel, I think Hawaii would be a good idea.

至於去哪兒旅行，我想夏威夷會是個不錯的選擇。

Everyone's going out today. As for me, I'd rather stay home.

今天大家都要出門。至於我，我比較想待在家。

比較

ⓐ as to...　　至於……；關於……（= concerning / about...）

As to money, we will simply have to borrow some from Andy.

至於錢，我們只好去向安迪借一些。

I'm at a loss as to what I should do.

我很迷惘，不知道該怎麼做。

ⓑ so as to...　　以免……，為了……（= in order to...）

We provide various products so as to attract more customers.

本公司提供各式各樣的產品以吸引更多顧客。

| ❶ [ au ] | however [ haʊˈɛvɚ ] |
|---|---|
| ❷ [ ju ] | computer [ kəmˈpjutɚ ] |

## 朗讀短文　**Read aloud the text**

🎙 請特別注意 [ au ]、[ ju ] 的發音。

I was an intern at a large technology company last summer. Before the internship started, I was very excited. **However**, after I started work, I was quite disappointed. I had to empty over fifty trash cans before everyone arrived in the morning. And after they clocked in, I had to make everyone coffee. That's all I did for three months. As for gaining **computer** skills, don't even ask!

## 換句話說　**Retell**

🎙 Retell the text with the help of the words and expressions below.

intern, technology, company, summer, internship, empty, clock in, gain, skill

## 討論題目　**Free Talk**

🎙 Talk on the following topic:

◆ Have you ever had an internship before? Describe the experience.

CH
4
職場與教育

253

朗讀 ▶
Lesson 51

# Practice Makes Perfect
## 熟能生巧

搭配筆記聆聽會話 **Listen to the text with the help of the notes given**

| play the violin | 拉小提琴 |
| --- | --- |
| a professional violinist | 職業小提琴家 |
| for now | 現在，目前 |
| practice | 練習 |
| orchestra | 交響樂團 |

再次聆聽並回答問題 **Listen again and answer the questions below**

Questions for discussion:

**1** What instrument does the woman play?

**2** What does the woman's teacher say?

**3** What will the woman do for now?

**A** Are you still playing the violin?

**B** Of course I am. In fact, my teacher says I will be a professional violinist someday.

**A** Really? Will you one day play at the Royal Albert Hall?

**B** Maybe. For now, I'll just keep practicing.

**A** I'm sure you'll be in a famous orchestra one day.

**A** 你還在拉小提琴嗎？

**B** 當然有呀。事實上，我的老師說有一天我會成為職業小提琴家。

**A** 真的嗎？你將來有一天會在皇家阿爾伯特音樂廳演奏嗎？

**B** 或許會。現在我將會不斷地練習。

**A** 我確信有朝一日你一定會進入知名的交響樂團。

**1 violin** [ ˌvaɪəˈlɪn ] *n.* 小提琴
viola [ vaɪˈolə / vɪˈolə ] *n.* 中提琴
cello [ ˈtʃɛlo ] *n.* 大提琴

**2 In fact, ...** 事實上，……；實際上，……
= Actually, ...
= As a matter of fact, ...

In fact, pigs are very clever and like to be clean.
事實上，豬很聰明，也愛乾淨。

**3 professional** [ prəˈfɛʃənl ] *a.* 專業的，職業的 & *n.* 專家；職業選手
pro [ pro ] *n.* 專家；職業選手

**4 violinist** [ ˌvaɪəˈlɪnɪst ] *n.* 小提琴家

🔖 **Notes**

通常以 -ist 結尾的字詞，為表「某學科的研究者」、「某樂器的演奏者」或「某工作的從事者」，如：

| linguist | 語言學家 |
| pianist | 鋼琴家 |
| novelist | 小說家 |
| journalist | 新聞記者 |

**5 royal** [ ˈrɔɪəl ] *a.* 皇家的

**6 hall** [ hɔl ] *n.* 大廳；走廊，通道
the city hall 市政府
a concert hall 音樂廳
a banqueting / banquet hall 宴會廳

**7 keep** [ kip ] *vi.* 繼續；保持（三態為：keep, kept [ kɛpt ], kept）

**Notes**

**a** keep 表「繼續」時，其後須接動名詞。

Keep working hard, and you'll realize your dream one day.

繼續努力，那麼有朝一日你就會實現夢想。

**b** keep 表「保持」時，其後須接形容詞作補語。

You should keep quiet when you are in the library.

你在圖書館時應該要保持安靜。

**8** **practice** [ `præktɪs ] *vi. & vt. & n.* 練習

practice + V-ing　　練習……

Practice makes perfect.

熟能生巧。(諺語)

Ella practices speaking English every day.

艾拉每天都練習講英語。

**9** **famous** [ `feməs ] *a.* 著名的，有名的

**10** **orchestra** [ `ɔrkɪstrə ] *n.* 交響樂團，管弦樂團

CH
4
職場與教育

口語新技能　**New Skills**

🎙 演奏樂器的說法

◆ 表示演奏樂器時，動詞應用 play，而樂器名詞前方須置定冠詞 the。

play the + 樂器名稱　　演奏某樂器

play the violin　　拉小提琴

◆ 替換看看：

| cello　大提琴 | drums　鼓 (常用複數) |
|---|---|
| flute　長笛 | guitar　吉他 |
| piano　鋼琴 | clarinet　黑管 |

## 🔖 Notes

表示從事某球類運動時，亦使用動詞 play，但球類名詞前方不置定冠詞 the。

play ＋ 球類運動名稱　　　　**從事某球類運動**

| play | basketball | 打籃球 |
| | baseball | 打棒球 |
| | volleyball | 打排球 |
| | badminton | 打羽球 |
| | tennis | 打網球 |
| | soccer | 踢足球 |
| | football | 打美式足球 |

## 簡短對答 Quick Response

◆ Make quick responses to the sentences you hear.

## 討論題目 Free Talk

🔖 Talk on the following topic:

◆ What instrument do you know how to play?

# You're Never Too Old to Learn
## 活到老，學到老

**搭配筆記聆聽短文** **Listen to the text with the help of the notes given**

| retire | 退休 |
| --- | --- |
| take Spanish classes | 上西班牙語課 |
| a community college | 社區大學 |
| regularly | 經常 |
| make a lot of progress | 進步很多 |

CH
4
職場與教育

**再次聆聽並回答問題** **Listen again and answer the questions below**

📍 Questions for discussion:

1️⃣ When will Grandpa retire?

2️⃣ Why does Grandpa want to learn Spanish?

3️⃣ Will the speaker learn Spanish, too?

Grandpa will be retiring next year. He plans on taking Spanish classes in a community college. He wants to learn Spanish because he will be living in Mexico. I will be visiting him regularly, so I'll try to learn Spanish, too. We will be talking to each other in Spanish. This way, I believe we will both make a lot of progress.

明年爺爺將退休。他計劃去社區大學上西班牙語課。他想要學西班牙語，因為他將住在墨西哥。我將經常去拜訪他，所以我也會試著學習西班牙語。我們彼此將用西班牙語交談。這麼一來，我相信我們都會進步很多。

**單字片語** Vocabulary and Phrases

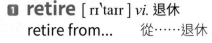

**❶ retire** [ rɪˋtaɪr ] *vi.* 退休
retire from...　　從⋯⋯退休

Angela retired from that company after 20 years of service.
安琪拉為那間公司效力二十年後退休了。

**❷ plan on V-ing**　　打算做⋯⋯
= plan to V

When do you plan on getting married?
= When do you plan to get married?
你們打算什麼時候結婚？

**❸ take** [ tek ] *vt.* 研修，修習 (某課程)
(三態為：take, took [ tʊk ], taken [ ˋtekən ])
take a computer course　　上電腦課

**❹ community** [ kəˋmjunətɪ ] *n.* 社區

**❺ college** [ ˋkɑlɪdʒ ] *n.* 大學
= university [ ˌjunəˋvɝsətɪ ]
a community college　　社區大學
go to college / university　　上大學

**❻ visit** [ ˋvɪzɪt ] *vt. & vi. & n.* 拜訪
visit sb　　拜訪某人
= pay sb a visit

We visited our grandparents last weekend.
= We paid our grandparents a visit last weekend.
我們上週末去探視我們的祖父母。

**❼ regularly** [ ˋrɛgjələlɪ ] *adv.* 經常；定期地
regular [ ˋrɛgjələ ] *a.* 經常；定期的
on a regular basis　　定期地
= regularly

To stay healthy, you should exercise regularly.
= To stay healthy, you should exercise on a regular basis.
要保持健康，你就應規律運動。

CH
4
職場與教育

**8** **try** [ traɪ ] *vi.* & *vt.* 嘗試；試圖
（三態為：try, tried [ traɪd ], tried）
try to V　　嘗試 / 試圖做……；設法……
I'm trying to make a chocolate cake.
我正嘗試做一個巧克力蛋糕。

**9** **progress** [ ˋprɑgrɛs ] *n.* 進步 (不可數)
make progress　　進步

---

## 實用詞句　Useful Expressions

🔑 We will be talking to each other in Spanish.
我們彼此將用西班牙語交談。

────────────────────────

◆ 介詞 in 與表某語言的名詞並用，可表「以……語言」，如：
in + 某語言　　以……語言
write in English　　以英語撰寫
talk in French　　用法語交談
The novel is written in English.
這本小說是以英語撰寫的。
They are talking in French.
他們正用法語交談。

◆ 各種語言的說法：
Spanish [ ˋspænɪʃ ] *n.* 西班牙語
English [ ˋɪŋglɪʃ ] *n.* 英語
French [ frɛntʃ ] *n.* 法語
Italian [ ɪˋtæljən ] *n.* 義大利語
Chinese [ ˌtʃaɪˋniz ] *n.* 中文
Japanese [ ˌdʒæpəˋniz ] *n.* 日語
Korean [ koˋriən ] *n.* 韓語
German [ ˋdʒɝmən ] *n.* 德語

## 發音提示 Pronunciation

| ❶ [ e ] | take [ tek ] | way [ we ] | make [ mek ] |
|---|---|---|---|
| ❷ [ v ] | live [ lɪv ] | visit [ ˋvɪzɪt ] | believe [ bɪˋliv ] |

## 朗讀短文 Read aloud the text

🎤 請特別注意 [ e ]、[ v ] 的發音。

Grandpa will be retiring next year. He plans on taking Spanish classes in a community college. He wants to learn Spanish because he will be living in Mexico. I will be visiting him regularly, so I'll try to learn Spanish, too. We will be talking to each other in Spanish. This way, I believe we will both make a lot of progress.

## 換句話說 Retell

🎤 Retell the text from the perspective of Grandpa with the help of the words and expressions below.

retire, plan on, take, community, college, visit, regularly, try, progress

## 討論題目 Free Talk

🎤 Talk on the following topic:

◆ Are you learning or have you learned any foreign language besides English?

# A Working Mom
## 職業婦女

搭配筆記聆聽會話 **Listen to the text with the help of the notes given**

| | |
|---|---|
| twins | 雙胞胎 |
| cope | 應付 |
| I'm sorry to hear that. | 很遺憾聽到你這樣說。 |
| attitude | 態度 |
| rub off on... | 影響…… |
| can't afford to... | 不能…… |

再次聆聽並回答問題 **Listen again and answer the questions below**

Questions for discussion:

**1** How many children does the woman have?

**2** Which one of the twins cries whenever the woman leaves?

**3** Does the woman want to quit her job?

Ⓐ Hi, Dana. How are the twins coping now that you're back at work?

Ⓑ One is doing fine, but the other cries every time I leave the house.

Ⓐ I'm sorry to hear that. What are you going to do about it?

Ⓑ I am hoping that Freya's attitude rubs off on Phoebe. I can't afford not to work.

Ⓐ I understand. Good luck.

Ⓐ 嗨，黛娜。妳的雙胞胎孩子在妳重回職場後應付得來嗎？

Ⓑ 一個是沒問題，但另外一個是每次我一出門就哭起來。

Ⓐ 很遺憾聽到妳這樣說。那妳現在要怎麼辦呢？

Ⓑ 我希望芙蕾雅的態度可以影響菲比。我不能不工作。

Ⓐ 我了解。祝妳好運。

**①** **twin** [ twɪn ] *n.* 雙胞胎之一 & *a.* 孿生的

The two girls are twins, but they look nothing alike.
這兩個女孩是雙胞胎，但她們看起來一點也不像。

**②** **cope** [ kop ] *vi.* 應付；對付；處理（與介詞 with 並用）

Dana is having a difficult time coping with the stress at her new job.
黛娜難以應付新工作帶來的壓力。

**③** **at work**　　在工作中

Nick hates being interrupted while at work.
尼克討厭工作時被打擾。

**④** **attitude** [ ˈætətjud ] *n.* 態度（與介詞 to / toward(s) 並用）

Peter holds a very optimistic attitude towards life.
彼得對人生的態度很樂觀。

＊ optimistic [ ˌɑptəˈmɪstɪk ] *a.* 樂觀的

**⑤** **rub off on...**　　對……產生影響
(rub 的三態為：rub, rubbed [ rʌbd ], rubbed)

Zoe's father doesn't like her new boyfriend Roy, and hopes that Roy's smoking habit will not rub off on her.
柔伊的爸爸不喜歡她的新男友羅伊，並希望羅伊的抽菸習慣不會對她產生影響。

口語新技能　**New Skills**

**①** 表示「既然」的說法

now that...　　既然……
＝ since...

🔑 **Notes**

now that 與 since 表「既然」時，視為連接詞。但由於 now that... 含有 now 一詞，故所引導的副詞子句應採現在式或現在完成式。

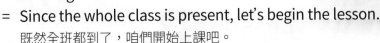

Now that the whole class is present,
let's begin the lesson.

= Since the whole class is present, let's begin the lesson.
既然全班都到了，咱們開始上課吧。

**2** 表示「祝你好運！」的說法

Good luck (to you)!

Good fortune (to you)! (較少用)

Best of luck (to you)!

Fingers crossed! (通常用於希望事情可以如對方所願，或祝某人在某事件中有所成就。)

God speed! (較少用，通常用於祝對方旅途順利、一路順風)

All the best!

Ⓐ I have an interview for my dream job tomorrow.
Ⓑ Good luck! / Best of luck! / Fingers crossed! / All the best!
Ⓐ 我明天要面試，是我夢寐以求的工作。
Ⓑ 祝你好運！

Ⓐ I'll be moving abroad next week.
Ⓑ Good luck to you! / Best of luck to you! / God speed! / All the best!
Ⓐ 我下週要搬到海外居住。
Ⓑ 祝你好運 / 一路順風！

**CH 4**

職場與教育

## 簡短對答 Quick Response

◇ Make quick responses to the sentences you hear.

## 討論題目 Free Talk

🔑 Talk on the following topic:

◇ Are you a working mom? Or do
you know any working moms?

267

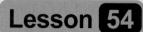

# Lesson 54
# A Different Way
# to Improve Your English
## 增進英語能力的另類方式

**搭配筆記聆聽短文** Listen to the text with the help of the notes given

| improve | 增進 |
|---------|------|
| confident | 有自信的 |
| suggest | 建議 |
| review | 評論 |
| describe | 描述 |

**再次聆聽並回答問題** Listen again and answer the questions below

 Questions for discussion:

1 What is Kevin good at?

2 What is Kevin less confident about?

3 What does the speaker suggest to Kevin?

短文聽讀　**Text**

　　My friend, Kevin, has been trying to find ways to improve his English. He is good at speaking and listening, but less confident about reading and writing. He loves to eat out at different restaurants, so I suggested he should read and write reviews in English for every place he eats at. He could describe the atmosphere, the location, the cost, and, of course, the food!

　　我的朋友凱文，一直在設法找尋增進英語能力的方法。他擅長英語口說及聽力，但對於閱讀及寫作比較沒有自信。他很愛去不同的餐廳吃飯，所以我建議他應該要針對每個他用餐的地方以英語閱讀並撰寫評論。他可以描述餐廳的氣氛、地點及價格，當然，還可以寫那家餐廳的食物！

**1 improve** [ ɪmˈpruv ] *vt.* 改善；增進

I'd like to improve my English speaking ability.

我想要增進我的英語口說能力。

**2 confident** [ ˈkɑnfədənt ] *a.* 有信心的；有自信的

be confident of / about...　　對……有信心

= have confidence in...

After the failure, John is not confident of himself anymore.

這次失敗過後，約翰對他自己已不再有信心了。

**3 review** [ rɪˈvju ] *n.* & *vt.* 評論

The movie deserves all the great reviews it is getting.

這部電影得到的佳評可謂實至名歸。

**4 describe** [ dɪˈskraɪb ] *vt.* 敘述；描寫；形容

The witness described the traffic accident to the police in detail.

那名目擊證人向警方詳述車禍發生的情形。

＊witness [ ˈwɪtnɪs ] *n.* 證人

**5 atmosphere** [ ˈætməsˌfɪr ] *n.* 氛圍；大氣；空氣

**6 location** [ loˈkeʃən ] *n.* 地點；(找到) 位置

The rent is cheap. In addition, the location is perfect.

除了房租便宜之外，地點更是棒得沒話講。

**7 cost** [ kɑst ] *n.* 價錢；費用；成本 & *vt.* 花費 (三態同形)

The cost of paper went up because lumber was in short supply.

因為木材的供應量短缺，所以紙張的價格上漲了。

＊lumber [ ˈlʌmbɚ ] *n.* 木材 (不可數)

實用詞句 **Useful Expressions**

**1** 表示「擅長……」的說法

be good at + N/V-ing　　擅長……

= be adept at / in + N/V-ing

= be skilled at / in + N/V-ing

= be proficient at / in + N/V-ing
Peter is good at playing several musical instruments.
= Peter is adept at / in playing several musical instruments.
= Peter is skilled at / in playing several musical instruments.
= Peter is proficient at / in playing several musical instruments.
彼得擅長演奏好幾種樂器。

**2** 意志動詞的用法

◆ 常見的意志動詞如下：

| suggest | 建議 |
| propose | 建議；提議 |
| recommend | 建議；推薦 |
| ask | 要求 |
| require | 要求 |
| demand | 要求 |
| order | 命令 |
| rule | 規定 |

◆ 意志動詞其後接 that 子句時，該子句只能用助動詞 should，而 should 在美式英語中，往往予以省略，直接用原形動詞。
Billy's teacher suggested that he (should) be quiet.
比利的老師示意他安靜一點。

CH 4 職場與教育

發音提示　**Pronunciation**

| **1** [ æ ] | has [ hæz ] | and [ ænd ] |
|---|---|---|
| | at [ æt ] | atmosphere [ ˈætməsˌfɪr ] |

| **2** [ p ] | improve [ ɪmˈpruv ] | place [ ples ] |
|---|---|---|
| | speaking [ ˈspikɪŋ ] | |

## 朗讀短文 Read aloud the text

📍 請特別注意 [ æ ]、[ p ] 的發音。

My friend, Kevin, has been trying to find ways to improve his English. He is good at speaking and listening, but less confident about reading and writing. He loves to eat out at different restaurants, so I suggested he should read and write reviews in English for every place he eats at. He could describe the atmosphere, the location, the cost, and, of course, the food!

## 換句話說 Retell

📍 Retell the text from the perspective of Kevin with the help of the words and expressions below.

improve, confident, review, describe, atmosphere, location, cost

## 討論題目 Free Talk

📍 Talk on the following topic:

◆ What do you do to improve your English skills?

# Lesson 55

# Passing with Flying Colors
## 高分通過考試

**搭配筆記聆聽會話** **Listen to the text with the help of the notes given**

| | |
|---|---|
| fail | (考試) 不及格 |
| top of the class | 全班第一名 |
| apologize | 道歉 |
| review | 複習 |
| prepare | 準備 |

**再次聆聽並回答問題** **Listen again and answer the questions below**

📌 Questions for discussion:

**1** Did the woman pass the test?

**2** How did the man do on the test?

**3** What does the man suggest to the woman?

## 實用會話 Dialogue

Ⓐ Hey, Tammy. How did you do on the test?

Ⓑ Not very well, James. I failed.

Ⓐ Oh, I'm sorry to hear that.

Ⓑ How did you do?

Ⓐ Err... I got 98%. Top of the class. Sorry.

Ⓑ Don't apologize for passing with flying colors! You worked hard, but I didn't even review the lessons.

Ⓐ Let's prepare together for the next test!

Ⓑ OK!

Ⓐ 嗨，譚美。妳考試考得怎麼樣？

Ⓑ 不太好，詹姆士。我考試不及格。

Ⓐ 喔，我很遺憾聽到這個消息。

**B** 那你考得好不好呢？

**A** 呃……。我考九十八分。是全班第一名。抱歉。

**B** 別為了考高分而道歉！你很用功讀書，而我卻連課程內容都沒複習。

**A** 我們下次一起準備考試吧！

**B** 好！

## 單字片語　Vocabulary and Phrases

**1** **fail** [ fel ] *vi.* 不及格；失敗 & *vt.* 使不及格；使失敗

Tammy didn't study at all; therefore, she failed the test.

譚美根本沒念書，所以她考試不及格。

**2** **top** [ tɑp ] *n.* 頂端 & *a.* 頂端的

at the top of...　　……的頂端

George is at the top of his class.

喬治在班上名列前茅。

**3** **apologize** [ əˋpɑləˌdʒɑɪz ] *vi.* 道歉；賠罪

apologize to sb for sth　　因某事向某人道歉

I must apologize to you for not answering your letter immediately.

我必須為沒有馬上回信給您而向您道歉。

**4** **pass (a test) with flying colors**　　高分通過 (考試)

pass [ pæs ] *vi.* & *vt.* 及格，通過 (考試)

color [ ˋkʌlɚ ] *n.* 旗幟；顏色

James passed the exam with flying colors because he was well-prepared.

詹姆士因為準備充分，所以高分通過考試。

**5** **review** [ rɪˋvju ] *vt.* & *n.* 複習 (功課)

Review the first five lessons before the exam.

= Go over the first five lessons before the exam.

考試前要複習前五課。

**6 prepare** [ prɪˋpɛr ] *vi. & vt.* 準備

prepare for... 為……做準備

All the students at the library are preparing for the final exams.

圖書館裡的學生都在準備期末考。

## 口語新技能 New Skills

📌 表示考試、測驗的說法

**a** quiz [ kwɪz ] *n.* 小考

a pop quiz 隨堂測驗／抽考

**b** test [ tɛst ] *n.* 考試，測驗；檢驗

a math test 數學測驗
an English test 英語測驗
a driving / road test 駕照路考
an aptitude test 適性測驗

### 📌 Notes

test 所指的測驗範圍較廣泛，除了指學校的單科測驗與一般常見的考試，亦可指各種檢驗或測試，如：

a blood test 抽血檢驗
a drug test 藥物檢驗
a pregnancy test 驗孕

**c** exam [ ɪgˋzæm ] *n.* 考試，測驗；檢驗
= examination [ ɪg͵zæməˋneʃən ]

midterm exam 期中考
final exam 期末考
entrance exam 入學考試

### 📌 Notes

exam 通常指較大型的考試，除此之外亦可指檢查，如：

a physical exam 體檢

## 簡短對答　Quick Response

◆ Make quick responses to the sentences you hear.

## 討論題目　Free Talk

Talk on the following topic:

◆ Do you prefer studying by yourself or with others?

# Taking a Gap Year
## 休個空檔年

### 搭配筆記聆聽短文 Listen to the text with the help of the notes given

| | |
|---|---|
| a gap year | 空檔年 |
| university | 大學 |
| confident | 有自信的 |
| relationship | 關係 |
| highly | 強烈地；非常 |

### 再次聆聽並回答問題 Listen again and answer the questions below

🔖 Questions for discussion:

❶ Where did the speaker go for his gap year?

❷ Who did the speaker meet while in Sydney?

❸ Does the speaker recommend taking a gap year?

I took a gap year to travel around Australia before I started university. I learned so much about myself during that time, and I became a more confident, stronger person. While I was in Sydney, I met a girl, Laura, and fell in love with her. As our relationship grew, we decided to continue traveling together to New Zealand. Now we are married! I highly recommend taking a gap year!

在我開始讀大學之前，我休了個空檔年，去澳洲旅行。在那段期間，我更加認識自己，並且變成一個更具自信、更堅強的人。我在雪梨時遇到蘿拉這個女孩子，並且愛上了她。隨著我們的關係升溫，我們決定一起去紐西蘭繼續旅行。現在我們結婚了！我強烈建議上大學之前先休個空檔年！

CH 4 職場與教育

**❶ a gap year** 空檔年，停學年，壯遊

gap [ gæp ] *n.* 間隙；空隙；空白

有些國家的高中畢業生，在上大學之前，會先休息一陣子，從正統教育中告假一段時間。「空檔年」可以為期一年或一年以上，是為了讓高中畢業生在進入人生的下一個階段前可以放鬆一下。在空檔年的這一段期間，這些準大學生可以去學習新技能或是去打工、做志工等，為他們的下一個人生階段做準備，更可以藉此好好地思考自己的過去、現在及未來。

**❷ travel around (...)** （在……）到處旅行

If I should become rich someday, I would travel around the world.
如果有一天我發大財，我要去環遊世界。

**❸ university** [ ˌjunəˈvɝsətɪ ] *n.* 大學

| | |
|---|---|
| go to university / college | 念大學 |
| a university / college student | 大學生 |
| apply for admission to a university | 申請某大學的入學許可 |

**❹ grow** [ gro ] *vi.* 增長；變得；成長 & *vt.* 種植
（三態為：grow, grew [ gru ], grown [ gron ]）

As time went by, we grew older and wiser.
隨著歲月的流逝，我們變老也變得更有智慧了。

**❺ continue** [ kənˈtɪnju ] *vt.* 繼續

continue + V-ing / to V 繼續……

Laura and her husband continued talking after the meal.
= Laura and her husband continued to talk after the meal.
蘿拉和她丈夫吃飯之後繼續交談。

**❻ married** [ ˈmærɪd ] *a.* 已婚的

unmarried [ ʌnˈmærɪd ] *a.* 未婚的（= single [ ˈsɪŋɡl ]）

Everybody knows that Harry is married.
每個人都知道哈利是已婚的。

**❼ highly** [ ˈhaɪlɪ ] *adv.* 極；非常；高度地

think highly of sb 看重某人

I think highly of Philip for his proficiency in English.
我對菲利浦的英文造詣給予高度的評價。

**8 recommend** [ ˌrɛkəˈmɛnd ] *vt.* 建議；推薦
recommend sb to V　　建議某人做某事

Our teacher recommended us to read the questions twice before answering them.
我們的老師建議我們在答題前要先把題目看兩遍。

## 實用詞句　Useful Expressions

**1 連接詞 while 的用法**

**a** while 表「當……」時，作連接詞，引導時間副詞子句。
While I was cleaning the drawer yesterday, I came across an old photo of my mother.
我昨天清理抽屜時，無意間發現一張我媽媽的舊照片。

**b** while 所引導的副詞子句中，若主詞與主句中的主詞相同時，該副詞子句可化簡為分詞構句。
While I was there, I had a good time.
= While (being) there, I had a good time.
我在那裡時很愉快。

**c** 課文第三句 "While I was in Sydney, I met a girl, Laura, and fell in love with her."（我在雪梨時遇到蘿拉這個女孩子，並且愛上了她。）也可改寫成：
While (being) in Sydney, I met a girl, Laura, and fell in love with her.

**2 表示「隨著……」的說法**

◇ as 作連接詞時可表「隨著」，表示兩個正在發展變化的情況，其句型如下：
As + 主詞 + 動詞, 主詞 + 動詞
As it grew darker, it became cooler.
隨著天色漸晚，天氣變涼了。
As kids get older, they become less attached to their parents.
隨著孩子的年紀漸長，他們變得愈來愈不會黏著父母了。

| ❶ [ e ] | Australia [ ɔˋstreljə ] | relationship [ rɪˋleʃənˏʃɪp ] |
| | became [ bɪˋkem ] | take [ tek ] |

| ❷ [ ð ] | that [ ðæt ] | with [ wɪð ] |
| | together [ təˋgɛðəˋ ] | |

## 朗讀短文 **Read aloud the text**

🔖 請特別注意 [ e ]、[ ð ] 的發音。

I took a gap year to travel around Australia before I started university. I learned so much about myself during that time, and I became a more confident, stronger person. While I was in Sydney, I met a girl, Laura, and fell in love with her. As our relationship grew, we decided to continue traveling together to New Zealand. Now we are married! I highly recommend taking a gap year!

## 換句話說 **Retell**

🔖 Retell the text with the help of the words and expressions below.

a gap year, travel around, university, grow, continue, married, highly, recommend

## 討論題目 **Free Talk**

🔖 Talk on the following topic:

◆ Have you or your friend ever taken a gap year?

## Lesson 57

# At a Job Interview
## 在工作面試

**搭配筆記聆聽會話** **Listen to the text with the help of the notes given**

| | |
|---|---|
| candidate | 候選人 |
| thesis | 論文 |
| tactic | 策略 |
| practical experience | 實際經驗，實務經驗 |
| quarter | 一季 |

**再次聆聽並回答問題** **Listen again and answer the questions below**

Questions for discussion:

**1** What was the woman's thesis on?

**2** Does the woman have any job experience?

**3** Is the man impressed by the woman?

🅰 So, why do you consider yourself the best candidate for the job?

🅱 I scored the highest mark in my class for my thesis on sales tactics. I have the practical experience to back that up, too. I achieved the largest increase in sales figures over the last four quarters in my previous job.

🅰 That's very impressive. When would you like to start working?

🅰 那麼，你為什麼認為你是這份工作的最佳人選？

🅱 我的銷售策略論文在班上獲得最高分。我也有實際經驗可以證實。前一份工作中，我成功使前四季的銷售數據有最大幅度的增長。

🅰 那很令人佩服。你想要什麼時候上工？

**❶ candidate** [ ˋkændəˌdet ] *n.* 候選人

**❷ score** [ skɔr ] *vt.* & *vi.* 得分 & *n.* 分數
score high / low on a test　考試得高 / 低分
George scored high on his English exam.
喬治英語考試得了高分。

**❸ thesis** [ ˋθisɪs ] *n.* 論文

**❹ sales** [ selz ] *n.* 銷售；銷量 (恆用複數)

**❺ tactic** [ ˋtæktɪk ] *n.* 策略
= strategy [ ˋstrætədʒɪ ]

**❻ practical** [ ˋpræktɪkḷ ] *a.* 實際的；務實的
We need someone with at least two years of practical experience.
我們需要至少有兩年實際經驗的人。
My father is a practical person.
我父親是個很務實的人。

**❼ achieve** [ əˋtʃiv ] *vt.* 達到 (= attain [ əˋten ])；
達成 (= accomplish [ əˋkɑmplɪʃ ])
What is the best way to achieve our goal?
達成我們目標的最佳方式是什麼？
Darren feels like he hasn't achieved anything in his life.
戴倫覺得自己在人生中沒什麼成就。

**❽ increase** [ ˋɪnkris ] *n.* 增加 & [ ɪnˋkris ] *vt.* & *vi.* 增加
be on the increase　正在增加
The country's population is on the increase.
這個國家的人口正在成長中。
The number of tourists is increasing steadily.
觀光客人數穩定上升中。

**❾ figure** [ ˋfɪgjɚ ] *n.* 數據 (常用複數)
sales figures　銷售數據

⑩ **quarter** [ ˈkwɔrtɚ ] *n.* 一季（等於三個月）；四分之一

⑪ **previous** [ ˈpriviəs ] *a.* 先前的
= **former** [ ˈfɔrmɚ ]

⑫ **impressive** [ ɪmˈprɛsɪv ] *a.* 令人印象深刻的

## 口語新技能 New Skills

🔑 表示「證實某事」的說法

> back sth/sb up　　證實某事；為某人作證
> There's little evidence to back up your theory.
> 幾乎沒有什麼證據可以證實你的理論。
> John backed me up when no one else believed me.
> 當沒有人相信我的時候，約翰幫我作證。
>
> 比較
> ⓐ back sb/sth up　　支持某人 / 某事
> 　 No one backed Henry up in the debate.
> 　 在辯論中沒有人支持亨利。
> 　 The manager backed up my proposal at the meeting.
> 　 經理在會議上支持我的提案。
>
> ⓑ back sth up　　備份某物
> 　 Did you back up your files?
> 　 你有將你的檔案備份嗎？

## 簡短對答 Quick Response

◆ Make quick responses to the sentences you hear.

## 討論題目 Free Talk

🔑 Talk on the following topic:

　◆ What was the most memorable job interview you've ever been to?

## Lesson 58

# Time Flies
## 時光飛逝

搭配筆記聆聽短文 **Listen to the text with the help of the notes given**

| | |
|---|---|
| by the end of this year | 到今年年底前 |
| get married | 結婚 |
| grandchildren | 孫子女 |
| yesterday | 昨天 |
| Time flies. | 時光飛逝。 |

再次聆聽並回答問題 **Listen again and answer the questions below**

CH
4
職場與教育

Questions for discussion:

1 Are Barbara and Terry co-workers?

2 How long have Barbara and Terry known each other?

3 How many grandchildren do Barbara and Terry have?

Barbara and Terry work together. Barbara has been working in the company for 30 years. Terry will have been working there for 35 years by the end of this year. They met at work 30 years ago, got married, and now have four children and six grandchildren. To both of them, though, the day they met feels just like yesterday. Time flies.

芭芭拉和泰瑞一起工作。芭芭拉已在公司任職三十年了。到今年年底前，泰瑞將在公司服務滿三十五年。他們三十年前因工作認識、結婚，而現在有了四個子女和六個孫子女。不過，對他們兩位來說，他們相遇的那天好似就在昨天。時光飛逝。

**❶ at work**　上班
at school　上學

Vincent is at work / school now.
文森現在在上班 / 課。

**❷ get married**　結婚
married [ ˈmærɪd ] *a.* 結婚的，已婚的
marry [ ˈmærɪ ] *vt.* & *vi.* 結婚，嫁，娶
（三態為：marry, married [ ˈmærɪd ], married）
a married couple　一對夫妻

Kelly and Alan will get married next month.
= Kelly will be / get married to Alan next month.
= Kelly will marry Alan next month.
凱莉跟亞倫將在下個月結婚。

We all know that Eric is married.
我們都知道艾瑞克結婚了。

**❸ children** [ ˈtʃɪldrən ] *n.* 孩子（為 child [ tʃaɪld ] 的複數）

**❹ grandchildren** [ ˈgrændˌtʃɪldrən ] *n.* 孫子女；外孫子女
（為 grandchild [ ˈgrændˌtʃaɪld ] 的複數）

**❺ yesterday** [ ˈjɛstəˌde ] *n.* 昨天，昨日 & *adv.* 在昨天
today [ təˈde ] *n.* 今天，今日 & *adv.* 在今天
tomorrow [ təˈmɔro ] *n.* 明天，明日 & *adv.* 在明天

**❻ Time flies.**　時光飛逝 / 光陰似箭。（諺語）

**❶** 介紹「介詞 for + 一段時間」的用法

for + 一段時間　持續一段時間
for one day / month / year　持續一天 / 一個月 / 一年
for a short / long time　很短 / 長的時間

CH
4
職場與教育

| for ages | 很久 |
| for a while | 有一陣子 |

 **Notes**

採完成式或完成進行式的句子中，若句中動詞具有持續發生的特性，可與
「for + 一段時間」並用。

I've been studying abroad for quite a few years.
我在國外讀書已有好幾年了。
Peter has been teaching English for thirty years.
彼得已經教了三十年的英語。
We haven't met for ages.
我們好久沒碰面了。

**2** 表示「想要做……」的說法

feel like + V-ing　　想要做……
I feel like going to the movies tonight.
今晚我想去看電影。

**Notes**

feel like 後亦可置名詞，此時 feel like 須譯成「感覺像」。
feel like + N　　感覺像……
I felt like a young person when I went back to school yesterday.
昨天重返學校時，我感覺自己像個年輕人。

發音提示　**Pronunciation**

| **1** [ ʌ ] | company [ ˈkʌmpənɪ ] | just [ dʒʌst ] |
|---|---|---|

| **2** [ g ] | together [ təˈgɛðɚ ] | got [ gɑt ] |
|---|---|---|
| | ago [ əˈgo ] | grandchildren [ ˈgrænd͵tʃɪldrən ] |

## 朗讀短文 Read aloud the text

🔖 請特別注意 [ ʌ ]、[ g ] 的發音。

Barbara and Terry work together. Barbara has been working in the company for 30 years. Terry will have been working there for 35 years by the end of this year. They met at work 30 years ago, got married, and now have four children and six grandchildren. To both of them, though, the day they met feels just like yesterday. Time flies.

## 換句話說 Retell

🔖 Retell the text with the help of the words and expressions below.

at work, get married, children, grandchildren, yesterday, Time flies.

## 討論題目 Free Talk

🔖 Talk on the following topic:

◆ What do you think about office romance? Should it be forbidden?

CH
4

職場與教育

291

# A Difficult Decision
## 困難的決定

**搭配筆記聆聽會話** Listen to the text with the help of the notes given

| | |
|---|---|
| impressive | 令人印象深刻的 |
| qualification | 資格 |
| a difficult decision | 困難的決定 |
| attitude | 態度 |
| concern | 擔憂 |

**再次聆聽並回答問題** Listen again and answer the questions below

Questions for discussion:

1. Is the man at a job interview?
2. Is the woman offering the man a job?
3. Is the man happy with the decision?

Ⓐ Of all the candidates, you are the most impressive. You have the best qualifications and you received the highest test score.

Ⓑ Thank you.

Ⓐ It has been a difficult decision, but we have decided to go with another candidate. We're afraid your attitude might be a concern for us. I wish you luck in your job search.

Ⓑ You must be kidding me.

Ⓐ 所有的應徵者當中，你是最令人印象深刻的。你資格最佳，也在測驗中獲得最高分。

Ⓑ 謝謝你。

Ⓐ 這是個很困難的決定，可是我們決定要錄取另外一位應徵者。我們擔心你的態度會對我們造成問題。祝你求職順利。

Ⓑ 你在跟我開玩笑吧。

**❶ qualification** [ ˌkwɑləfəˈkeʃən ] *n.* 資格，條件（常用複數）

Do you have the qualifications to be an engineer?

你有擔任工程師的資格嗎？

**❷ receive** [ rɪˈsiv ] *vt.* 收到，得到

Teresa received her education in the US.

泰瑞莎在美國接受教育。

**❸ difficult** [ ˈdɪfəkʌlt ] *a.* 困難的

= tough [ tʌf ]

= hard [ hɑrd ]

**❹ decision** [ dɪˈsɪʒən ] *n.* 決定

decide [ dɪˈsaɪd ] *vt. & vi.* 決定

make a decision　　做決定

**❺ go with sb/sth**　　選擇某人 / 某物

After hours of discussion, we decided to go with Kyle's proposal.

經過數小時的討論，我們決定要採用凱爾的提案。

**❻ attitude** [ ˈætətjud ] *n.* 態度

**❼ concern** [ kənˈsɚn ] *n.* 擔憂；關心 & *vt.* 擔心；關心

My concern is that you won't be able to finish your work on time.

= I'm concerned that you won't be able to finish your work on time.

我擔心你無法按時完成工作。

**❽ wish** [ wɪʃ ] *vt.* 希望；祝福 & *n.* 願望

wish sb sth　　祝某人……

make a wish　　許願

**❾ search** [ sɝtʃ ] *n. & vt. & vi.* 搜尋

be in search of...　　搜尋……

= search for...

They are in search of a good doctor to treat their child.

他們正在尋找好的醫生來治療他們的孩子。

Emily is searching for the best pizza in town.

艾蜜莉在尋找鎮上最好吃的披薩。

📌 表示「你在跟我開玩笑吧」的說法

**You must be kidding (me).**　　你在跟我開玩笑吧。
kid [ kɪd ] *vt.* & *vi.* 開玩笑 (三態為：kid, kidded [ ˋkɪdɪd ], kidded)
**Carl was just kidding when he said he wants to quit.**
卡爾說想辭職時是在開玩笑。

---

📌 **Notes**

本句常用於表示懷疑或難以置信。亦可用下列句子取代：
**You've got to be kidding (me).**　　你一定是在跟我開玩笑。
**Are you kidding (me)?**　　你在跟我開玩笑嗎？
**You must be joking.**　　你一定是在說笑。
＊joke [ dʒok ] *vi.* 開玩笑

---

🅐 I heard your favorite restaurant is closing down.
🅑 You must be kidding me.
　= You've got to be kidding me.
　= Are you kidding me?
　= You must be joking.
🅐 我聽說你最喜歡的餐廳要關門大吉了。
🅑 你在跟我開玩笑吧。

簡短對答 **Quick Response**

◆ Make quick responses to the sentences you hear.

討論題目 **Free Talk**

📌 Talk on the following topic:

　◆ Have you ever been rejected at a job interview?

# A Born Leader
## 天生的領袖

### 搭配筆記聆聽短文 Listen to the text with the help of the notes given

| | |
|---|---|
| take charge | 負責 |
| organized | 有條理的 |
| confidence | 信心 |
| drive | 幹勁 |
| political party | 政黨 |

### 再次聆聽並回答問題 Listen again and answer the questions below

Questions for discussion:

**1** Is John the kind of person that always leads others?

**2** Is John a confident person?

**3** What does John do now?

John is the person who always takes charge. Among all his friends, he is the most organized and has the greatest confidence. He has the most energy and the least need for sleep! He has the biggest drive to succeed in whatever he is doing. It is no surprise, therefore, that John is now the leader of the largest political party in the country. He is truly a born leader.

約翰總是負責任的那位。在他的朋友之中,他最有條理,而且最有自信。他充滿最多的活力,並且需要最少的睡眠!他有最大的幹勁想要在他所做的任何事上獲致成功。因此,毫不意外地,約翰目前是國內最大政黨的黨主席。他真的是天生的領袖。

**❶ take charge (of...)** 　負責 (……)
charge [ tʃɑrdʒ ] *n.* 負責，責任 (不可數)

Kimberly took charge of the office temporarily.
金柏莉暫時掌管辦公室事務。

**❷ organized** [ ˈɔrɡənˌaɪzd ] *a.* 有條理的，有組織的
Benny is not a very organized person.
班尼不是個很有條理的人。

**❸ confidence** [ ˈkɑnfədəns ] *n.* 信心
have confidence in... 　對……有信心

I have confidence in our new campaign.
我對我們新的活動有信心。

**❹ energy** [ ˈɛnədʒɪ ] *n.* 精力，體力 (不可數)；能源

**❺ drive** [ draɪv ] *n.* 幹勁，衝勁 (不可數)
have the drive to V 　有幹勁做……

Tim has the drive to work around the clock.
提姆有幹勁可以日以繼夜地工作。

**❻ succeed** [ səkˈsid ] *vi.* 成功
succeed in + N/V-ing 　成功地……

The scientist succeeded in developing a new type of medicine.
這位科學家成功研發出新種類的藥物。

**❼ leader** [ ˈlidə ] *n.* 領袖

**❽ political** [ pəˈlɪtɪkḷ ] *a.* 政治的
a political leader 　政治領袖

**❾ party** [ ˈpɑrtɪ ] *n.* 黨團
a political party 　政黨

**❿ born** [ bɔrn ] *a.* 天生的
a born athlete 　天生的運動家
a born musician 　天生的音樂家

**1** 表示「毫不意外地」的說法

　　It is no surprise...　　毫不意外地，⋯⋯
= It comes as no surprise...
　　It is no surprise that Nelly got married before us.
= It comes as no surprise that Nelly got married before us.
　　娜莉比我們早結婚很不足為奇。

　　It was no surprise when William got promoted.
= It came as no surprise when William got promoted.
　　威廉獲得升遷時我一點也不意外。

**2** 介紹副詞 truly 的用法

　　truly [ ˈtrulɪ ] *adv.* 真正地
= really [ ˈrɪəlɪ ]
　　truly 常置於句中修飾形容詞或動詞，並用以強調以及加強語氣。
　　This view is truly breathtaking.
= This view is really breathtaking.
　　這風景真美得讓人歎為觀止。
　　I truly value your opinion.
= I really value your opinion.
　　我真的很重視你的意見。

| | | |
|---|---|---|
| **1** [ i ] | least [ list ] | succeed [ səkˈsid ] |
| | need [ nid ] | leader [ ˈlidə ] |
| | sleep [ slip ] | |

| | | |
|---|---|---|
| **2** [ aɪ ] | organized [ ˈɔrgənˌaɪzd ] | surprise [ səˈpraɪz ] |
| | drive [ draɪv ] | |

CH
**4**
職場與教育

請特別注意 [ i ]、[ aɪ ] 的發音。

John is the person who always takes charge. Among all his friends, he is the most organized and has the greatest confidence. He has the most energy and the least need for sleep! He has the biggest drive to succeed in whatever he is doing. It is no surprise, therefore, that John is now the leader of the largest political party in the country. He is truly a born leader.

### 換句話說  Retell

Retell the text with the help of the words and expressions below.

take charge, organized, confidence, energy, drive, succeed, leader, political, party, born

### 討論題目  Free Talk

Talk on the following topic:

◆ Do you consider yourself a leader or a follower?

## Lesson 01

🎙 再次聆聽並回答問題 **Listen again and answer the questions below**

**1** She wants to go to a convenience store.

**2** The police station is next to the convenience store.

**3** Yes, the map is in an app on her cell phone.

🎙 簡短對答 **Quick Response**

**Q1** Is there a convenience store near your house?

**A1** Yes, there is a convenience store nearby.

**Q2** Do you have a map app on your phone?

**A2** Yes, I have a map app on my phone.

🎙 討論題目 **Free Talk**

My school is a ten-minute walk from my house. I usually go there on foot. The fastest way to get there is to take a right at the alley, and walk down it for about five minutes. Then, take a left and cross the street. Keep going for another five minutes, and the school gate is on the left. Although the school's not far from my house, I do wish I didn't have to walk every day, especially when it is raining.

## Lesson 02

🎙 再次聆聽並回答問題 **Listen again and answer the questions below**

**1** No, the speaker does not have to work today.

**2** The speaker must clean his / her room first.

**3** The speaker wants to order pizza.

🎙 換句話說 **Retell**

I don't have to go to work because today is Sunday. I can play video games and watch TV all day long, but I must clean my room first.

There are so many empty pizza boxes that I can't see the TV. Also, I must take out the garbage. Then, I can play video games, watch TV, and order more pizza!

## 討論題目 Free Talk

On weekends, I like to sleep in. Then, I do some house chores. Afterwards, I like to make myself a cup of coffee and listen to some music to relax.

## Lesson 03

## 再次聆聽並回答問題 Listen again and answer the questions below

**1** They can't dine out because they don't have much money.

**2** They have a few eggs, mushrooms, and vegetables.

**3** He likes to eat his wife's omelets.

## 簡短對答 Quick Response

**Q1** Are you going to eat out tonight?

**A1** Yes, I'm eating out tonight.

**Q2** Do you like to dine out?

**A2** No, I prefer to stay at home and cook.

## 討論題目 Free Talk

In my fridge, there are a few pieces of bread, a dozen eggs, some milk, ham, and butter. I can make a sandwich out of this food. It'll be very easy. First, I will need to make a fried egg. Then, I'll spread the butter on the bread. Then, I'll place the fried egg and ham in between the two slices of bread. And there you have it: a simple yet delicious sandwich. Oh, I can pour myself a glass of milk, too!

🎙 再次聆聽並回答問題 **Listen again and answer the questions below**

**1** Yes, the speaker loves sweet food.

**2** The speaker likes to eat tiramisu the most.

**3** The dentist tells the speaker to eat less sugar.

🎙 換句話說 **Retell**

I have a sweet tooth. I will eat anything with sugar in it, like chocolate cake, ice cream, or fruit salad. My favorite food, though, is tiramisu. My dentist said that I should eat less sugar, but I can't help it. I want everything to be sweet. Maybe I don't have a sweet tooth. Maybe I have sweet teeth!

🎙 討論題目 **Free Talk**

Yes, I have a sweet tooth. I love eating anything sweet. My favorite dessert is brownies. I love them so much that I have to eat one each day. In fact, all of my friends know about my love for brownies, so on my birthday, they got me birthday brownies instead of a birthday cake!

🎙 再次聆聽並回答問題 **Listen again and answer the questions below**

**1** The speaker was awake because the baby was crying.

**2** The speaker drank coffee.

**3** The speaker drank too much coffee.

🎙 換句話說 **Retell**

I was awake last night because our newborn baby kept crying. I was exhausted today, so I drank a large cup of coffee. And then another. And then another. And then another! Now, the baby is asleep, but I am wide awake! Oh, I drank too much coffee!

📌 討論題目 **Free Talk**

Yes, I like to drink coffee. In fact, without a cup of coffee to start my day, I feel tired and drowsy for the rest of the day. That's why I must have a cup of coffee in the morning. Sometimes, I drink another cup in the afternoon to go with my afternoon snacks. I never drink coffee at night. It makes me restless when I'm supposed to fall asleep.

**Lesson 06**

📌 再次聆聽並回答問題 **Listen again and answer the questions below**

**1** He dreamed of cockroaches in his bed.

**2** No, it was just a dream.

**3** He thought the dream was scary.

📌 簡短對答 **Quick Response**

**Q1** Are you scared of cockroaches?

**A1** Yes, I am scared of cockroaches.

**Q2** Did you have a nightmare last night?

**A2** No, I did not have a nightmare last night.

📌 討論題目 **Free Talk**

I had a nightmare two nights ago. It was about zombies. In the dream, I was in a hospital. There was no one else around. As I wandered around alone in the hospital, I came across a group of zombies. They started chasing me as soon as they saw me. I ran for my life, but I ended up at a dead end. Luckily, just as the zombies were about to eat me, I woke up. I was so scared that when I woke up, I was sweating heavily!

## Lesson 07

🎙 再次聆聽並回答問題 **Listen again and answer the questions below**

1 The speaker was in the park.

2 He was checking his phone while walking.

3 He bumped into a tree.

🎙 換句話說 **Retell**

I was sitting in the park, people watching and waiting for my friend to arrive. I saw a guy walking and checking his phone at the same time. First, he nearly walked into a trash can. Then, he tripped over a seat. Finally, he bumped into a tree and banged his head! He was using his phone the whole time! There must be a lesson in there somewhere!

🎙 討論題目 **Free Talk**

Yes, I've walked and texted at the same time before. When I first got my new phone, I was so excited I couldn't put it down. My eyes were practically glued to the phone. I was texting my friends and checking social media all the time. One day, I was crossing the street. I was so focused on texting that I forgot to look out for cars. And, surprise, surprise, I got hit by a car. Fortunately, I only got some minor injuries. Ever since that day, I've never walked and texted at the same time again.

## Lesson 08

🎙 再次聆聽並回答問題 **Listen again and answer the questions below**

1 She is the speaker's sister.

2 She is going to university.

3 She will leave her big bed and big desk behind.

## 📌 換句話說 Retell

Next month, my sister, Mandy, will move out. She is going to university to study history. She asked whether I will miss her. And I said, "Of course! Will you leave your big desk and big bed here?" She said she would. I suppose I won't miss her that much after all!

## 📌 討論題目 Free Talk

I moved out of my house when I went to university. At first, it felt great being away from home. There wasn't anyone telling me what to do. I could eat whatever I wanted, and do whatever I wanted to do. However, after a few weeks, I started to miss home. I missed my mother's cooking. I missed watching games with my father. I missed playing with my dog. I thought I wouldn't go back home until the semester was finished, but now I go home every week.

## Lesson 09

## 📌 再次聆聽並回答問題 Listen again and answer the questions below

**1** No, she did not answer her phone.

**2** She was sleeping.

**3** She was dreaming about winning one million dollars.

## 📌 簡短對答 Quick Response

**Q1** Are you a heavy sleeper?

**A1** Yes, I am a heavy sleeper.

**Q2** Did you sleep well last night?

**A2** Yes, I slept well last night.

## 📌 討論題目 Free Talk

I usually have no trouble sleeping. However, sometimes I drink too much coffee during the day, which makes it hard to fall asleep at night. In that case, I like to do some yoga or stretches before I go to bed. Listening to soothing music and lighting a scented candle can also help me fall asleep easier. The last thing one should do is to lie in bed and scroll through one's phone. Not only does it hurt your eyes, but it doesn't help with sleeping at all.

## Lesson 10

🎙 再次聆聽並回答問題 **Listen again and answer the questions below**

1. A wizard was in his dream.
2. The wizard said he would go to Mars someday.
3. He wants to be an astronaut.

🎙 換句話說 **Retell**

Andy has had many strange and crazy dreams. Last night, he had a dream about a wizard that could predict the future. The wizard told Andy that someday he would catch a spaceship to Mars. The wizard also said that Andy would be the first president of Mars one day. Now, Andy wants to be an astronaut and realize his dream!

🎙 討論題目 **Free Talk**

Yes, I would love to travel to space someday. I've always loved watching space movies. It's thrilling to see the astronauts take off in a space rocket. My favorite moment is when they finally enter space and see the vast galaxy. I'd love to see the breathtaking view myself. I know it's not yet common for the general public to travel to space, but I'm hoping my dream will be realized in my lifetime.

## Lesson 11

🎙 再次聆聽並回答問題 **Listen again and answer the questions below**

1. She is looking for a new apartment.
2. One is close to a subway station, and the other one is close to a park.
3. The rent for both apartments is too expensive.

## 換句話說 Retell

My friend, Jane, is looking for a new apartment. She is considering two apartments. They are both conveniently located. One is close to a subway station, and the other one is close to a park. The catch is, however, that Jane can't afford either of them. Apparently, the rent for each one is too steep. She should think carefully about the decision and look before she leaps.

## 討論題目 Free Talk

If I were renting an apartment, I would first consider the location. For me, the apartment should be near a convenience store. And I would prefer there to be a gym nearby. Of course, the rent should be reasonable and within my budget. And it'd be great if the apartment is beautifully furnished so that I only need to bring my personal items when I move in. I would also prefer a great view of the mountains or the skyline from the balcony. I guess I have pretty high standards when it comes to apartments!

### Lesson 12

## 再次聆聽並回答問題 Listen again and answer the questions below

1 Yes, he is stronger than her.

2 No, he cannot lift the box by himself.

3 She suggests unpacking the box into two small boxes.

## 簡短對答 Quick Response

Q1 Are you strong?

A1 Yes, I am strong.

Q2 Do you often help other people out when they're struggling?

A2 Yes, I often help other people out.

Whenever I'm struggling with things, I'm not afraid to ask for help. Of course, I always try to solve the problem by myself first. However, I believe that when you've tried everything and the problem is still there, it's time to ask others for help. For instance, I encountered a problem at work once. I searched the company database and records, but couldn't find anything that was helpful. Eventually, I sought help from my manager, and she helped me solve the problem in just five minutes! From that experience, I learned that asking for help can be quite an efficient way to resolve issues.

## Lesson 13

### 再次聆聽並回答問題 Listen again and answer the questions below

1. The speaker dreamed about flying.
2. The speaker is scared of flying.
3. The speaker has to travel a lot for business.

### 換句話說 Retell

I dreamed about flying last night. Actually, it was more of a nightmare because I'm scared of flying. In the dream, I was on board the plane by myself, and it was in total darkness. You would think I'd be used to flying by now, since I have to travel a lot for business, but it still terrifies me!

### 討論題目 Free Talk

I have a fear of heights. I've been afraid of heights for as long as I can remember. Whenever I'm standing on the edge of a cliff or walking on a bridge, my legs start shaking and I get dizzy. This has stopped me from going on a few adventures. For instance, I rarely go on roller coasters, so I usually have to stay behind and watch over my friends' belongings while they have a thrilling ride on the roller coaster. I wish I didn't have this fear of heights, so I could experience more adventures in my life.

### Lesson 14

🎙 再次聆聽並回答問題 **Listen again and answer the questions below**

❶ He dislikes fruit and vegetables.

❷ Because he has bad eating habits.

❸ Yes, he agrees with his mother.

🎙 換句話說 **Retell**

Jordan is a picky eater. He doesn't like fruit or vegetables. Due to his bad eating habits, he is often tired or sick. His mother told him that he should make himself eat healthy foods. She also said that when he gets older, fruit and vegetables would have a positive effect on his health. Deep down, Jordan knows that his mother is right.

🎙 討論題目 **Free Talk**

Yes, I am a picky eater. I hate eating certain fruits and vegetables. For instance, I've never tried eggplant, and I never will. I understand that there are some people who love it. However, I feel disgusted just by looking at it. Why does it have to look so mushy? Judging from its appearance, I always assume that it's not going to taste good. Therefore, I've never tried eggplant before. I also dislike bananas. The reason is pretty much the same. I just don't like their mushy texture. To be honest, I'm not a big fan of their smell, either.

### Lesson 15

🎙 再次聆聽並回答問題 **Listen again and answer the questions below**

❶ He feels as sick as a dog.

❷ No, he said he's as blind as a bat.

❸ She is taking him to the doctor's.

## 簡短對答 Quick Response

**Q1** Do you have a headache?

**A1** No, I don't have a headache.

**Q2** Do you like to see the doctor?

**A2** No, I don't like to see the doctor.

## 討論題目 Free Talk

The last time I saw a doctor was a couple of months ago. I was crossing the street when a car hit me. As I fell to the ground, I hit my head. After going to the hospital and getting examined, the doctors concluded that I had suffered a minor concussion. I had to stay at the hospital overnight for observation. I guess I was pretty lucky that I didn't have any serious injuries, and the driver offered to pay for all my medical expenses.

## Lesson 16

## 再次聆聽並回答問題 Listen again and answer the questions below

**1** The speaker's dad gave the speaker the gold watch.

**2** The speaker dropped it in the bath.

**3** Yes, he fixed the watch.

## 換句話說 Retell

When I graduated, my father gave me an expensive gold watch. Two days later, though, I accidentally dropped it in the bath. The battery was as dead as a doornail. I was panicking when I took it to the watch shop, but the watchmaker said it wasn't as bad as all that. He called the next day and said the watch was fixed. It was as good as new!

After I started working, I bought my first designer bag with my own salary. I was very proud of myself and thought of it as a milestone. I only take the bag out with me on special occasions. One day, I went to a fancy restaurant with my friends. I accidentally spilled red wine on the bag, and the stain couldn't be removed. I was so mad at myself for being so clumsy. My friends could tell that I was extremely upset. A few months later, on my birthday, they bought me the same bag as a present. Let's just say, I have the best friends anyone could ever ask for.

## Lesson 17

再次聆聽並回答問題 Listen again and answer the questions below

1. The speaker will move into the new house next week.
2. Yes, the new house is bigger than the old one.
3. No, the rent for the new house is not cheaper than the old one.

換句話說 Retell

Next week, I will move into my new house. It is more than three times the size of my old house. It has twice as many bedrooms and bathrooms. The kitchen of the new house is four times as big as my current one. Unfortunately, the rent is double the amount I'm paying now. I might need to find a housemate to share the cost.

討論題目 Free Talk

When I was still a student. I rented a house in the suburbs with my friends. The house came with three bedrooms, three bathrooms, and a front and back yard. Since I shared the rent with my friends, I was able to cover the cost with my part-time job. After graduation, I moved to the city. At first, I wanted to find a place with a rent close to what I used to pay, but it turned out to be impossible. The apartment that I'm living in now is half the size of my old house, and there's only one bedroom, one bathroom, and needless to say, there's no yard. And I'm barely able to pay for the rent with my full-time job!

## Lesson 18

**再次聆聽並回答問題 Listen again and answer the questions below**

1. She likes bags, shoes, wine, and chocolates.
2. He wants to ask his wife's sister.
3. No, he's bad at choosing presents.

**換句話說 Retell**

I'm not sure what to buy for my wife's birthday. She likes bags and shoes, but I don't know what color to buy. She likes wine and chocolates, but I don't know what type to buy. I somehow always end up buying the ones she dislikes. I guess I should ask her sister. I'm so bad at choosing presents.

**討論題目 Free Talk**

My best friend Amy loves wearing make-up. In fact, she has a collection of lipsticks. According to her, a girl can never have too many lipsticks, so I guess I'll buy her a lipstick for her birthday. The problem is, however, I don't know what shade of color to buy. All of her lipsticks look like the same color to me, but she insists that they're all different. Maybe I'll just ask her what shade she wants.

## Lesson 19

**再次聆聽並回答問題 Listen again and answer the questions below**

1. He wakes up at nine o'clock on Sundays.
2. He meets his friends at their favorite restaurant.
3. She works on Sundays.

**Q1** Do you work on Sundays?

**A1** No, I don't work on Sundays.

**Q2** What time do you wake up on Sundays?

**A2** I wake up at eight on Sundays.

## 討論題目 Free Talk

On Sundays, I like to go to the park to exercise. I take my pet dog with me sometimes for a walk. He also loves to go to the park.

**Lesson 20**

## 再次聆聽並回答問題 Listen again and answer the questions below

**1** No, this is not the first time.

**2** He wants to book a table at a nice restaurant for Sally's birthday.

**3** He spent his money on new clothes.

## 換句話說 Retell

Hey, Dad. It's Nick calling. I know I said I wouldn't ask again, but can you lend me some money? I'd like to book a table at a nice restaurant for Sally's birthday next week, but I spent the rest of my money on new clothes. I promise I will pay you back this time. I hope Mom is well. Love you!

## 討論題目 Free Talk

Yes, I have borrowed money from my parents. Once, when I was in middle school, I asked my mother for money. I told her I wanted to buy some books. Apparently, she thought I was going to buy some classic novels. She was so happy that I was finally going to start reading that she gave me the money immediately. The truth was, however, I wanted to buy comic books. It goes without saying that my mother was furious when she saw me bringing home those comic books.

🎙 再次聆聽並回答問題 Listen again and answer the questions below

**1** He is drinking beer.

**2** He says it's always raining.

**3** He says the beer tastes awful.

🎙 簡短對答 Quick Response

**Q1** Is there anything wrong?

**A1** No. Nothing's wrong.

**Q2** Have you ever tried beer?

**A2** No, I've never tried beer.

🎙 討論題目 Free Talk

These days, I'm often worried about my school exams. I have six exams next week on different subjects. It's stressful just to think about them, especially the math exam. I find it very difficult to understand math, and I'm always worried that I might fail the exam. I guess I need a tutor to help me.

Lesson **22**

🎙 再次聆聽並回答問題 Listen again and answer the questions below

**1** The speaker met his former classmate.

**2** Yes, he thinks she liked him in high school.

**3** Yes, the woman is single.

🎙 換句話說 Retell

Yesterday, I ran into my former classmate at the train station. He was my crush in high school. I'm sure he had a crush on me, too. I told him I wasn't dating anyone, and I wanted to see him again. He was on top of the world, and I was, too!

參考答案

📍 討論題目 Free Talk

Yes, I have run into an old friend before. After graduation, I had left my hometown to live in a different city. I felt alone because I was away from my friends and family. One day, while I was eating by myself at a diner, I heard someone calling my name. I turned around and saw a familiar face. It was my friend from high school! I was so happy to see him that I treated him to dinner. We chatted until it was closing hours. It was nice to have an old friend around in a strange city.

Lesson 23

📍 再次聆聽並回答問題 Listen again and answer the questions below

**1** He was chatting with Mark last night.

**2** Yes, he called last night.

**3** She was chatting with Becky last night.

📍 簡短對答 Quick Response

**Q1** Where were you last night?

**A1** I was out with my friends last night.

**Q2** Did you go home last night?

**A2** Yes, I went home last night.

📍 討論題目 Free Talk

No, I rarely stay out late with my friends. Even though I like chatting with my friends, I prefer to get home before 10 p.m. I like to leave some time just for myself at night. It's when I can truly relax. I remember one time, I stayed out late with my friends and didn't get home until midnight. The next day, I had a terrible headache from lack of sleep. And I wasn't in the mood to do anything. I do love my friends, but I guess I just love my beauty sleep more.

## Lesson 24

### 再次聆聽並回答問題 Listen again and answer the questions below

**1** No, the speaker's friends all have different hobbies.

**2** Yes, the speaker has a friend who is teetotal.

**3** No, it is difficult for the speaker to plan activities.

### 換句話說 Retell

All of my friends have completely different hobbies and interests. One loves to go rock climbing, while another is scared of heights. One loves to play soccer, but another will only watch the game on TV. One goes to a bar every weekend, but another is teetotal. And one likes to go running, while another has to be forced just to go anywhere. This makes it very difficult for me to plan activities!

### 討論題目 Free Talk

My friends have various hobbies. One of my friends, George, is very athletic. He likes to play basketball, and he goes jogging every day. Another one of my friends, Katie, is a moviegoer. She loves to watch all genres of movies. In fact, she goes to the theater so much that she became a VIP customer. And another one of my friends, Timmy, is an aspiring chef. He is always cooking and baking. I love how my friends have different hobbies because it keeps me healthy, entertained, and well-fed!

## Lesson 25

### 再次聆聽並回答問題 Listen again and answer the questions below

**1** She plans to visit her grandparents.

**2** He will watch the fireworks with his buddies.

**3** She might go meet the man after the visit.

## 簡短對答 Quick Response

**Q1** Do you like watching fireworks?

**A1** Yes, I like watching fireworks.

**Q2** Have you ever seen the sunrise?

**A2** Yes, I have seen the sunrise.

## 討論題目 Free Talk

For last year's New Year's Eve, I invited a couple of friends over. We planned to cook dinner together, so they all brought some food with them. We ended up cooking a big meal that included a hot pot, curry, some fried chicken, and noodles. After the hearty meal, we had a couple of beers and watched the New Year's Eve concert. We were having so much fun we almost missed the countdown. Then, we watched the fireworks from the balcony. It was great spending the end of the year and starting a new year with my dearest friends.

## Lesson 26

## 再次聆聽並回答問題 Listen again and answer the questions below

**1** He thinks skipping meals is a bright idea.

**2** He wants to lose weight quickly.

**3** You might overeat at the next meal.

## 換句話說 Retell

My friend, Graham, thinks it is a bright idea to skip meals. He wants to lose weight quickly; hence, he says skipping meals is a good way to eat less. However, I read in an article that skipping meals could cause health problems. In addition, since you're so hungry, you're likely to overeat at the next meal. I'll have to tell Graham the next time I see him!

I've tried a lot of methods to lose weight. From my experience, one of the most effective ways is the 16/8 diet plan. It involves eating only during an 8-hour window and fasting for the remaining 16 hours. Of course, during that 8-hour period, you should eat a healthy diet instead of consuming junk food. Also, exercising regularly is a must if you want to successfully reduce body fat. One thing to keep in mind, though, is that while a method might work for me, it might not work for you. Therefore, it's important to find a method that truly suits you.

## Lesson 27

**再次聆聽並回答問題 Listen again and answer the questions below**

1 Yes, she is married.

2 She goes away with her husband at least once a month.

3 Yes, he thinks it's a good idea.

**簡短對答 Quick Response**

Q1 Are you married?

A1 No, I'm not married.

Q2 Do you often go on vacation?

A2 No, I seldom go on vacation.

**討論題目 Free Talk**

In my opinion, a good way to keep the love alive is to give each other personal space and privacy. Even though it's nice to be around our loved ones, it does get exhausting seeing them 24/7. And, to be honest, it does get a bit suffocating doing everything together. Therefore, it's important to have some time for ourselves. This way, we can develop our own interests and hobbies, and when we meet again at home, we'll have more things to share with each other!

## Lesson 28

### 再次聆聽並回答問題 Listen again and answer the questions below

**1** No, the speaker never cooked before going to college.

**2** Because the speaker ran out of money.

**3** No, they didn't get sick from the food.

### 換句話說 Retell

I had never cooked before going to university; as a result, I spent the first three weeks of the term eating out. I was just enjoying that lifestyle when I realized I had started to run out of money. Therefore, I began watching videos about cooking on a budget. I made curry for my housemates the following weekend. Thankfully, none of them got food poisoning! I guess there's a first time for everything.

### 討論題目 Free Talk

Yes, I consider myself a good cook. I started developing a passion for cooking when I moved out of my parents' house. Since I couldn't afford to eat out every day, I decided to cook for myself. Over time, I learned how to cook fried rice, pasta, curry, beef stew, and many more dishes. Sometimes I like to change the recipe to eat healthier. I often invite my friends over for a meal. I'm not trying to brag, but the dishes that I serve all get very high reviews from them. I'm sure I'll continue cooking in the future. Who knows, maybe I'll even open up a restaurant!

## Lesson 29

### 再次聆聽並回答問題 Listen again and answer the questions below

**1** She was sick.

**2** Yes, she is feeling better.

**3** Yes, she thinks the cold was worse than usual.

## 簡短對答 Quick Response

**Q1** Have you ever had a cold before?

**A1** Yes, I've had a cold before.

**Q2** Do you always go see a doctor when you catch a cold?

**A2** No, I don't always go see a doctor.

## 討論題目 Free Talk

The last time I caught a cold was two years ago, and it was as bad as a cold can be. It started out with a runny nose and sneezing; then, I started coughing and got a severe headache. I thought if I rested for a few days and drank lots of water, the symptoms would disappear. One or two days later, though, I started to run a fever. My temperature was so high my roommate had to get me to a hospital. Under the care of the doctor and nurses, I had a speedy recovery.

### Lesson 30

## 再次聆聽並回答問題 Listen again and answer the questions below

**1** He will save $5,000 by the end of the year.

**2** He plans to buy an engagement ring.

**3** He plans to go to Paris.

## 換句話說 Retell

By the end of the year, Jonas will have saved $5,000. He will have put aside enough money to buy his girlfriend an engagement ring. He plans to take her to Paris and propose under the Eiffel Tower. Then, he plans on taking her for a candlelit dinner on a cruise on the Seine. Jonas is such a romantic!

## 討論題目 Free Talk

Yes, I have tried to save money in order to buy something expensive before. It was during my first year of college. Once the term started,

I realized nearly everyone had a laptop. At first, I thought I could do things the old-fashioned way and get by with my pen and notebook. However, after a few classes, I realized that college was nothing like high school. There were so many notes to take, so many articles to read, and so many papers to write. In the end, I took a part-time job in order to put aside some money to buy a laptop.

**Lesson 31**

📍 再次聆聽並回答問題 **Listen again and answer the questions below**

**1** Because he feeds it too much.

**2** No, her dog is not friendly.

**3** Yes, the postman is scared of her dog.

📍 簡短對答 **Quick Response**

**Q1** Do you keep a dog as a pet?

**A1** No, I don't keep a dog as a pet.

**Q2** Are you a dog person or a cat person?

**A2** I'm a cat person.

📍 討論題目 **Free Talk**

I would like to keep a parrot as a pet. Since most people keep dogs or cats as pets, I think it'd be cooler and more special to keep a parrot. I would name my pet parrot Hook, as in Captain Hook from the story *Peter Pan*. And on Halloween, I would dress up as a pirate and have Hook stand on my shoulder. Together, we would surely win the office's costume contest. And while my friends train their pet dogs to shake hands and fetch a stick, I would teach my pet parrot to sing and talk. I'm so excited just thinking about it!

## Lesson 32

🔑 再次聆聽並回答問題 Listen again and answer the questions below

**1** They have been apart for more than three months.

**2** He moved away to study abroad.

**3** She will jump on a plane and surprise him.

🔑 換句話說 Retell

My boyfriend and I have been apart for more than three months. While I stayed here to work, he moved overseas to study abroad. When he first moved away, we called each other at least twice a day. Now, it's less than three times a week. I can't help feeling like we are drifting apart. So, I'm going to jump on a plane and surprise him. Actions speak louder than words!

🔑 討論題目 Free Talk

Yes, I have been in a long-distance relationship before. A few years ago, I received a job offer to work in the US. It was a once-in-a-lifetime opportunity, so I accepted the offer. At that time, I was in a steady relationship with my boyfriend. We both hated being apart, but we found ways to make it work. We called each other every day and talked about everything. I introduced him to my colleagues and friends in the US. He also called me whenever he was having a gathering with his friends. For us, the best way to cope with a long-distance relationship was to try our best to include each other in our lives.

## Lesson 33

🔑 再次聆聽並回答問題 Listen again and answer the questions below

**1** No, he doesn't want to watch it.

**2** He thinks it is cheesy and boring.

**3** No, she doesn't like it.

📍 簡短對答 **Quick Response**

**Q1** What kind of movies do you like?

**A1** I like action films.

**Q2** What kind of movies do you dislike?

**A2** I don't like horror or thriller movies.

📍 討論題目 **Free Talk**

I love watching movies. My favorite movie is *The Avengers* because it's exciting and full of action. Also, I love superheroes. I wish I had superpowers like them, so I could help fight bad people and save the world.

**Lesson 34**

📍 再次聆聽並回答問題 **Listen again and answer the questions below**

**1** He is going to see a concert.

**2** No, she doesn't like concerts.

**3** She is going to make a few calls.

📍 簡短對答 **Quick Response**

**Q1** Have you ever been to a concert?

**A1** Yes, I have been to a concert before.

**Q2** Do your friends like to go to concerts?

**A2** No, they don't like to go to concerts.

📍 討論題目 **Free Talk**

The last concert I went to was my favorite band's. It was held at a stadium. The tickets were sold out, so the stadium was full of people. Everyone was hyped for the concert, especially at the opening of the concert. Seeing the band perform live left me in awe. I was excited beyond words. The highlight of the concert was when the band performed my favorite song. It was a performance I'll never forget.

🎙 再次聆聽並回答問題 Listen again and answer the questions below

&#x2460; The name of the restaurant is Albert's Restaurant.

&#x2461; Yes, the waiter thinks the chef's pizza is good.

&#x2462; For drinks, the waiter recommends red wine.

🎙 換句話說 Retell

Welcome to Albert's Restaurant. I'm Leah Roberts, your chef. The soup is the best in town. The pizza is also to die for! Here is a menu for you. The food is on the left, and the drinks are on the right. For drinks, I recommend our red wine. It goes well with any of our dishes.

🎙 討論題目 Free Talk

Yes, I have a favorite restaurant. It's a small diner for Chinese dishes. It's my family's tradition to have dinner there every weekend. In fact, we've been there so many times that we've become friends with the chef. The chef's fried rice is to die for. My favorite dish, however, is the steamed dumplings. They're juicy and full of flavor. I highly recommend this restaurant to everyone.

**Lesson 36**

🎙 再次聆聽並回答問題 Listen again and answer the questions below

&#x2460; She is watching a basketball game on TV.

&#x2461; He is cooking dinner.

&#x2462; He is quitting alcohol.

🎙 簡短對答 Quick Response

Q1 Do you like to watch basketball games?

A1 Yes, I like to watch basketball games.

參考答案

325

Q2 Do you like to drink wine?

A2 No, I do not like to drink wine.

📌 討論題目 Free Talk
_____

Today, I plan to study English. I'm traveling abroad to the United States next month, so I want to prepare myself for it. My goal is to improve my English speaking and listening skills so that I won't have any trouble talking to the locals. I study for two hours each day. Also, I listen to English podcasts and watch English news broadcasts. During my free time, I even watch English-speaking shows. In fact, I'm putting so much effort into learning that I'm even speaking English in my sleep!

Lesson 37

📌 再次聆聽並回答問題 Listen again and answer the questions below
_____

1 No, she doesn't know where Andy is.

2 They will take the train.

3 She wants to leave without Andy.

📌 簡短對答 Quick Response
_____

Q1 Have you ever been late before?

A1 Yes, I have been late before.

Q2 Have you ever missed a train or a flight before?

A2 No, I have never missed a train or a flight before.

📌 討論題目 Free Talk
_____

If my friends were late, I would wait for them. I would also ask my friend the reason. If it were a reasonable reason, for instance, their car broke down or they had a car accident on the way, I would be quick to forgive them. However, if the reason were unacceptable, like they overslept, didn't catch the bus, or their car ran out of gas, I would be quite annoyed. In fact, I wouldn't hesitate to tell my friend that I was unhappy with them.

## Lesson 38

🎙 再次聆聽並回答問題 **Listen again and answer the questions below**

1. The speaker will go on a road trip with Tom.
2. Chicago is the final destination of their road trip.
3. The gas will be expensive.

🎙 換句話說 **Retell**

Next week, I'm going on a road trip with Tom, my best friend. We are starting from LA and driving all the way to Chicago. It will be the trip of a lifetime! Tom and I will share the driving, so we won't be too exhausted. Also, we will share the cost because the gas will be really expensive. However, it will be worthwhile!

🎙 討論題目 **Free Talk**

Yes, I've been on several road trips before. My favorite one was with my family when I was a child. We drove for two hours to a beautiful beach. My mother made sandwiches and packed some refreshing fruit so that we could have a picnic there. After the picnic, my father helped me build a huge sandcastle. We also swam for a while in the ocean. At night, we stayed at a beach house, where we saw the stars and listened to the waves. It was a great experience!

## Lesson 39

🎙 再次聆聽並回答問題 **Listen again and answer the questions below**

1. No, she is not in Mexico.
2. She will fly to Mexico on Monday.
3. Her mom and dad will go with her to Mexico.

## 🎗 簡短對答 Quick Response

**Q1** Have you ever been to Mexico?

**A1** No, I've never been to Mexico.

**Q2** Do you like flying?

**A2** Yes, I love flying.

## 🎗 討論題目 Free Talk

Yes, I have traveled abroad before. It was during a summer vacation when I was in college. I flew all the way to New York to meet my internet friend, Sarah, who I've been chatting to for many years. She was born and raised in New York, so she offered to show me around the famous city. We went to all the famous tourist spots and even visited some secret destinations. Even though I was nervous about traveling abroad before I departed, I ended up having a fantastic time with Sarah.

**Lesson 40**

## 🎗 再次聆聽並回答問題 Listen again and answer the questions below

**1** It is on Friday night.

**2** No, she will be late.

**3** He will save some spaghetti and pudding for her.

## 🎗 簡短對答 Quick Response

**Q1** Do you often have to work overtime?

**A1** No, I rarely work overtime.

**Q2** Do you like to eat spaghetti?

**A2** Yes, I like to eat spaghetti.

🔖 討論題目 **Free Talk**

Yes, I have hosted a dinner party before. It was when I moved into a new house. I invited a few friends over for a housewarming. Before the guests arrived, I ordered some pizza and sandwiches, and I also prepared some drinks. I even decorated my house with balloons. I guess I was very excited for the party. Once my friends arrived, we had so much fun together that we decided to take turns hosting dinner parties each month.

**Lesson 41**

🔖 再次聆聽並回答問題 **Listen again and answer the questions below**

**1** Yes, Lisbon is a great place to visit.

**2** You can take the tram in Lisbon.

**3** Yes, the locals are friendly.

🔖 換句話說 **Retell**

Lisbon is a great city to visit. There is a castle overlooking the city. You can take a ride in the famous tram up into the old town. You can hear the traditional music drifting out of the bars. You can taste the awesome seafood. You can also feel the warmth of the friendly locals. Before you know it, you'll be back in Lisbon again.

🔖 討論題目 **Free Talk**

The city I would love to visit again is New York. I went to New York a couple of years ago. Even though I stayed there for only a few days, I was completely mesmerized by the vibrant city. I love how you can spend the day strolling in the museums or going window shopping in SoHo or Times Square. And at night, you can go to the bars or a nice restaurant for a relaxing evening. It'd be great to have more time to experience all the different aspects of the city.

📌 再次聆聽並回答問題 **Listen again and answer the questions below**

**1** She is cutting down on caffeine.

**2** She prefers to drink water.

**3** Yes, she wants some ice for her drink.

📌 簡短對答 **Quick Response**

**Q1** Do you prefer water or juice?

**A1** I prefer water.

**Q2** Do you like to add ice to your drinks?

**A2** No, I don't like to add ice to my drinks.

📌 討論題目 **Free Talk**

Yes, I like to drink coffee. I must have at least one cup of coffee per day. In the morning, before eating my breakfast, I always brew coffee. Smelling the sweet aroma of the coffee beans can help wake up my brain and make me feel more energetic. For my first cup of coffee, I always take it black. However, if I'm feeling the need for a second cup in the afternoon, I prefer to take it with cream; otherwise, I won't be able to sleep at night.

📌 再次聆聽並回答問題 **Listen again and answer the questions below**

**1** They are most likely at a restaurant.

**2** She bought him a watch and a shirt.

**3** The man is paying for the meal.

📌 簡短對答 **Quick Response**

**Q1** Do you often dine out with your friends?

**A1** Yes, I often dine out with my friends.

**Q2** Do you often offer to pick up the check?

**A2** No, I seldom offer to pick up the check.

## 🔔 討論題目 Free Talk

Yes, I have treated my friends to a meal before. I lived abroad for work after graduation, and I hadn't returned home for a few months. Once my friends heard the news that I was coming back to visit, they all cleared their schedules to have dinner with me. I was really grateful because I knew they were all busy with work and family. During our meal together, we had so much fun chatting and catching up. At the end of our meal, I offered to get the check because I was so happy to see them.

## Lesson 44

## 🔔 再次聆聽並回答問題 Listen again and answer the questions below

❶ The speaker is spending the holidays with her boyfriend's family.

❷ No, the speaker was not close to his family at first.

❸ The speaker will go surfing with him.

## 🔔 換句話說 Retell

I'm becoming increasingly excited about the vacation! My boyfriend and I will spend the holidays with his family in Bali. I used to feel a bit awkward around his family, but recently, we've become closer and closer. As a matter of fact, I'm going to play tennis with his brother, go surfing with his dad, and work on my tan with his mom. I can't wait!

## 🔔 討論題目 Free Talk

If I were on a vacation at a summer resort, I would try all kinds of beach activities. I've always wanted to learn surfing, so I would take surfing lessons. I would also like to go snorkeling to see the amazing ocean life. Another activity I would like to try is paddle boarding. I've seen videos of people paddle boarding on the ocean before dawn and arriving at a secluded destination just in time to see the sun rise over the horizon. Even in videos, the view was to die for! Therefore, I've put it on my bucket list to go paddle boarding and see the sunrise with my own eyes.

**Lesson 45**

🔖 再次聆聽並回答問題 **Listen again and answer the questions below**

1 He has been skydiving twice.

2 Yes, he thinks it's safe.

3 She wants him to call her every day.

🔖 簡短對答 **Quick Response**

Q1 Have you ever been skydiving before?

A1 No, I've never been skydiving.

Q2 Do you call your parents every day?

A2 No, I don't call my parents every day.

🔖 討論題目 **Free Talk**

I've always wanted to try freediving. It's a form of underwater diving. In freediving, divers have to rely on holding their own breath, whereas in scuba diving, divers use breathing equipment to breathe underwater. Overall, freediving gives you more freedom when underwater. I want to try it because I've always wanted to explore the ocean. It goes without saying that our ocean is more polluted than ever, so I would like to have the chance to see the underwater world while it is still possible.

🎙 再次聆聽並回答問題 Listen again and answer the questions below

**1** He will take the plane.

**2** No, he will have breakfast on the plane.

**3** They will meet on Saturday.

🎙 簡短對答 Quick Response

**Q1** Have you ever been on a plane before?

**A1** Yes, I've been on a plane before.

**Q2** Do you like to eat in-flight meals?

**A2** No, I don't like to eat in-flight meals.

🎙 討論題目 Free Talk

The last time I traveled by plane was when I flew to Hong Kong for a business trip. The flight was interesting because it was extremely short. The flying time was less than 90 minutes, which was shorter than the drive from my house to the airport! While flying, it was obvious that the flight attendants were busy from the start to the end. They helped passengers board the plane, served us meals, assisted with passengers' individual requests, and prepared the cabin for landing. At the same time, they kept a professional attitude by smiling and being welcoming and helpful.

Lesson **47**

🎙 再次聆聽並回答問題 Listen again and answer the questions below

**1** No, he doesn't think it's good.

**2** No, it's more difficult to use than his old one.

**3** Yes, it's cheaper than his old one.

參考答案

**Q1** Do you have your own phone?

**A1** Yes, I have my own phone.

**Q2** Is your phone cheap?

**A2** No, it's not cheap.

📌 討論題目 Free Talk

My phone comes with many features. One of the features that I find really useful is the GPS function. Whenever I'm going to places I'm not familiar with, I simply open my maps app and let technology lead the way. The app is rarely wrong about the location and the route. To be honest, I don't even bother memorizing street names anymore. My friends tell me I rely too much on it, but who can blame me when it's so simple and convenient!

**Lesson 48**

📌 再次聆聽並回答問題 Listen again and answer the questions below

**1** The speaker had lunch at twelve.

**2** The speaker met a supplier at three.

**3** The speaker is going out with her boss for dinner.

📌 換句話說 Retell

I had a busy day today. I had a breakfast meeting at eight this morning, lunch with a client at noon, and coffee with a supplier at three. I'm having a few drinks with my colleagues at 6 p.m., and my boss is treating me to dinner at 8 o'clock. Now that I think of it, today is just a day of eating and drinking!

📌 討論題目 Free Talk

My day at work is usually pretty busy. In the morning, I clock in at 8 a.m. Then, I have a morning meeting with my team at 8:30. After the meeting, I have to meet with a couple of clients. Sometimes, the meetings take so long that I don't even have time for lunch! In the afternoon, I have another meeting with my boss. To put it simply, my day at work is full of meetings, meetings, and more meetings!

## Lesson 49

再次聆聽並回答問題 **Listen again and answer the questions below**

1 They are going to study English.

2 She wants to go to the library.

3 He doesn't want to go to the cafeteria.

簡短對答 **Quick Response**

Q1 Where do you usually go to study?

A1 I usually stay at home to study.

Q2 Do you like to go to the library?

A2 Yes, I like going to the library.

討論題目 **Free Talk**

For me, the best way to prepare for a test is to pay attention in class and take plenty of notes. If there is anything I don't understand, I ask my teacher or classmates. After school, I review my class notes and try to organize them. The most important thing, however, is to get plenty of sleep! That's why I always go to bed before 10.

## Lesson 50

再次聆聽並回答問題 **Listen again and answer the questions below**

1 The speaker had the internship at a large technology company.

2 No, the speaker was not satisfied with the internship.

3 No, the speaker did not gain computer skills.

### 🔖 換句話說 Retell

Last summer, I worked as an intern at a large technology company. I was very excited before the internship started. However, after I started work, I found it to be fairly disappointing. Before everyone arrived in the morning, I had to empty more than fifty trash cans. And after they clocked in, I had to make coffee for everyone. That's all I did for three months. As to gaining computer skills, don't even ask!

### 🔖 討論題目 Free Talk

Yes, I've had an internship before. When I was a student, I applied for an internship at a start-up. I've always thought the company's founder and CEO seemed very wise and inspiring. Without a doubt, I looked forward to working for him. However, once my internship started, I was a bit disappointed because he turned out to be mean and bossy. I guess that's one way to run a company.

## Lesson 51

### 🔖 再次聆聽並回答問題 Listen again and answer the questions below

1. She plays the violin.
2. Her teacher says she will be a professional violinist someday.
3. She will keep practicing for now.

### 🔖 簡短對答 Quick Response

**Q1** Do you play the violin?

**A1** No, I don't play the violin.

**Q2** Have you ever heard an orchestra perform?

**A2** Yes, I have heard an orchestra perform.

I only know how to play the piano. I had piano lessons when I was young. My piano teacher was very strict. She was always telling me to practice, practice, and practice! Whenever I made mistakes, she would scold me. Even though I loved playing the piano, I was always nervous when meeting my teacher. However, under her guidance, I did improve a lot, and I even won first place in a piano contest. I guess her teaching method worked on me after all.

## Lesson 52

### 再次聆聽並回答問題 Listen again and answer the questions below

1. He will retire next year.

2. Because he will be living in Mexico.

3. Yes, the speaker will learn Spanish, too.

### 換句話說 Retell

I'll be retiring next year. I plan on taking Spanish classes in a community college. Since I'll be moving to Mexico, I want to learn Spanish. My granddaughter will visit me regularly, so she will try to learn Spanish, too. We will talk to each other in Spanish. This way, we will both make great progress.

### 討論題目 Free Talk

Besides English, another foreign language that I've learned is French. Ever since I was a child, I've always wanted to learn French. To me, French is such a romantic language. Therefore, I took French classes when I was in university. I learned French for two years. However, since I've never had a chance to actually go to France, I haven't had many opportunities to talk to French native speakers. In fact, the only words that I'm brave enough to say are *bonjour* and *merci*.

參考答案

🖈 再次聆聽並回答問題 **Listen again and answer the questions below**

**1** She has two children.

**2** Phoebe cries every time she leaves the house.

**3** No, she doesn't want to quit her job.

🖈 簡短對答 **Quick Response**

**Q1** Do you have children?

**A1** No, I don't have children.

**Q2** Would you like to have twins?

**A2** No, I don't want to have twins.

🖈 討論題目 **Free Talk**

My colleague, Rita, is a working mom. She gave birth to a boy last year and took a year off to care for her baby. This year, she came back to work. We all thought she would be quite anxious about leaving her baby with a nanny, but, as it turns out, she is quite relieved to take a break from her baby. She said she couldn't stand all the screaming and crying. And, surprisingly, she missed working. It's amazing how she can strike a balance between family and work.

🖈 再次聆聽並回答問題 **Listen again and answer the questions below**

**1** He is good at English speaking and listening.

**2** He is less confident about reading and writing in English.

**3** The speaker suggests that he should read and write restaurant reviews in English.

🖈 換句話說 **Retell**

I have been trying to find ways to improve my English. I'm good at speaking and listening, but not that confident about reading and writing. I love to eat out at different restaurants, so my friend suggested I should read and write reviews in English for every restaurant I eat at. It's a great idea. I could describe the atmosphere, the location, the cost, and, of course, the food!

## 🔖 討論題目 Free Talk

To improve my English skills, I take half an hour to study every day. During this time, I mainly focus on learning and reviewing English grammar. Additionally, I like to read news articles in English during my commute to improve my reading skills. My favorite way to improve my listening skills is to watch TV series or listen to podcasts. As to improving my speaking skills, I just chat with my American friend, Sarah. However, we're always gossiping, so I guess I should find a proper teacher to discuss serious topics with.

## Lesson 55

## 🔖 再次聆聽並回答問題 Listen again and answer the questions below

1. No, she didn't pass the test.
2. He passed the test with flying colors.
3. He suggests they prepare for the next test together.

## 🔖 簡短對答 Quick Response

**Q1** Do you often fail tests?

**A1** No, I rarely fail tests.

**Q2** Do you often review lessons after class?

**A2** Yes, I often review lessons after class.

## 🔖 討論題目 Free Talk

Most of the time, I prefer to study by myself. It is more efficient for me to study without the disturbance of others. Being alone helps me stay more focused; this way, I can concentrate more and absorb more information. I had a study group with my friends in the past. I thought it'd be great for us to discuss questions and come up with answers together. However, we ended up chatting and gossiping. I learned more about my friends' relationships than the history of the Roman Empire! Long story short, I never went to another study group again.

## Lesson 56

再次聆聽並回答問題 Listen again and answer the questions below

**1** The speaker went to Australia for his gap year.

**2** The speaker met Laura while in Sydney.

**3** Yes, the speaker recommends taking a gap year.

換句話說 Retell

Before I started university, I took a gap year to travel around Australia. During that time, I learned so much about myself, and I became a more confident, stronger person. I met a girl, Laura, while I was in Sydney, and I fell in love with her. As our relationship grew, we decided to continue to travel together to New Zealand. Now, we are married! I highly recommend taking a gap year.

討論題目 Free Talk

One of my friends, David, has taken a gap year before. He took a gap year once he graduated from high school. To be honest, we all thought he just wanted an excuse to travel around the world. However, to our surprise, he signed up to be a volunteer for an international charity organization. During the gap year, he built houses for refugees, helped those suffering from hunger, and taught children living in orphanages. When he returned home, we could all tell that he had become more mature, more responsible, and more sympathetic.

## Lesson 57

🎙 再次聆聽並回答問題 **Listen again and answer the questions below**

**1** Her thesis was on sales tactics.

**2** Yes, she has job experience.

**3** Yes, he is impressed by her.

🎙 簡短對答 **Quick Response**

**Q1** Do you have any job experience?

**A1** Yes, I have job experience.

**Q2** Have you ever written a thesis before?

**A2** No, I've never written a thesis before.

🎙 討論題目 **Free Talk**

I had a job interview a couple of months ago. The interview was done online through a video conference call. I had never had an online interview before, so I was quite nervous. I made an effort to clean up my room to make sure the background of the video call would be tidy and clean. I also checked the lighting so that my face would be clear enough. I bought new headphones with a microphone so that my voice would sound clear. On the day of the interview, the interviewer didn't even turn on the camera, so I was the only one with the camera on. I felt so awkward because I didn't know where to look. It was definitely an odd interview experience for me.

## Lesson 58

🎙 再次聆聽並回答問題 **Listen again and answer the questions below**

**1** Yes, they are co-workers.

**2** They have known each other for 30 years.

**3** They have six grandchildren.

參考答案

## 換句話說 Retell

Barbara and Terry are colleagues. Barbara has been working in the company for 30 years. By the end of the year, Terry will have been working there for 35 years. They met at work 30 years ago and got married. Now, they have four children and six grandchildren. To both of them, however, the day they met feels just like yesterday. Time flies!

## 討論題目 Free Talk

I don't think office romances should be allowed. Being in a relationship with a colleague can complicate a lot of things. For instance, my colleagues, Rita and Josh, have been dating for a year. When their relationship is stable, they are a great team, always finishing projects on time and always coming up with new ideas. However, whenever they have a fight, they refuse to talk to each other or even see each other. When this happens, the rest of us have to share the workload and take over their projects. To be honest, we're all a bit frustrated by this situation.

## Lesson 59

### 再次聆聽並回答問題 Listen again and answer the questions below

**1** Yes, he is at a job interview.

**2** No, she is not offering him a job.

**3** No, he is not happy with the decision.

### 簡短對答 Quick Response

**Q1** Have you ever been to a job interview?

**A1** Yes, I have been to a job interview before.

**Q2** Have you ever interviewed a job candidate?

**A2** No, I have never interviewed a job candidate before.

🗨 討論題目 Free Talk

I have been rejected at a job interview before. When I was in college, I wanted to have a part-time job so that I could pay the rent. I saw the café near my house had a job opening for the waiter position. I immediately went there and asked the manager about it. After answering a few questions from the manager, I was asked to wait on a few tables for a trial. To my embarrassment, just when I picked up a tray full of drinks, I tripped over a customer's foot and dropped the entire tray on the customer. Needless to say, the manager rejected me right after that incident.

Lesson 60

🗨 再次聆聽並回答問題 Listen again and answer the questions below

1 Yes, he is the kind of person that always leads others.

2 Yes, he is a confident person.

3 He is the leader of the country's largest political party.

🗨 換句話說 Retell

John always takes charge. Out of all his friends, he is the most organized and has the greatest confidence. He has the most energy and has the least need for sleep! He also has the biggest drive to succeed in everything he does. It comes as no surprise that John is now the leader of the country's largest political party. He is truly a born leader!

🗨 討論題目 Free Talk

I consider myself more of a leader. I'm not afraid to speak my mind and make decisions. In fact, whenever there's a problem at work, I'm always the one to take the initiative to solve it. And if there's an issue that we need to discuss, I'm always the first one to share my opinions or ideas. I'm the kind of person that likes to see progress

參考答案

343

and hates it when things are stalled. However, at times, I prefer being a follower. For instance, when my husband is asking me what's for dinner, I like to let him decide.

# Notes

國家圖書館出版品預行編目（CIP）資料

英語輕鬆學：學好初級口語就靠這本！/
賴世雄作. -- 初版. -- 臺北市：常春藤有聲出版股
份有限公司, 2022.12　面；　公分.
-- ( 常春藤英語輕鬆學系列；E67 )
ISBN　978-626-7225-10-3（平裝）
1. CST：英語　2. CST：口語　3. CST：會話
805.188　　　　　　　　　　111020277

**常春藤英語輕鬆學系列【E67】**

# 英語輕鬆學：學好初級口語就靠這本！

| | |
|---|---|
| 總 編 審 | 賴世雄 |
| 終　　審 | 陳宏瑋 |
| 執行編輯 | 許嘉華 |
| 編輯小組 | 鄭筠潔・Nick Roden・Brian Foden |
| 設計組長 | 王玥琦 |
| 封面設計 | 謝孟珊 |
| 排版設計 | 王穎緁・林桂旭 |
| 錄　　音 | 劉書吟・李鳳君 |
| 朗讀播音老師 | Terri Pebsworth・Michael Tennant |
| 講解播音老師 | 奚永慧・呂佳馨 |
| 法律顧問 | 北辰著作權事務所蕭雄淋律師 |
| 出 版 者 | 常春藤有聲出版股份有限公司 |
| 地　　址 | 臺北市忠孝西路一段 33 號 5 樓 |
| 電　　話 | (02) 2331-7600 |
| 傳　　真 | (02) 2381-0918 |
| 網　　址 | www.ivy.com.tw |
| 電子信箱 | service@ivy.com.tw |
| 郵政劃撥 | 19714777 |
| 戶　　名 | 常春藤有聲出版股份有限公司 |
| 定　　價 | 499 元 |

常春藤　www.ivy.com.tw
愛上英語的第一站

 **常春藤** 英語集團 　讀者問卷【E67】
英語輕鬆學：學好初級口語就靠這本！

感謝您購買本書！為使我們對讀者的服務能夠更加完善，請您詳細填寫本問卷各欄後，寄回本公司或傳真至（02）2381-0918，**或掃描 QR Code 填寫線上問卷**，我們將於收到後七個工作天內贈送「常春藤網路書城熊贈點 50 點（一點＝一元，使用期限 90 天）」給您（每書每人限贈一次），也懇請您繼續支持。若有任何疑問，請儘速與客服人員聯絡，客服電話：（02）2331-7600 分機 11～13，謝謝您！

線上填寫
免郵寄最環保

姓　　名：＿＿＿＿＿＿　性別：＿＿＿＿　生日：＿＿＿年＿＿＿月＿＿＿日

聯絡電話：＿＿＿＿＿＿　E-mail：＿＿＿＿＿＿＿＿＿＿＿＿＿＿＿

聯絡地址：☐☐☐☐☐☐＿＿＿＿＿＿＿＿＿＿＿＿＿＿＿
　　　　　＿＿＿＿＿＿＿＿＿＿＿＿＿＿＿＿＿＿＿＿＿

教育程度：☐國小　☐國中　☐高中　☐大專／大學　☐研究所含以上
職　　業：**1** ☐學生
　　　　　**2** ☐社會人士：☐工　☐商　☐服務業　☐軍警公職　☐教職　☐其他＿＿＿

**1** 您從何處得知本書：☐書店　☐常春藤網路書城　☐FB／IG／Line@ 社群平臺推薦
☐學校購買　☐親友推薦　☐常春藤雜誌　☐其他＿＿＿＿＿＿＿＿＿＿

**2** 您購得本書的管道：☐書店　☐常春藤網路書城　☐博客來　☐其他＿＿＿＿＿＿

**3** 最滿意本書的特點依序是(限定三項)：☐試題演練　☐字詞解析　☐內容　☐編排方式
☐印刷　☐音檔朗讀　☐封面　☐售價　☐信任品牌　☐其他＿＿＿＿＿＿＿

**4** 您對本書建議改進的三點依序是：☐無（都很滿意）☐試題演練　☐字詞解析　☐內容
☐編排方式　☐印刷　☐音檔朗讀　☐封面　☐售價　☐其他＿＿＿＿＿＿＿

原因：＿＿＿＿＿＿＿＿＿＿＿＿＿＿＿＿＿＿＿＿＿＿＿＿＿

對本書的其他建議：＿＿＿＿＿＿＿＿＿＿＿＿＿＿＿＿＿＿＿＿

**5** 希望我們出版哪些主題的書籍：＿＿＿＿＿＿＿＿＿＿＿＿＿＿＿＿＿

**6** 若您發現本書誤植的部分，請告知在：書籍第＿＿＿＿＿頁，第＿＿＿＿＿行

有錯誤的部分是：＿＿＿＿＿＿＿＿＿＿＿＿＿＿＿＿＿＿＿＿＿

**7** 對我們的其他建議：＿＿＿＿＿＿＿＿＿＿＿＿＿＿＿＿＿＿＿

感謝您寶貴的意見，您的支持是我們的動力！　常春藤網路書城 www.ivy.com.tw